Digging deeper will put them
in the killer's crosshairs ...

REMAINS

CINDY BONDS

Scrivenings
PRESS
Quench your thirst for story.
www.ScriveningsPress.com

Published by Scrivenings Press LLC
15 Lucky Lane
Morrilton, Arkansas 72110
https://ScriveningsPress.com

Printed in the United States of America

Paperback ISBN 978-1-64917-407-9

eBook ISBN 978-1-64917-408-6

Editors: Elena Hill and Linda Fulkerson

Cover design by Linda Fulkerson - www.bookmarketinggraphics.com

All characters are fictional, and any resemblance to real people, either factual or historical, is purely coincidental.

And the peace of God, which surpasses all understanding, will guard your hearts and your minds in Christ Jesus. ~ Philippians 4:7

PROLOGUE

"What's wrong?" The high-pitched whimper echoed as streams of tears tracked down chubby, bright red cheeks. "Where're you going?"

Wiping the little girl's face, she gave Jacqueline a tight hug. "Nothing's wrong, honey. But I do have to go. Remember, I'll be back soon."

Rushing down the stairs, Jacqueline's quick footsteps tip-tapped on the wooden steps from behind.

"But Rach ..." Jacqueline pulled out her name, but there was no time to stop.

Just being here, saying goodbye—it was too dangerous.

God, please watch over them. Keep them safe.

Pushing through the door and into the frigid Chicago air, Rachel gripped her arms. Snow clouds hung low. The stormy morning matched her grieving heart. If only none of this had happened. If only she'd left sooner.

Jacqueline's muffled scream brought her back to reality. Rachel turned, but the girl was gone from the doorway. She scanned the area. It was eerily quiet. The only sound, the wind whirling through the barren branches of the trees.

After one last look at the empty window, she dashed down the paved pathway beside the house. Pausing, she snuck a look around the corner. Gabby's car sat parked on the other side of the road, puffing plumes of smoke into the gray sky.

"Hurry!"

With a nod to Gabby, she sprinted across the yard to the street. A burning sensation sliced through her side as the muffled echo of a gunshot hung in the dense air.

"No, God. Please," she whispered, falling forward. Gabby's scream resounded.

Her hands couldn't stop the fall as the curb entered her sight, her weight pressing down, her body useless to stop it.

1

Seven years later

"Sir, I'm headed to the gym to get him now. He doesn't have good cell service there." Detective Greer Bennett strode into the Lexington City Gym, irritated and cold. "In fact, I'm probably about to lose service too."

"Get out there now, Bennett. Homeland is already on it, and I'm not so keen in giving up before we even start."

"Yes, sir."

Her frown deepened as the click sounded.

Pushing through the doors to the basketball courts, her nose wrinkled as she pocketed her cell phone and unzipped her jacket. Although it was in the forties and robust fall weather outside, it was a balmy eighty degrees in the gym.

"Hey, Greer."

She nodded to Paige with a smile. "How're you feeling?" Climbing the steps, she took a seat next to Paige, who rolled her eyes.

"Oh, just great. Rick insisted I come with him today and as it turns out, all the other wives had something much better to do. So, I've been shopping." Paige waved her phone with a wink as she let out a laugh. "I'll have everything ready for this baby one way or another."

"Serves him right. But unfortunately, we have a case."

"I figured that's why you're here." She turned her attention to the game. "Rick!"

Glancing over the court, Greer tried to keep her eyes off Thomas, but as usual, it didn't do much good. His large size and big grin were too hard to ignore.

"Yeah?"

Her gaze shifted to her partner.

"Greer says it's time to go."

Rick tossed the ball behind him as he jogged up to the stands. "What's up?"

"Mansfield has been trying to call you for the past hour. He's hot."

Rick shrugged as he wiped his face off. "He's always hot. What's going on?"

"Something at an empty lot in Pine Valley. Apparently, it's big because Homeland already has a man there. The sheriff needs some help and requested you."

Greer gripped Paige's hand to help her stand. Rick took over, walking his six-month-pregnant wife down the steps.

"And next time you make her come and sit on these awful bench seats just to watch you play ball, I'm going to come down here and school you."

"That last time was a lucky shot."

"Yeah, sure."

"Greer."

Following Paige off the bleachers, she turned. Her jaw clenched as Thomas jogged toward her, that big grin on his face.

Forcing a smile, she nodded and shoved her hands in the jacket pockets. "How's it going?"

"Things are about the same. You?"

"I'm good. Look, I've got to go—"

"Yeah, same old, same old."

She frowned at his condescension "See ya around, Thomas."

Before she could get to the outer door of the gym, a hand gripped her arm. Yanking free, she found Thomas's frame in her space.

"I'd like to talk sometime. Anytime. Call me."

Forcing her eyes to his, she sighed. She had been drawn to him like a moth to a flame when they first met six months ago. As those icy blue eyes stared, it was hard to keep from being drawn in once again.

"Nothing's changed. You want something I can't give. Let's just leave it."

He pushed in, lightly taking ahold of her waist. "I don't want to leave it."

"So, you've changed your mind?"

He shrugged. "Not sure, but I am certain I'm not ready to just walk away."

"It's been almost a month. And I can honestly say, I'm not ready to go back down that road." She swallowed hard as his eyes flitted around her face, landing often on her lips. "I have to go."

Pulling back, she turned and all but ran to the front of the gym, high-tailing it outside to find Rick standing outside his car and talking to Paige.

"If you ever leave me like that again—"

"Look," Rick held up his hands in defense. "I can't stop him, G. He's going to keep talking until you listen."

"I'm done listening."

"Rick, stop it. She's made her decision, and you should tell him that." Paige's voice quivered, and Greer stooped over to look in the window.

Paige wiped her face and blew out a deep breath.

"You okay?"

Paige just waved her off. "Hormones. I'm fine. But I am upset that things didn't work out for you. He seems like such a good guy."

She sighed and straightened. "He is, just not the guy for me."

With a nod to Rick, she headed for the car. Slamming the door, she started the engine and turned up the heat. Chewing on the inside of her cheek, the past few months rushed through her mind. "God, tell me I made the right decision."

After the disaster in Nashville, moving back to Lexington last year seemed the best idea. Poised to partner with her old high-school friend in the town she graduated in, the pieces started to fit. Her life finally felt whole again.

Then Thomas entered the picture.

Blowing out a deep breath, she held her head in her hand as Rick slipped into the car.

"Let's go."

"You're not even going to change?" She eyed him with a wrinkled nose.

Rick shrugged. "I smell fine."

With a shake of her head, she put the address that would lead them to the scene in the GPS—well outside the city in the rural community of Pine Valley.

Chit-chat about baby supplies and the status of the high school football team evolved into a more personal discussion.

"Look, whatever happened between you and Thomas, you need to fix it. I'm tired of all the questions about you every Saturday."

She clenched her jaw a moment. "He wanted to get engaged."

"Okay. So, you don't want to get married?"

"We dated a month. He never even told me he loved me,

and I'm not all that sure I could say I loved him. My work interfered with half our dates, and we had to plan around his EMT schedule. We weren't close enough to get engaged."

"I get that. But you two seemed to click."

"Well, yeah, we did. But honestly, I think a lot of that was the newness of everything. You remember that, right? When you first start dating someone, and it's all new and attraction, and that's pretty much it. We didn't know each other well enough to know if we wanted the same things and the future ..." she trailed off, feeling an ache.

The thing was, at thirty-four, she wanted a future. She wanted to get married, maybe even have a family. But she wasn't willing to just give in because an amazingly handsome guy she wasn't even sure she loved was willing to give that to her after a handful of dates.

"You know, he ended things. I didn't want to talk about marriage just yet, it was too soon. After a few days of fighting, I told him I couldn't keep arguing about it and to drop it for a few more months. He said he wanted more, and if I wasn't ready, he needed to move on."

"Really? He made it out like you ended it."

"Of course, he did." She turned right into the empty lot.

The police tape fluttered in the wind as she parked the car.

"Did Mansfield say why Homeland was here?" Rick nodded at the black SUV parked on the other side of the drive.

She shook her head and stepped into the brisk fall air. "Nope. Guess we're about to find out."

Zipping up her jacket, her body shivered in the cool breeze.

They showed their credentials to the officer, and he let them by.

"Hey, Patrick. How's it goin'?" Rick led the way, smiling at the small-town sheriff who slid from his car to meet them.

"Ricky, glad you're here. I would hate to have to deal with some young city detective."

Rick clutched his chest. "I'm still young."

She chuckled. The man smiled.

"Well, you brought a friend."

She stuck out her hand. "Detective Bennett."

He shook it. The older sheriff looked to be in his sixties and had probably been in this rural community for decades.

"Nice to meet you, miss. Sheriff Patrick Tindall at your service."

"What in the world did you dig up?"

The man's gaze slowly left hers and turned to the backhoe sitting in the distance.

"Well, we had a new buyer come in here, wanted to put in one of those dollar shops. Anyway, the digging crew called about an hour ago. Said they found something shady. When I got here, it looked like some bones had been uncovered, so I called in the ME. He called a forensic somebody, and suddenly, Homeland is here, and I'm just trying to keep up."

She stood at the edge of the dug-out trench, whitewashed bones stuck out of the dark red dirt.

"Where's the forensic anthropologist?"

Patrick shrugged at Rick's question.

"She was here earlier. Said she had to get more equipment or something."

"She needed specialized digging equipment that you didn't have on hand." The deep voice echoed on the breeze from across the trench.

Her eyes leveled on a man in designer jeans and a sports coat. Six foot or so, the sports coat stretched tightly over his broad shoulders. Sunglasses covered his eyes as his dark hair fluttered in the fall breeze.

"And you are?"

"Special Agent Sullivan."

Federal. Great.

His square jaw clenched as he walked around the trench. Without a word, he pulled out his credentials to show them.

"Nice to meet you, Agent Sullivan. I'm Detective Rick Myers." Rick grinned and shook the man's hand.

Sullivan didn't give her a second glance as he spoke to Rick. "I have a guess who this is, but until we get a positive ID, I'm left waiting. I'd appreciate being kept in the loop. Although, I don't plan on going anywhere."

"Sure, anything we can do to help. Right, G?"

The man was hard to read behind those sunglasses, but his stiff body language spoke volumes.

"Are you going to read us in?" she questioned.

He shook his head. "Nope, if it's who I think it is, it's my case."

She stepped in front of Rick to gain the guy's attention. "This is *our* case, and unless your director has affirmed your position, which I'm guessing he hasn't ..." her eyebrow rose as Sullivan's jaw clenched harder, "then we will, out of respect for your situation, allow you to hang around. But we're not obligated to share any information."

Pulling his sunglasses off, his green eyes darkened. "Is there a reason for your hostility?"

"Not hostile, just protective. It's not the first time other agencies have asked for the same allowances and then pushed us off without the least bit of courtesy."

"I won't," he growled.

"Sure. Last time a Fed took Rick here out to dinner, offered him a steak while his men took over the entire scene and body. He had no idea until he got back to work."

Rick hit her back, and she turned.

"That was a long time ago when I was fresh. It won't happen again." Rick glared.

She turned back to face the agent. "No, it won't."

Stepping back to the scene, the icy gaze of both men sent chills up her neck.

"I don't work that way. Law enforcement deserves respect—any law enforcement."

Shaking her head at Sullivan's comment, she slipped on gloves and sat on the edge of the hole.

"What do you think you're doing?"

Glancing up, she ignored the agent's stern tone. Swinging her gaze to Patrick, she asked, "So, pictures have been taken and measurements made, correct?"

"Yes, ma'am. Did it all myself and already got the okay from the ME to move the body after the forensic woman gives the all clear." He smiled, and she slid down the edge.

"Easy there, Greer. Don't—"

She silenced Rick with a stare. "I think I can handle it. Besides, you three are a little too heavy-footed to get details."

A chuckle from the sheriff made her smirk. Carefully easing around the body, she wedged herself between the trench walls and the scene markers.

Sweeping a gloved hand around the hip bone that stuck up on its side, she knelt low to get a good look at the brushed-away dirt that revealed the hip structure.

"Female, I'm guessing younger than thirty, mid-to-late twenties maybe?" She peered up to the agent. "That meet your requirements, Agent Sullivan?"

He nodded, sliding the sunglasses back in place.

Pushing hers back to hold her hair, she scanned the remains. Fragments of fabric, probably clothes, stuck up in between the bones and the dirt. The rubber sole of a boot barely shone through the dirt from the edge of the taped-off scene. She rose to tip-toe around for a better look. Stepping outside the scene, she had only about a foot of space as she wiped off the tread and dug around the boot.

"Find something?"

Ignoring Rick's call, her gut churned. There was something more here, something she wasn't going to like. Those boots weren't feminine, and with the angle ...

Grunting, she pulled at a large rock, turning it over to reveal a smooth surface underneath the dirt.

The limited space in the area left her trying to heave the large rock. She rolled it underneath to sit on. Her fingers worked their way into the space, clearing the smooth surface. The brittle white texture under her fingers confirmed her suspicions.

"There's another body."

2

G reer studied the remains buried in the red clay dirt. "I can't imagine these remains belong to the first victim, seeing how she seems to be complete and the angle would be wrong."

"If it's mine, there will be three more besides her."

Agent Sullivan stood on the ridge above.

"Okay. Serial killer?"

That was usually FBI jurisdiction.

He shook his head, then squatted and held his hand down. "Come on. Get out of there, and I'll run it by both of you."

"You just said we wouldn't be read in."

He shook his head and motioned with his hand.

Ignoring her first instinct to blow the man off, his actions were far too curious. Maybe she had misjudged him.

She stood and held up her hand, then hung on tight, using her feet to guide herself upward as he pulled. His arm wrapped around her waist to lead her from the hole, and she quickly stepped away, trying to ignore the cologne that immediately filled her senses. She had to admit, the guy smelled good.

"Come on. We can't do much until the anthropologist gets

back, but I can give you basics." He nodded toward his car, and she pulled off the gloves, turning to Rick.

"What changed?" she whispered as Rick came up beside her.

"I have no idea. Although, I'm certain it's not your pleasant demeanor," he mumbled as he stepped ahead.

Yes, everything she said had come out harsh. But her experiences with federal agencies never ended well. Bigger agencies assumed locals couldn't do their jobs, so they moved in and took over. And the last time that happened, people died.

Swallowing the memories, she followed the men to an SUV.

Sullivan opened the door and tossed his sunglasses on the seat. Turning, he appeared with a file folder and handed it to Rick.

"Before moving to Homeland, I worked in the FBI on a cartel task force. There's one case I never solved. When I moved to Homeland, I told them this case would bring me out, and they reluctantly agreed, probably because it was a long shot it would ever be discovered."

She stood next to Rick and peered over his arm.

The file contained information on the Bolstero Cartel, a stiff-arm crew from the last decade that had moved in and out of the headlines. The case was dated seven years ago.

"I guess I don't get it, Agent Sullivan. Why would you want to go back to the FBI just to work this kind of case?" Rick relented the file as she pulled it in close and read through the names.

"Rachel Sullivan."

Sullivan's jaw clenched.

"Relative?"

He nodded. "She was caught in the middle, the DEA tried to use her as a mole, and that's what got her killed."

"And you know that because?"

"Because she's in that hole," he growled.

Greer nodded and returned to the file. "Says here without a body, there was never a trial."

Anger burned on his reddening face.

"Hermann Bolstero was the leader and under investigation. She went in as a mole and began passing off information, but it was never enough. When she disappeared, I did some digging. Bolstero ran a trucking company, allowing him and his money to appear legit. The day she disappeared, along with a few other people connected to Bolstero, a truck supposedly broke down in this area.

"He had trackers on all his trucks. The notes I found said a truck broke down here, but the tracker went offline for three hours. When it came on, it was at a gas station a few blocks away. It left only a few hours later. Why would the tracker break down suddenly? And what caused the truck to leave after only a few hours if there was a breakdown?"

She closed the folder and crossed her arms. "That's not in here. How did you get that information?"

He shrugged. "I told you. I dug around."

"Man, that's awful. But if you're not FBI anymore, how is Homeland going to take this case? It's not their thing."

Sullivan narrowed his eyes at her before turning to Rick. "I have a provisional license with the FBI to continue working should this case come to court. I know the players, the background, everything about this case."

"But with that, I'm sure you would have to not only prove the identities, but also prove Bolstero's involvement. This was years ago."

"That's why I would like to be kept in the loop. I have more than enough information on Bolstero to make him pay for what happened."

"Why didn't the FBI peg him another way? I don't recall Bolstero ever being convicted of any crime. With the DEA involved, I'm guessing it was drugs. You're telling me that in all the years he's been in business, he's never been convicted of anything? Even with a mole present?"

Sullivan blew out a breath and straightened from the SUV.

"They tried to make things stick, but he had a slick lawyer, and there were always technicalities. Instead of prosecuting Bolstero, the lawyer did his best to determine who the mole was. She said she was being careful, but she never should've been in that situation."

"Never should've been in that situation? You mean she didn't work for the DEA?"

"No. She was never an agent. She was coerced to work for them, and that position cost her her life."

A van pulled into the lot, idling close to the hole. A woman in a white plastic suit slid from the seat with a phone to her ear.

"I got it, thanks." The newcomer shoved the phone into her pocket, then turned to them. "Okay, you two guys, come unload everything. No sense a woman doing so much when you two can handle it."

"I'm Detective Bennett." Greer stuck out her hand and the woman took it.

"Dr. Shaver. I was here earlier. Seems like an interesting find. You have an idea who it might be?" Dr. Shaver nodded to the folder in Greer's hands.

"Possibly. I took a dive in there a minute ago, found more than one set of remains."

The woman frowned for a moment, then her eyes lit as she grinned. "Wouldn't happen to be Greer Bennett, would it?"

Greer smiled and nodded.

"Well, good grief. Why am I here?"

She chuckled. "Because you're the expert, not me. I've been out for a while."

Shaver nodded. "What did you assume?"

"Female, under the age of thirty. Mid-to-late twenties?"

"I agree. Where was the other set?"

Greer followed Dr. Shaver to the scene as the men finished unloading the digging equipment.

"See that rock? I moved it over and found the indention of bone underneath. It fits our case file, but I want to see what you have to say. Your unbridled opinion." She winked at the woman who nodded emphatically.

"Make the case fit the evidence, you're right. Let me get to work."

"Here's my card, call or text me. I'd like to be kept updated as much as possible."

Dr. Shaver took the card and dug out one of her own. "Here's my email. I don't keep my cell phone on me when I work, but it's there too. Let me know if you need anything. I'll be sure and give you updates. Nice to meet you Dr., I mean *Detective* Bennett."

Dr. Shaver worked a small rung ladder into the ground and then placed it gently over the side, carefully climbing down to the remains.

The men walked up beside Greer as Dr. Shaver got to work.

"It'll take her the rest of the day to remove the body. I wouldn't plan on an ID until tomorrow at the earliest."

"That long?" Sullivan's green eyes narrowed, frustration etched on his features as he stared into the trench.

"I'm sorry, but with the decay and the possibility of trace evidence, all that dirt will have to be sifted through a layer at a time. If you can get the dental records of your potential victims to Dr. Shaver, I'm sure that will speed things up."

He nodded, his gaze focused on the hole and the remains barely sticking up from the earth. To lose someone he loved and never know for sure what happened was a hard thing to carry around for all these years. And now, to have the answer so close ...

Greer bit the inside of her lip, shoving down her own feelings.

Not now, God, I can't deal with that now.

"Patrick, looks like you'll have a boring day." Rick's voice made her turn.

Patrick chuckled. "It's fine by me. I can handle sitting here in the cool breeze. I have some lures that need to be fine-tuned, anyway."

"You're going to mess with lures?" Agent Sullivan's heated voice cut through.

"So far, no one knows about this place or what's been discovered. Patrick's force is small. If this gets to the media, we might have to do some more drastic protocols to keep the evidence safe. But right now, I think we'll be fine." Rick's easy tone didn't seem to help the situation as the agent huffed and marched to his car.

"I don't think he likes me much." Patrick chuckled.

"He's got a personal interest." She crossed her arms, shivering.

Patrick and Rick continued their conversation about fishing and lures as her mind drifted. Agent Sullivan paced next to his SUV with a phone to his ear, rubbing the back of his neck.

Memories fell heavy on her chest, and she took a deep breath. It wasn't the same, not really. Her father had disappeared when she was six. But her mother had always said he'd run away with someone else, someone he loved more than them.

Swallowing the lump in her throat, images of the gravesite she helped to excavate five years ago flashed in her mind. Finding her father's body in a grave outside Nashville had effectively put an end to her forensic career. She transitioned into the Police Academy. If only she had found out why he had to die.

"Greer, ready?" Rick's voice pulled her to the present.

She nodded. "Let me get this back to the agent."

Crossing the field, she held out the file. "Here's your file back. Give me your number, and I'll keep you apprised."

He shook his head. "Keep it. I'll send you my number."

"You have my number?"

He nodded, looking over her shoulder. "Yours and your partner's. How well do you know this doctor?"

She shrugged. "I don't. But I'm sure she'll do a great job. There's not too many of them around, you know. It takes a lot of passion and expertise to get to that level of forensics."

He leaned back against his SUV.

"You staying here?"

He nodded, his gaze flicking to hers for a second.

"Okay. Hope you have good cell service." She made her way to the car, sliding in the seat behind the wheel.

"You good?" Rick asked.

She nodded, then started the car and put on her seatbelt, tossing the file to him. "Dr. Shaver will keep us updated. Can't do much until we get an ID."

Driving back in silence, Rick's prying eyes pricked her skin. "What is it now?"

"What's got you so quiet?"

"I'm not quiet. Just thinking."

"About?"

She groaned at the tone of his playful voice. "What do you think?"

"Agent Sullivan or Thomas. It's hard to tell."

"Neither."

He chuckled. "Well, the way you were looking at the agent earlier, I just wondered."

Her head snapped around to see his grin. "What? What're you talking about?"

"I asked you if you were ready like three times. You never answered. You just stared at Sullivan."

"I wasn't staring. I was thinking, and he was in my way."

Rick sat there grinning.

"Don't go there. The case—it hits home a little, and I feel bad for him. What he's going through."

"Sorry, didn't think about it that way. Have you been making any progress?"

"No. It's a dead-end case, and I've been too busy," she said.

His hand gripped her wrist. "Let me know if you ever want any help."

"Thanks," she whispered, working to focus on the road ahead.

"But you know, the guy didn't have a wedding ring on."

"Rick, seriously?"

His laughter filled the car as she drove back to the office.

3

Clenching his jaw, Agent Gage Sullivan watched the sedan exit the parking lot.

"He's in gym clothes and she has an attitude. Great combination." He slid into his seat.

Propping the car door open, the cool breeze hit him. He leaned his head back and closed his eyes. Rachel. He had finally found Rachel. The evidence was overwhelming. It had to be her.

"God, you owe me." Opening his eyes, Gage focused on the hole.

Ten years ago, he left the Marines and applied to the FBI just to keep an eye on Rachel. A school-teacher-turned-homeschool-teacher to a criminal. It was a life she didn't deserve, and he had failed miserably at keeping her safe. Now he was here digging up her grave.

Scanning the scene, the memories came rushing back. Seven years ago, he'd searched Pine Valley for any trace of Bolstero's trucks or anyone who might've seen a truck come through. He'd ended up here, but his search was cut short when the owner showed up and kicked him off, unimpressed by his badge.

Kinda like Detective Bennett.

She was angry. What made her so arrogant?

A tone sounded from his phone and he picked it up. With a smirk, he read the text.

> Just so you know, I have your number too. Here's Dr. Shaver's email address. Send the dental X-rays and it'll speed up the process once she gets the remains to the office.

Seemed Detective Bennett didn't like to be bested.

> Got it.

Glancing over at the sheriff, he frowned as he sent out another text.

> Your sheriff looks more like he's focused on his need to sleep.

> You worry too much, Special Agent. Rick says he's a good guy. Old, but dependable.

Shoving the phone in the cup holder, he slid down from the truck as the deputy spoke with the sheriff, then turned around and left. With a sleepy sheriff and absent deputy, at least Gage was here to help protect the scene.

The call had come early this morning and he drove from Louisville at breakneck speed to get here before the investigation began. Thankfully, one of his buddies at the switchboard heard the call about remains in Pine Valley.

Weaving through the trees, he ended up behind the trench with a good view of the road. A large white SUV pulled into the lot, throwing gravel and dust.

One man got out of the passenger side, and the sheriff met him at the side of his cruiser. The two exchanged a few words, then the man motioned toward the sight.

Gage started back around the trench, hoping he was imagining the anger on the man's red face. The sheriff put a hand on his gun, and Gage picked up his pace, pulling his weapon.

A single gunshot rang out. The sheriff dropped.

Knowing the anthropologist was in the trench, Gage went looking for the shooter.

A rifle barrel retreated into the SUV's back window, and Gage reached for his phone.

"Ugh," he muttered.

It was still in the car.

Keeping low to the ground, he slunk through the brush as another man emerged from the SUV. The two approached the trench, guns raised. Pausing, Gage aimed his weapon.

"Homeland! Freeze!"

The gun swung toward him, and he fired, hitting the first man and sending the second running back to the SUV. He sprinted up to the trench, hiding at the van's side as he watched for the SUV.

"You, okay?" Peering inside, he saw the woman kneeling, hands over her head.

"What's happening?"

"Stay down," he hissed.

He swung his gun toward the SUV as the gun barrel appeared again. Firing at the windshield, his bullets pinged off the glass.

Gage dove just as a shot fired past his shoulder. Crouched, he aimed once more, hitting the back window where the rifle sat. The SUV's tires spun on the gravel, gritting dust and debris as they finally caught traction.

Firing, he edged up to the sheriff. The SUV backed out and

then fled down the road. After emptying his clip, Gage knelt down and felt for the sheriff's pulse.

"I'm alive, just bruised up," the man said through deep breaths.

"Good." Gage pulled the sheriff to sit. "Hit the vest?"

The sheriff nodded as he leaned back against the tire, pale and breathing heavy.

"I need to call it in."

"I just did." Dr. Shaver stood outside the trench, her focus on the body at her feet as her phone fell from her hand.

4

"I can't believe this," Greer muttered as they sped down the road, lights on and siren blasting.

"It's not on the wire yet, I just checked. How did anyone know what was found?"

"Dr. Shaver didn't give me much. Have the others arrived yet?"

Rick shook his head. "No, we'll probably beat them."

Her hands clenched in her lap as her stomach churned and her head pounded. The only person who would attack a crime scene filled with remains would be the man or men responsible for the remains in the first place.

Was Hermann Bolstero really behind all this?

Who else would have the info before anyone else?

SIRENS ANNOUNCED the arrival as Gage stood. Detective Bennett only glanced at him as she sprinted to the trench.

"Dr. Shaver?" She took off down the ladder.

"Hey, where's the sheriff?" Detective Myers sounded from behind.

"Ambulance already took him. He's okay. The bullet struck the vest."

"Good. He's a good man," Myers commented.

The detective's focus went on the dead man, lying next to the trench.

"I got to him before he had the chance to fire on the doctor."

"Where were you?" Myers scanned the area.

"I went walking through the woods, trying to get a feel for the place. See if there was anything I missed last time I was here."

"And when was that?"

He turned. Detective Bennett stood, frowning and arms crossed. Did the woman ever smile?

"Right after Rachel disappeared, seven years ago. I did my research on this place. It was cleared five years ago when the bank took hold."

"Earl Graves. He passed away, and his family couldn't cover the taxes, so the bank got it. We did our research too."

Gage turned back to Myers and shook his head. "I was here off and on for months after Rachel disappeared. I searched every place I could think of where bodies might be dumped. Honestly, I assumed they chose the river."

"But you said you were here." An edge filled the tone of Detective Bennett's voice.

Gage clenched his jaw and swung his attention back to Bennett as he set his hands on his hips. She sure liked to argue.

"I was. Guy ran me off with a gun. He said he didn't care that I had a badge, no one was trespassing on his land."

"Could be someone paid him to use his land."

She was probably right.

"If you had mentioned that to the FBI, they could've

investigated, found out if Mr. Graves had an unusual amount of money in his possession."

"Greer." Myers's stern voice hung in the air, ignored.

"Can't do anything now, though. Especially since he's dead, and the land was passed over. What else did you discover, Agent Sullivan?"

Fisting his hands at her need to chastise him, he worked to ease his tone. "Is there a reason you're giving me the fifth-degree?"

She stepped into his space. "I find it interesting that anyone at all knew about this situation. Rick had just checked the wire. Nothing was leaked. We didn't do it, the sheriff didn't have a reason to do it, and Dr. Shaver just told me she didn't tell anyone why she needed the equipment. So, that leaves you." Her amber eyes seared into his as her jaw clenched.

"Why would I risk it?"

"I don't know."

Letting his anger ease, he studied her, curious how she was going to react when he told her about the sheriff.

"Before the ambulance arrived, Sheriff Tillman informed me that the man who confronted him was the same one who bought the land from the bank. Niko Manus. He's also the man who ran away and jumped back in the SUV after I shot his associate." He motioned toward the dead man by the trench. "So, it seems there is one other way someone else would know."

Her face crimson, she gave a nod. "I'll check it out." She pushed past him and headed to the sedan.

She was inside and on the highway within seconds.

"I'll just, um—did you get an ID on the man you shot?"

Gage tore his eyes from the car to look at Myers. Nodding, he handed over the evidence bag with the wallet in it.

"Carmen Durant? Never heard of him or the Niko guy," Myers commented. "Did Patrick say why the man was mad?"

He shrugged. "Didn't say much except the name of the man he knew. He was hurting pretty bad."

"It didn't go through, did it?"

"No, but point-blank range with a rifle, even with a vest it's going to bust some ribs."

Myers nodded. "Yeah. Hope Greer takes it easy on him."

Gage frowned, crossing his arms as he leaned back against the SUV.

"Look, she's been burned too many times by other agencies. There's some bad blood there. I've already talked to her about being so hateful, but honestly, I can't blame her."

"Why?"

Myers' gaze searched around the empty scene. "Right before we became partners, she had a big case come up while in Nashville. Her team had the guy on the ropes and got enough info to lead them to a huge bust—drugs, guns, you name it.

"She personally called all the proper authorities, covered her bases, but right when her team were about to breech, sirens and lights went off, and everything broke loose. Several officers were injured, including a good friend of hers."

Gage's stomach dropped. "Who was it?"

"FBI. They didn't communicate to the proper agents, and even though she called to make sure the Bureau didn't have a stake involved, they decided she couldn't handle it and came anyway. She lost some good people because of the chaos that occurred from them coming in without warning."

Her obvious irritation made a little more sense. But still, he wasn't FBI anymore, and it wasn't the agency backing him.

"She'll cool off and apologize."

That didn't seem likely.

"Well, since I don't have a car, let's see what we can discover about the location of Mr. Manus. And let me see your gun. I'll have someone out here ASAP to get you cleared for the shooting."

After handing over his weapon, Gage leaned back and mulled Detective Bennett's past encounters. As much as he understood her anger, he still didn't appreciate her personality. Short tempered and jumping the gun—there was no way he could work this case with her.

But she was sure great to look at. With that dirty blonde hair that curled on the ends and bright amber eyes, she was definitely a head-turner. If only her personality matched her looks.

He smiled to himself. Yeah, that would be an unbeatable combination. Too bad she already had a disdain for him.

He straightened and shook the thought from his head. This case was about to get complicated, and he sure didn't need the hot-tempered detective on his brain while he tried to finally convict Hermann Bolstero for his crimes.

He wouldn't let anything mess with his investigation, give the defense even one thing to hold against them in court. He wanted Bolstero in jail for what he did, and nothing could stop him. Even an attractive and bitter detective.

5

Heated and irritated, Greer marched through the hospital, flashing her badge and trying to ignore the embarrassment of putting her foot in her mouth in front of Agent Sullivan. He must think she was an idiot.

Blowing out a deep breath, she knocked on the door and entered. "Sheriff Tillman?"

"Come on in here. It'll make me feel better to see a pretty face like yours, detective."

She chuckled and stepped inside, walking up to the hospital bed. "What happened here, sir?"

He waved her off with a smirk. "Just a shot to the vest. Everything else is precautionary."

"Patrick?"

A soft voice made her turn. An older woman rushed inside, tears streaking her face as she wrapped her arms around the sheriff.

"Freeda? Who told you to come here?"

She playfully slapped the man's shoulder. "You old goat! Why didn't you call me? Missy from the ER called and said they were admitting you because you were shot."

He chuckled and pulled at the woman's arm. "It hit my vest, hon. I'm fine."

"Then why are you being admitted?"

Patrick blew out a breath with a wince. "Broke a rib, fractured another. Guy was standing much too close. But it could've been worse." He winked at his wife as she sat on the bed next to him.

"Well, I'm glad that's all it is."

The woman glanced up.

"I'm Detective Bennett, ma'am. I'm investigating the shooting."

The sheriff's wife nodded as she stood. "Freeda Tillman, Patrick's wife. So nice to meet you."

Greer smiled and took the woman's frail hand. "Your husband is a good man." She winked at Patrick.

"He's a goat, never telling me anything, pestering me to no end."

Greer pushed her hand over her mouth to cover her grin.

"But he's my husband, for better or worse." Freeda leaned over and kissed his forehead.

"I'm the worse, if you didn't get what she was saying." Patrick winked.

Greer laughed out loud.

"Let me go call David. He'll be worried." Freeda exited the room as Patrick frowned.

"No need in telling him. I'm fine." He shook his head. "David's my son. Say, you're not looking, are you?" Patrick's eyes roamed her hands.

"No, sir. Sorry. I actually need to talk to you about the man who shot you."

He sighed. "Never trusted them much, but our town needs business."

She leaned against the foot of the bed, pulling out her phone to take notes. "So, you knew him?"

"Niko Manus. He bought that place and another property here in town. They're building gas stations, I think ..." He trailed off, stroking his chin. "Anyway, he showed up all upset, angry that I sent the construction guys home. I told him it was a crime scene, and he wasn't going to get anything done until the bodies could be removed."

She nodded along as she typed. "Is he the one who shot you?"

"Naw, just kept on jabbering, getting madder and madder. I had my hand on my gun, just in case. Then I felt the shot. It slammed into my chest, and I fell hard. Took my breath away for a bit—probably why they didn't shoot me again. Even with the vest, I guess they thought I was dead."

"So, you didn't see the shooter?"

"Nope, just a rifle barrel out of the back window, shooting at that Homeland fellow. I tried to lift my arm to shoot, but I was so winded, I could hardly take a breath."

"A rifle that close, you got lucky," she said as she typed.

"Well, at least we have a name, and that's better than nothing. I just wish I could've stopped them."

She leaned into the bed. "I get his anger, but shooting a sheriff? Seems a bit of an overreaction."

"Criminals do things we normal folk don't understand. Act without thinking then clean up the mess later."

She nodded. "I'll email over the report for you to sign. You know how it works."

He returned her nod. "Sure do. You know, you should smile more, hon. You might find yourself with a ring on that finger."

"Thanks for the advice." Stepping out of the room, she made her way to the nurses' station. "I need an email address for official paperwork."

She typed it into her phone and headed toward the elevator.

Nothing felt right. Why would Niko Marcus, idiot criminal

or not, risk killing a sheriff? Construction couldn't start back without the sheriff's go ahead. It's not like they would suddenly show up and start work unless the scene was released.

The questions rattled around her head as she strode from the elevator, slamming into a bulwark.

"Oh, sorry."

"For what?"

Heat rising on her face, she peered up at Agent Sullivan.

"I ... what're you doing here?"

He shrugged. "Same as you."

"I have his statement."

Sullivan entered the elevator and pushed the button without a word.

Stunned, she turned around to see Rick with a growing grin, standing in the lobby.

"What are you two doing here, and who's at the scene?"

"I've got four men standing guard, and we're here to see Patrick."

"I've got his statement. We can go."

"I want to see him. You can sit here red-faced and wait for me after leaving me like you did." Rick stormed away as she stared after him.

With a groan, she collapsed on one of the chairs in the lobby, irritated and embarrassed. She never should've rushed off like she did, but she was too embarrassed to just stand there while Sullivan glared.

God, what is wrong with me?

The answer was way too obvious. She was too prideful and hung on to everything. Letting go of what the FBI did to her seemed impossible—and then with the missing sister of the agent and then thinking about her dad ...

Pulling it together had to happen now, or the rest of this case would destroy the little bit of sanity she had left.

"Thanks for checking on me, young man." Sheriff Tillman nodded at Gage as Detective Myers came through the door, taking the sheriff's attention. "I was wondering where you were."

"Sorry, just talking to my partner."

Tillman let out a whistle. "One of you is sure missin' out."

"Now come on, Patrick. You know I'm married."

Huh? He had missed that.

"Then you're up, Homeland." Tillman winked as he shook his head.

"No thanks."

"Besides, I've got a baby on the way."

Tillman's attention was pulled away as the two talked about due dates and ultrasounds. Gage shook his head and edged to the window.

He wondered why Manos would do something so foolish as attack the sheriff in broad daylight. It didn't make any sense to shoot the sheriff and then try and take out Shaver. What would they do then?

"You ready, Agent Sullivan?"

He nodded and turned back to the men.

"Let me know when you catch them. I'm curious about what's going on in my town." Tillman narrowed his eyes, shifting between Gage and Myers.

As they left, Myers's phone rang. He answered it in the elevator.

"Hey, babe."

Gage rolled his eyes.

"What do you mean?" Myers straightened as his voice rose. "I'll be right there, I'm twenty minutes away. Don't do anything!"

He took off running out the elevator as Detective Bennett rose from the lobby chairs.

"What's going on?"

Gage followed her out in a jog as Myers frantically searched the lot.

"Come on, I'll drive."

"No, give me the keys." Myers snatched them from her grasp. He hit the panic button then followed the sound.

"Rick? I need to drive. You're too upset."

Bennett did her best to negotiate as Myers drove off, tires squealing.

"What?" She turned to him. "What happened? What's wrong?"

"His wife called."

Her eyes widened. "And?"

He shrugged. "That's all I know."

With a groan she pulled her phone from her pocket and dialed. "Come on, drive me to the office so I can get my car."

"I'm going back to the scene."

Phone to her ear, her jaw dropped. "You won't drive me in? You get that's my partner and my partner's wife?"

He nodded. "I understand, but I've got a job to do, and he headed in the opposite direction of the scene."

"Paige, call me now. What's going on?" She hit a few more buttons, then let out a groan. "Busy signal. Are you saying you won't help me?"

"I can give you a ride to the scene. Surely you can catch a ride from there."

"Seriously?"

Climbing into the SUV, he turned on the car and waited. A few moments later, she appeared, scooting inside and slamming the door.

He backed out and let her simmer as the silence overcame the cab.

A few minutes into the drive, she cleared her throat.

"I am sorry about earlier. I let my misconceptions cloud my judgement."

"*Humph.*" He shook his head.

"What?"

He shrugged. She didn't do so well with apologies.

"Are you normally so quiet?"

He clenched his jaw, weighing his words. She didn't seem too eager a listener, but he sure didn't want to be on her bad side. Even if Myers was willing to share, she still didn't act interested in being in his corner. And he had to be in on this case.

"Quiet, yes. As far as Myers, I'm sorry, but after the attack, I can't risk anything happening."

"Rick said he posted a four-man team."

"That's not enough."

"You might be right."

He snapped around to see her looking out the window, chewing on the inside of her cheek. "What? Why?"

She shrugged. "The media now knows. An officer was shot, and an ambulance and police cars lit up the scene. If it wasn't that Bolstero guy in the first place, he'll know about the bodies and will do what it takes to cover it all back up again."

Turning back to the road, he sighed.

"I'll have an escort ready to take whatever Dr. Shaver has back to her office so we can get an ID. Are you planning on staying the whole night?"

He nodded.

"Okay, then I'll keep the four-man crew for now. You have my number. You can call if you feel like something's off."

He pulled into the lot.

Why the sudden change in her attitude? Guilt?

Again, she chewed on the inside of her cheek, focused on

the men at the scene before sliding from the car. Guilt didn't fit. He knew that way too well.

He got out and followed her to the two cruisers.

"Keep everyone out. No pictures, no reporters, nothing."

"Detective Myers already informed us."

"I need a cruiser to get back to the office. Detective Myers had an emergency."

One of the officers held up his keys.

"I'll have them return your cruiser when the others come to replace you." She turned to him. "Did you get a phone call?"

"Yeah. Gave my statement and signed a form online. Your investigative team said they'd run the shooting brief to your captain."

"You need a backup?"

"Nope."

"I'll have a new shift here at three in the morning."

He nodded as she rushed to the cruiser and pulled out of the driveway. Guilt or not, he would take it.

Turning to the trench, his stomach dropped. That feeling of dread worked its way up his spine as he stared. It would be an unbearable night.

6

Rushing inside the hospital lobby on the other side of town, Greer hurried up to the obstetrics floor to search for Rick.

The elevator door opened, and she found Rick pacing the floor.

"Rick?" She ran up and gave him a hug.

"Sorry, I'm sorry." His breaths heavy, he squeezed her shoulders.

"It's fine. Just tell me what's going on. No one answered any of my calls."

"She was having some blurred vision and a few back cramps. The doctor got worried it could be Preeclampsia, so she admitted her for a while."

"But she's okay now?"

He nodded. "They've done some tests, and everything looks good."

Greer swallowed the lump in her throat and followed him into the room. Paige's mother and father stood by the bed.

"Greer? What're you doing here?" Paige was pale, her eyes droopy.

She gave her friend a hug. "What do you think? Rick gets all nuts, and I know it's about you." She winked as Paige chuckled.

"I didn't mean to scare him. I was just worried."

"You should've called the second you started having problems instead of on the way to the ER."

"Well, it's all good now."

Paige's mother and father started in on a conversation as she pulled Rick to the side of the room.

"You taking some time?"

His gaze shifted between her and Paige. "She said not to, to save it for when the baby comes. But I don't know."

"It's up to you."

She smiled, seeing the concern in Rick's eyes. It made her hope a man would be that worried for her well-being someday.

"I'll be back tomorrow. They're discharging her in a few hours. As long as she feels good in the morning, I'll be back in."

She nodded and gave a wave to Paige as she left the room, pulling her ringing phone off her belt.

"Bennett."

"How's Myers?"

She frowned at Agent Sullivan's grizzled tone. "His wife is fine. Tests came back normal. Is there a reason you didn't call his cell?"

"Have been, never answered. Glad it's all good."

There was a pause, and as soon as she started to speak, the call ended.

"Rude. Good grief." She shoved the phone back in her pocket.

SITTING IN HER OFFICE, Greer yawned and tapped the phone screen. It was almost eleven, and although she'd been working through the aspects of the case, there was nothing to be found.

Diving into the construction company first seemed the best angle. Since Manos assumed he could cover up the murder of a sheriff and forensic anthropologist for that land, they might all be into something shady together. But *nada*.

Her phone buzzed.

"Bennett."

"You sound tired."

"You sound bored, Agent Sullivan. Is that why you keep calling me?"

"*Humph.* I've been sitting in a car or on the ground for the past twelve hours. You could say I'm bored."

"You want the details I've uncovered?"

"Yes."

She sat up and pulled out a notepad. "Manos is still in the wind, but his assets have been frozen. So, he's either underground or found a way out before we could stop him."

"I'm betting in the wind. Guy took off like a shot."

The sound of a car door slamming echoed through the line.

"The man you shot, Carman Durant, has ties to a few illegal gambling situations, served a little jail time, but nothing for murder. The construction company looks like a bust too."

"Why the construction company?"

Leaning back in the chair, she let out a sigh. "With the attack on the sheriff, I wondered if maybe the construction company had some ties to your cartel or something else shady. If I was part of that crew, I would ask to speak to the sheriff to make sure everything had been cleared before I started back, wouldn't you?"

Why was she so forthcoming with what she found? She let the silence settle refusing to feed him more information.

"I had the same thoughts. Did you check out the money that set it up?"

"The construction company?"

"Yeah, their backers."

She shook her head. "Nothing popped. At least, nothing to me."

"Send me the list."

"Send me your email."

"You don't have it?"

She smirked. "No, I don't have it."

"Okay."

The call ended, and she stared at her phone. Did he really just hang up on her again?

What a jerk.

After getting his text, she typed in his email and attached the spreadsheet and the names of the backers. Then she typed at the top of the page:

Nice talking to you, although your phone manners need some work.

Sending the email, she shut down her computer and turned off the lights. Waving at the night shift officers, she wearily left the building and headed to her car in the lot across the street.

Her phone beeped, and she pulled it off her belt.

Seems we both have manners that need some improvement.

With a grunt, she shoved the phone back on her belt. Pausing, she gazed through the dusty haze of lights that lit the private lot. Something small and white sat on her windshield. Her body tensed.

Her alert went up as she pulled her weapon. Goosebumps pricked her neck as her stomach dropped out. Carefully weaving through the row of cars, she stopped and pulled out her phone, speed-dialing Rick.

"Yeah?"

"What?"

"You called me." The grizzled voice of Agent Sullivan came out, and she groaned as she shoved the phone in her pocket.

Someone was watching, waiting.

"Bennett?" Sullivan's voice echoed in the night air as she slowly approached her vehicle.

A shiver ran down her neck. She tried to turn but ended up in a chokehold. With a yell, she pulled at the arm with her free hand, then elbowed the man in the sides with no effect.

"Stay off the case. Leave it alone," the deep voice asserted into her ear as her hands pulled on the arm cutting off her air.

7

"Bennett!" Gage yelled into the speaker to no avail as he flew down the highway.

It made him physically sick to hear her being attacked over the phone, so far away that he couldn't help. The muffled sound of her grunting had turned into complete silence.

"Hands."

Her voice sounded forever away, but he could hear the sternness in her order. At least the command proved she had a gun aimed at her attacker. Switching to hold her call, he put in the number for the station.

"Lexington PD."

"Get backup to the parking lot. Detective Bennett needs assistance."

"Uh, what?"

"Get someone out there now!" He hung up and switched back to the phone call.

"Put it down."

A muffled voice sounded, but he couldn't understand what was being said. He took the exit off the highway just as gunshots sounded through the speaker.

"Bennett!"

The call ended.

Ten minutes later, he slammed his brakes in front of the police station and parked on the road. Jumping from the car, he sprinted across the lot, his heart pounding. The lights and officers caught his attention as he weaved through to find Bennett leaning against her sedan.

Coming to a stop, he paused and took a breath. Arms crossed, she appeared unharmed as she spoke to an officer.

Her gaze hit his.

Ambling up to the scene, he shoved his hands in his pockets.

"What're you doing here?"

"You called me, remember?"

"It was a mistake. I thought I hit Rick's number. I must've hit redial."

He gave a nod, studying her for injury as she straightened. "Where's the shooter?"

Her jaw tightened as a sigh escaped. "He got away. There's a note though."

Her gloved hand took the offered bag from the police officer. "All it says is 'Stay away.' I guess it could mean anything."

He pulled it from her hands. "You know what it means."

She snatched it back. "I do work other cases, Agent Sullivan." She handed the bag over to the CSI team that had arrived.

He followed her away from the car as she yanked off the gloves.

"You do have video surveillance here, right?"

"Of course. But he managed to fog up the cameras with some kind of paint or foam. We don't have a shot of his face."

Her focus was past his shoulder as she spoke, her fingers mindlessly rubbing back and forth on her neck. With a frown, he stepped closer, lifting her chin to see the bruise already forming across her throat.

She swatted at his hand, then stepped back.

"Did you get checked out?"

"I'm fine."

"I heard gunshots. You or him?"

"Both. He fired first, missing me by a mile, and I followed him out of the lot that way." She pointed toward an alley that wrapped to the back side of the lot. "There was a car, and he jumped in. I shot out the back glass, but the license plate was covered."

"Make or model?"

"Older sedan, probably a Buick or Oldsmobile? White." She rotated her head, rubbing the back of her neck as she spoke.

"Where's Myers?"

Her eyes cut to his for a second before she glanced away. "I … I didn't call him. He's got too much going on right now. I'll let him know in the morning."

As she turned to walk away, she suddenly stopped. "Dr. Shaver." With a groan, she pulled out her phone and put in a call to the anthropologist. "Dr. Shaver? Sorry to wake you. It's Detective Bennett. Have you seen anything suspicious?"

She motioned to a uniformed officer. "Find Dr. Sarah Shaver's address and set up a protection detail at her residence."

"Yes, ma'am." The officer ran off as Bennett continued speaking to the doctor.

"No, I just want to be careful. I had a note on my window to stay away. Someone might be trying to scare me off the case, and I want to make sure you're adequately protected. If you see anything suspicious or strange, let the officer outside know or call me." She held her forehead, her eyes closing for a moment as she spoke.

The woman was tired. But the way she moved, taking

charge of the scene, there was no way she would leave until it was all detailed and complete. At least, he figured that fit her personality—in control, on top of everything, and leading the charge.

He muffled a smile.

"Thanks." She hung up and headed back to the car. "Go back to your scene, Agent Sullivan. Nothing you can do here."

She pushed past him, her dress pants sitting nicely on her curves as the sleeves of her button-up top sat rolled up on her arms. The jacket she had worn earlier was draped over another sedan, and her hair was now piled up on top of her head.

He shook his head and strode back to his SUV. As he opened the door, he paused. There was no way he could leave. If she wasn't calling Myers to watch her back, he needed to stay. Not that she would let him—she seemed way too eager to get him out of here.

Sliding into the seat, he turned off the overhead light and sat in the dark with the door open. If his partner was being threatened, he wouldn't let him out to dry. So, if she wasn't going to call Myers, the same applied here. Now that there were adequate officers at the trench, it was much more secure, and a new shift would coming in soon.

Detective Bennett was a hot-tempered, stand-offish detective who would rather jump off a cliff than allow someone like him to be involved in an investigation. But after what Myers mentioned about her past and seeing her move around the crime scene, he found an in-control detective with experience and a need for answers.

With a smirk, he leaned back as he continued to watch her work. His mind drifted, and he shook his head.

"Don't do it, man."

But it was too late. The beautiful woman he had found attractive with a bad personality suddenly took a turn and had become the woman he found to be a winning combination.

Now, how was he going to be able to work with her? And would she agree to work with him?

8

G lancing over her shoulder, Greer noticed the black SUV still parked in the road.

"What does he think he's doing?" She signed the evidence forms and handing them back to the officer. "Be sure and find the slug he shot at me. We might be able to match it to another case or weapon in the system."

"Yes, ma'am."

The techs searched each car in the lot, attempting to light up the shadows of the cars using flashlights. It would take all night to find the slug like this.

Standing in the spot she was attacked, Greer went through the motions and aimed her finger in the direction of the shooter, trying to calculate the angle.

"High or low?"

She jumped at Agent Sullivan's voice. "I thought I told you to go back to your scene?"

He simply shrugged. "High or low?"

With a sigh, she turned back around and tried to remember where the sound of her attacker's bullet echoed from.

"I can't even remember." She chewed on her cheek for a moment. "I want to say to my right?" She turned to the empty lot. "Great, we'll be looking all night."

Agent Sullivan pulled out his phone. "Come on."

Using his cell phone's light app, he swept it across the ground. With a grunt, she turned on her flashlight and followed, jogging to catch up.

"I might be wrong. I can't really remember, and if a car was driving by, it could've messed up what I heard."

"I don't think a car was driving by."

"Why not?"

"I've been here almost an hour, not one car has driven by." He suddenly stopped and turned to look at the scene. "He had a handgun?"

"Yeah, missed by a mile."

He nodded and narrowed his eyes. "He was by the bumper of the red car two spots ahead of yours?"

She nodded as his gaze flicked to hers for a second. He looked over the path, tracing the route with his hand, stopping at newspaper stand within the lot. Shining his light, the cracked glass revealed a tear in the newspaper that sat against the frame.

"I think we found it." He took a few pictures with his phone as she called the techs over.

He shined his light inside while they both leaned down. In the back, a bullet was sticking out, wedged in the metal.

She smiled. "Great!"

His eyes widened a moment before he straightened, then they moved out of the way for the techs to get to work.

"Hopefully, that will give us something, because there's no way I can pick him out of a lineup." She started back across the street when Sullivan stepped in beside her, bumping into her shoulder.

"What did he look like?"

"Black stocking hat pulled down low with a black hoodie on, almost covering his eyes, scraggly beard. Caucasian. About five eleven and maybe two or two-twenty. He was muscled though," she trailed off and rubbed her neck, wincing at the bruise that would probably show in full force tomorrow morning.

"You were lucky."

She scoffed. "What, you don't think I could defend myself?"

Taking hold of her wrist, he gently pulled her to a stop. "No, because if he wanted to hurt you, I think he would've. He's looking to scare you, deter you. He had that handgun the whole time, why grab you? If he really wanted you gone, he would've shot you the second you came out of the station. You need to be more careful."

She pulled her arm away. That was the most he had spoken since discussing the case.

"You really should go back to your crime scene. Rick and I will be out early."

As she walked away, she felt his presence from behind. Stopping suddenly, she turned and found him towering over her.

"What?"

"Did the doctor say anything?"

Her anger eased at the look on his face. He was hurting. His brows knit together, his green eyes empty and desperate.

"No. She said it was too late to get started on what she had. She managed to pull two bodies out that were in proximity and intertwined. In the morning, she'll run the dentals against what you sent her first, then move on to other databases. If she calls, I'll call you. Deal?"

He gave a nod and trudged to his SUV.

An hour later, Greer watched through the window as the crime scene tape was removed and she finished filing her paperwork. Tomorrow, well today, now that it was well after one in the morning, would be a long day.

Descending the stairs of the building, Sullivan's black SUV sat right across from her car.

With a groan, she hustled across the street, gripping her jacket and shivering under the cold breeze. Sliding into the car, she turned the key and jacked the heat up. Her phone's ringtone went off. Looking up, the glare of Agent Sullivan appeared as her lights lit the front glass.

He nodded.

"Yes, Agent Sullivan?"

"You should've had someone escort you out."

"Why? You really think the same guy would try again right in front of the police station?"

"Criminals aren't that smart. Besides, he attacked you once in front of the station. I don't think he's deterred."

She rolled her eyes and put the car in gear. "I'm going home. Go back to your crime scene."

Hanging up, she backed out and headed to the highway. Glancing in her mirror, she found the SUV following.

"Go easy, he's being, nice. He came to help you and didn't hang up earlier when you called."

Hearing him call her name during her ordeal had given her strength. She knew he was listening and that hopefully he would call in some backup, which he did.

She sighed. Maybe she should've thanked him for that.

The problem was, it seemed ill-advised to trust someone she didn't know, especially someone who had formally worked for the FBI. Her mind suddenly kicked into gear.

"He wants in on the case."

Hitting the steering wheel, she sped up and gritted her teeth. All he wanted was to make sure she would keep him involved. Well, he was sucking up to the wrong person. Rick would be his contact from now on. She didn't even want to look at him.

Turning on her street, her eyes narrowed at the truck sitting in front of her home.

"You have got to be kidding me."

Parking in the garage, she walked out in disbelief.

"Hey." Thomas met her in the driveway as Sullivan's SUV drove past and parked across the street.

"What're you doing here?"

"I heard through the grapevine you were attacked. You didn't call. You could've called me." He reached out, and she stepped back.

"Look, I don't need to call you. We're not a couple anymore."

"Are you sure you're okay?"

Cutting her eyes to the SUV, she motioned to the garage. "Let's go inside."

Through the garage, she shut the door and then saddled up to the bar in the adjoining kitchen. Tossing her keys on the Formica countertop, she leaned in and watched Thomas.

He stood with his arms crossed. "Just because we're not together right now doesn't mean I don't care about you."

She sighed. "Thomas, why the push to get married? We had only gone out on a handful of actual dates and were attracted to each other, but that's not the basis for a marriage. Can you honestly say you love me?"

He collapsed on the barstool and swung it around to face her. "Well, I'm not saying I don't love you."

"Not the same thing. When I do get married, I plan on doing it once, for keeps."

He narrowed his eyes. "Greer, have you ever wanted more in your life?"

"We've discussed my past enough for you to know the answer to that."

"Well, what if I told you once we get married, you could have pretty much whatever life you wanted?"

The pit of her stomach dropped out. "What does that mean?"

He stepped around the bar in front of her, leaning back against the edge. "I have an inheritance. It comes to me when I'm forty or when I get married, whichever is first. Honestly, I'm tired of waiting. You and I, we have something. Do you not think we could make it work?"

Her face heated. "An inheritance? You want to get married for money?"

"Not just money. My father's estate, his yacht, his foundations, and stock interests. More money than you would probably know what to do with."

"I can't believe this. I thought you were this great, stand-up guy with morals, with the same ideals as me, and you—you want to get married so you never have to work ever again. Why don't you just grab the next woman you see and marry her?"

"It doesn't work that way." His tone went stern. "My step-mother has already started an appeal to get me kicked out. I mess up once, just once, and I'm out. My lawyer has insisted this isn't a get rich quick scheme. I can't just make a deal with someone."

"I think it's time for you to leave."

"Greer."

"No. You need to go." Hustling past him, she unlocked the front door and flung it open. "Don't worry about coming by again."

He paused in front of her, and she held up her hand.

"Don't. This is over. I'm not willing to settle for money. No matter how well we get along."

Jaw clenched, he took off out the door.

Leaned against the doorframe, she crossed her arms and watched him leave. Thomas had been a good friend, a man she cared about deeply. Love? No, but it really hurt when he left the first time.

But this? How did she not see this? When he proposed so soon, pressuring her so much about marriage so quickly, it was strange. But she never thought it would be something like this.

Her gaze went to the street, Sullivan's SUV still parked. Glaring at the driver's side window, knowing Sullivan was in there even if she couldn't see him, she pointed down the street, mouthing "Leave."

The car didn't move.

With a grunt, she pulled the door to and wrapped her arms around her body as she marched across her lawn and to the road. The SUV door opened, and Sullivan slid out, slamming the door and striding toward her.

"What do you think you're doing?"

"Walking you back to your house." He pulled at her arm to turn her around.

"Hey." She pulled away, stopping in the middle of the street.

His head on a swivel, he pushed into her personal space. "I know you understand the tactics of a protection detail. But for a woman who was just assaulted and threatened, you're not taking things very seriously. Get inside."

Too irritated to argue, she brushed past him, stomping to her house with him in tow. Climbing the steps, she opened the door and tried to slam it shut, but his hand gripped the edge and pushed it open.

"You need to leave. I don't like being watched."

"You were attacked."

"I'm fine. In fact, I bet you're drawing much more attention to the situation by being here."

"I'm not the one arguing in the yard at one in the morning."

Fisting her hands, she barely contained the anger pulsing through her body. "Leave."

His gaze moved from hers, glancing down and he nodded, turning to step through the front door.

"And I mean leave this street. I don't want to see you here again, Agent Sullivan."

He barely paused as she spoke, then slammed the door shut on his way out.

Anger rushed through as her body shuddered, heat flooding her cheeks and neck.

Who did he think he was? He wasn't even here for the FBI or Homeland, that badge sure meant nothing to her.

Shucking off her jacket, she threw it on the couch before locking all the doors and setting the alarm. Stomping down the hallway, she then kicked her shoes off in her closet and slammed the door.

She started the shower then paused at the reflection in the mirror. Sheriff Tillman's words echoed in her head and a wave of sadness rushed over.

Did she really not smile?

With a groan, she undressed and eased under the warm water. The heat warmed her body as she leaned into the tile, working to slow her mind and the pounding in her heart.

"God, ease my mind."

This town was where God had waited on her. In the muck and sadness of her life, she found peace and happiness. If it hadn't been for God's intervention, there was no way she would've been able to handle the life changes that hit her after college.

Sighing, she shook off the memories and decided sleep was more important than a walk down memory lane. After drying and dressing, she brushed her teeth and hair and settled in bed for the night.

"Lord, please watch over Rick and Paige and the baby, keep them safe and protected." The hurt look on Sullivan's face washed through her mind. "And give Sullivan some peace, Lord. He sure needs it."

9

"Well, you did a great job, man. Just great." Gage climbed back up into the SUV.

In his haste to get her inside, he let the anger of her attitude get to him. Then there was that guy she was arguing with in the driveway.

Who was he? Their voices had been loud enough to hear her mention they were no longer together. Why would any guy let her get away?

"Possibly her anger issues."

Sighing, he leaned his chair back and kept his eyes focused on the road ahead of him. The only problem, that's not really where his focus sat.

"Good grief, let it go."

It had been at least three years since he had a date, one of the many reasons he'd moved to Homeland last year. Before that, he had lots of dates—first dates. Seemed he could rarely get in for a second, much less a third.

This job was supposed to change that. Rubbing his pained shoulder—another reminder of how far he'd fallen, how much he'd given up after losing Rachel.

Shaking his head, he settled in for the night. There was no way he would leave Bennett without protection. Because no matter what she said, there was something going on, and she was the target now. A target he wasn't willing to let out of his sight.

As Greer strode into the office, coffee in hand, Rick met her at the door.

"Why didn't you call me?"

She furrowed her brow and shushed his heated tone. "It's way too early, and I haven't finished my coffee."

"It's almost nine. What happened, Greer?"

She pushed past him with a yawn and sat at her desk. "Look, you were busy. There was nothing you could do anyway. The guy took off, and that was that."

Rick hovered.

"I'm sorry. I tried to call you, but I hit the wrong number."

"Who did you call?"

She sighed. He would never let her live it down.

"I had just gotten a phone call from Agent Sullivan. I thought I hit your speed dial, but apparently, I hit redial." Groaning at the chuckle, she glared. "That's enough. Have you done any police work today?"

"Actually, while you slept in, I found Manos."

"Really?"

Rick nodded as he leaned against the desk. "Yep, they're bringing him in as we speak. Apparently, he thought he could get away by taking a bus with a fake ID."

She chuckled and sat her coffee down, then leaned back to look at him. "Rick, do you think I smile enough?"

He shrugged. "What's enough?"

"I don't know."

"This about Thomas?"

"No, but he was waiting for me when I got home. I finally got everything out of him about why he was so intent on getting married."

"Oh?"

"Apparently, he has an inheritance. He can't access it until he turns forty or gets married, whichever comes first. He said he's tired of waiting."

"Ouch." Rick grimaced. "Well, how much?"

She rolled her eyes.

"You were worried you had made the right choice—now you know."

"Yeah, but how did I miss that?"

"You don't ever get the full picture, G. You know that."

She sighed as she pulled her buzzing phone from her belt. "Bennett."

"Any word?"

She huffed at Agent Sullivan's stiff tone. "Oh, good morning to you, Agent Sullivan. Look, you need to lose my number. Don't think I didn't notice this morning. If you want to talk, you can talk to Rick."

She tossed Rick her phone as she stood and grabbed her mug, making her way to the breakroom for more coffee. Between Rick pestering her about Sullivan, and Sullivan pestering her about being attacked, coffee was the only thing that would keep her from going off again.

"Lord, give me some grace. Please."

"Uh, what's going on Agent Sullivan?"

Gage rubbed his forehead at Rick's irritated voice. "Look, I was going to call, but I figured ... with your wife."

"She's fine. What is it you need to talk to me about?"

"You hear about last night?"

"Yes, but obviously not all of it."

"No, not all of it. I think she's being targeted."

"Why?"

"She accidentally called me before she was attacked. I heard the scuffle and called in backup. When I got there, she'd blown off the fact the guy targeted her car with a note and was waiting on her. I think there's much more going on."

Rick was silent for a moment. "Thanks for the heads up. What did she mean by this morning?"

"She wouldn't call you, wouldn't let anyone help. I followed her home and stayed outside her house until early this morning. Obviously not early enough," he added.

"I appreciate that. She won't accept my help, and as far as being targeted, this case is the only heavy thing we've had lately."

"I've got a bad feeling something else is up. Guy attacks her from behind then later decides to shoot at her and misses by a mile? It doesn't make sense."

Rick sighed. "Yeah, I see your point. Call me if you need anything more, I'll run interference. Least I can do for you."

"Not a problem. Well, not a big one." He smiled as Rick laughed. "Talk to you later."

"Yeah, bye."

The quietness he had discovered with Homeland had been his refuge—his escape from the demons he felt came out when he spoke when that wit of his got him into trouble.

But being here, right now, an end in sight and the discovery of Rachel, he really had no idea how to deal.

Then he went and opened up his big mouth once more. When was he going to learn?

10

"Glad you got in your chuckles for the day." Greer sat back down at the desk.

Rick stood, handing her the phone. "Look, you should've called me. In any case, I'm glad he put up with you long enough to watch over you. He thinks you're being targeted."

"I'm not being targeted. That guy would've probably put a note on both our cars, but yours wasn't there."

"Agent Sullivan seems convinced." Rick stared at her for a moment. "What's with giving him such a hard time?"

"You know why."

"I know your past and why you're here. But that doesn't include Sullivan. In case you haven't noticed, he's with Homeland and is here for his sister—without the FBI task force behind him. You need to be nicer."

She scoffed. "He's arrogant and rude."

"Pot, kettle."

"Cut it out. Has he not been rude to you?"

Rick shrugged. "Not really. Just quiet. You should appreciate that." Rick smirked as she threw a waded-up ball of paper at him. "Hey, just speaking the truth."

"I would appreciate a quiet partner. That sounds great." She chuckled.

"Hey, Myers? Where you want him?"

A state trooper entered with a cuffed and obviously unhappy Mr. Manos.

"Interrogation one. I'll be right there."

Greer raised an eyebrow. "*You'll* be right there?"

"Let me take a shot. I know the area and how the small town works better than you. I might be able to play a card or two for sympathy. And we both know you're not in a mood to give anyone sympathy."

She nodded as she logged on to her computer. "Better get something about the shooter, or Patrick will come after you."

Rick's chuckle echoed down the hall as she grinned.

THE MORNING FELT WASTED as Greer leaned back with a yawn. She had struck out with every phone call trying to locate other men who were associated with Manos' business.

He was a quick study, buying up all the properties in small, rural areas. And here in Tennessee, land was ripe for the picking. Putting up small dollar shops and hiring as few workers as possible, he was making a killing.

Cupping her chin, she wondered why he lost his cool about the property. Nothing could be done until the scene was cleared. Why was it such a big deal to him?

"Well, we got a few things," Rick said as he fell into his chair opposite her.

"What'd he say?"

"He won't give us the shooter's name. He's worried about being labeled a snitch and getting taken out in prison."

"So, whoever it is has connections. That's not good. Maybe

he's not really running the company and has a boss he reports to."

"I thought of that, but he says it's all his money that provides the funds to purchase land and build." Rick shrugged. "Anyway, he said the reason things went south is because the person he bought the land from threatened him. Told him if he didn't clear out the cops, he would be the next one in that trench."

"But the bank owns the land. I followed up with them this morning just to see if anyone had called and asked about it."

He shook his head. "That's his story."

"You bet it's a story." She leaned back in her chair.

"The lawyer is still talking to him. I've told him he's an accomplice to attempted murder of a county and federal agent. The judge won't go easy, and the only way he gets a lesser sentence is if he gives us the shooter."

"No details about the seller?"

"Nope, says that's a dead end too. They'll outright kill him and his family."

"Great, just great. We have no connection between the landowner and the Bolstero cartel. So, until we get the ID on the remains, I'm not sure what else we can do."

"Myers, a word."

She puckered at the sound of Mansfield's tone. "He doesn't sound happy."

"Yeah, well, I can see his point. I'm not thrilled either. The doctor call?"

She shook her head, glancing at the clock that read a little before eleven. "Nope, I'll give her a little longer." Her cell rang as Rick stood. "Speak of the devil."

Rick nodded and headed toward Mansfield, who was waiting in the hallway.

"Hey, Dr. Shaver. Good to hear from you."

"You too. After last night, I've been worried all morning."

"Sorry. Like I said, it was just a precaution."

"Yeah, well, I'm not usually involved in any precautions. Anyway, I wanted to let you know I got a match for two of the bodies. Rachel Sullivan and Havier Martinez."

She closed her eyes a moment, feeling an ache move through her chest.

"You still there?"

"Yeah, I'm here. Thanks for the heads up. Do you have any ideas on cause of death?"

"The female was blunt force trauma. But the other, looks like something more … torturous. I found nicks on the bone in several places, and based on the staining of the cervical vertebrae, I'm going to guess a nick to the carotid artery. I'm getting a second opinion."

Greer sighed. "Okay, time of death?"

"I'm going to call in a specialist about the fibers and a few other items we found in the grave. Hopefully, that'll give us a definitive timeline. The date on Rachel Sullivan's records said seven years ago?"

"Yes, seven years." she confirmed.

"That seems about right. All right, well, I should have the other two ready soon."

"Really? You were up early."

A throaty chuckle echoed over the line. "Daybreak. I couldn't really sleep last night anyway, so as soon as the sun came up, I was there and ready. My intern and I had the other two bodies loaded by nine. They were intertwined like these first two. I still have to do some sifting through the dirt, but I'll be confirming the dentals of the other two as soon as we finish cleaning them up."

"Thanks. I appreciate you working so diligently on this."

"Well, that guy deserves a break."

"What guy?"

"The Homeland guy. He saved my life and told me the other day he suspected his sister was there."

"Rachel was his sister? I didn't realize that."

"I'll be glad to get him the body for some closure. When I figure everything out, I'll call or email you."

"Thanks." Greer hung up and snatched the keys from the desk.

Time for a drive.

Telling Agent Sullivan about his sister wasn't what she wanted to do. As much as she would rather Rick handle this, he was busy, and Sullivan deserved an answer—in person.

After stopping for a quick snack at her favorite bakery, she headed to the crime scene thirty minutes away. Pulling in, she parked, then took a deep breath. His SUV was facing the road, the windows down on both sides. Sullivan sat in the driver's seat with his head back and an arm out the window.

Agent Sullivan lacked tact. Although, he probably thought the same of her. He annoyed and aggravated her to no end. But right now, it wasn't about her feelings or their turf war. It was about his sister. His murdered sister.

She grabbed the drinks and the bag of pastries and made her way to the passenger side of the SUV.

Silence greeted her as she slid inside, shoved the drinks in the cupholder, and settled on the seat.

"It's her."

She nodded as she set the bag in between them. Pulling out her favorite glazed donut, she sat back and took a bite. The silence lingered as she let him absorb the truth. Taking a sip of her iced mocha, Sullivan let out a deep breath and slid down from the SUV.

With the windows down and the chilly October air moving through, she zipped up her jacket and ignored the shiver.

"Hey, yeah, got confirmation. Can you call? ... Thanks."

Swallowing the last bite, she felt the pain of losing someone and not having any details—nothing except the bitter information from her mother and the remains to put into the ground.

What kind of father just leaves? And if he didn't leave on his own, what kind of enemy did he have?

The sound of the door made her jump, jarring her from the memories.

"You good?"

"Yep." She kept her gaze out the window.

"The other body?" He dug through the bag and pulled out a large fritter.

"Havier Martinez." She cleared her throat. "Dr. Shaver's got a few things from the dirt she wants to look at to confirm the timeline."

"You think I'm wrong?"

She shook her head without looking up, taking a sip of her drink. "Nope, I think you're spot on. But we need to build a case."

He sighed. "Sorry, it's ... I don't know what it is. I knew it was her, but to hear it confirmed, it's a hit."

"I get it. It's still a surprise when that last bit of doubt is erased." She leaned forward and searched for another donut from the bag.

"You talk to your boss?"

"Rick is right now. Getting everything in order for you to officially hand off the case to us."

"Hand off?" His heated tone caused her to sigh. "This is *my* case."

She faced him, taking a breath at the red rushing on his cheeks. Wanting this to go well, she paused before she spoke.

"I get that this is your case. But you're a brother of the victim. You can't be involved. Remember you said the guy's lawyer was slick? Anything you touch will be compromised.

Rick and I will handle the case, and you will be there to guide us. You know this case better than anyone else."

He turned to stare out the window, his face and neck red. Clenching his jaw, he nodded.

"You'll be in this with us, Sullivan. We won't leave you out."

She grabbed her drink and opened the door, sliding down out of the SUV and into the chilly air.

"WELL, HOW DID HE TAKE IT?"

"Better than I thought he would." Greer tossed the keys on the desk. "I told him we'd let him in, but we had to do the casework."

Rick nodded. "Good. Mansfield was pretty clear, Sullivan can be there, but if he gets a hold of anything, it can mess with the outcome."

She collapsed in her chair. "So, cold case file, huh? I don't think I've ever worked one."

He chuckled. "Around here, we take it on as if it were brand new. Start from the beginning."

"And the beginning is Hermann Bolstero."

11

P acing the wood line, Gage found himself at ease, and yet, frustration loomed. To finally lay Rachel to rest was a blessing. How many families with missing members don't get to accomplish that?

But Bolstero was at the center of it all, and his gut told him the fight to prosecute wouldn't be easy—if even possible—after all this time. But the man had to pay for what he did.

Shaking his head, he pulled the ringing phone from his pocket.

"Sullivan."

"Hey, Mom and Dad want to know when they can set up the service."

He blew out a deep breath at his brother Max's question. "It's an active crime scene, the case will be re-opened, so I'm not sure when that can happen. How are they doing?"

"Actually, they're pretty relieved."

He turned at the sound of a car pulling into the drive. It was another black SUV. "Look, I've got to go. I've been told I'll be in on the investigation, so as soon as I know something I can talk to you about, I'll give you a call."

"Sounds good. Later, man."

"Yeah." He hung up as men in suits got out and headed his way.

The sight of a familiar face made him shake his head as he approached them.

"Gage Sullivan. Never thought I'd see the day I would have to tell you, you were right."

He chuckled and nodded. "How's it going, Dwight?" He shook hands, and Dwight pulled off his sunglasses.

"It was going good until we were sent out here to see what the fuss was all about. This is my partner, Ross Shepherd."

Gage nodded, his gaze quickly moving back to Dwight. "You taking the case?" He hated to think that would happen, but at least if it did, Dwight was a good enough guy that he would keep Gage in the loop.

Dwight only shrugged. "Not sure. Boss just wants me to ask around and see what they've got so far. It's a pretty cold case. But if you're right, and there's a shot at Bolstero, you know we'll be on top of it."

"I can give you the unofficial situation."

Dwight nodded and took out his phone. "Shoot."

"Land was being excavated by a construction company when they found human remains. Sheriff and then a forensic anthropologist showed, and she just identified two of the bodies based on dental records."

"Who?"

"Havier Martinez and," he paused, swallowing the lump in his throat, "my sister, Rachel."

Dwight's gaze shot up to him. "Sorry, man."

"At least she's been found. Saves my mom and dad from wondering anymore."

"Did they look into the previous owner and the construction company?"

He nodded. "For those details, you might want to talk to

Detectives Myers and Bennett. I'm not willing to step on toes when they've told me they'll be keeping me in the loop."

"Okay, we'll head that way. Any more bodies in there?"

"I know there are more, I'm assuming two. I sent the dentals of the four I assumed it would be, so we'll see if I'm right."

Dwight nodded, then shoved his hands in his pockets. "I'm really sorry. This is rough. But we'll get him."

Gage sighed. "I want to think so. But I'm not so sure this case is going to go down like you think. The detectives are— let's just say they're not fans of the FBI. Watch yourself."

Dwight just grinned. "You know me. I turn on the charm, and it's all good. Is one of them female?" Dwight's eyebrows rose as Gage nodded confirmation. "Then we're in."

He chuckled, wanting to warn his friend, but really wanting to see what happened between him and Bennett.

"I'll follow." Nodding to the men, Gage headed to his SUV, cranked the engine and waited for Dwight and his new partner to back out.

Chuckling to himself, he followed the FBI to the PD thirty minutes away.

"This should be good."

"Excuse me?" Greer felt her face flame as the smooth-talking FBI looked her over, making her skin crawl. "I think you need to step back."

"Look, I'm just here to see what you have." Special Agent Dwight Carver flashed his grin again.

Crossing her arms, she took an even breath to calm herself. "Even if we had something, which besides the IDs Sullivan told you about, we don't. And it's not my place. You can speak with my captain."

"It would be a lot quicker—"

"No." She cut off the other FBI guy with a glare. "I'm not interested in quicker. See, around here, we do things by the book. If you want this case, you're going to have to discuss that with my boss. Then, if you don't get it, you leave." She glared between the men as Rick came up behind them.

"Problem?"

"FBI, They want the case," she said between gritted teeth.

"Oh, then right this way. Captain's been waiting." Rick gave her a wink and showed the men the way to Mansfield's office.

The agents followed Rick as she went back to her desk. A chuckle came from Sullivan, and she paused. Hand over his mouth, she could see the laughter in his eyes. Huh? Maybe buttoned-down Agent Sullivan wasn't so surly after all.

"What's so funny?"

He shook his head as he pocketed his hands. "Nothing."

"Then why are you laughing? You realize they take the case, you might not be in ..." It suddenly dawned on her. "You know one or both of them?"

Sullivan nodded. "Dwight and I used to be partners."

She collapsed in her chair. "What a wonderful pleasure that must've been."

"It's just that, Dwight is usually pretty smooth. Thinks highly of himself when it comes to ladies."

Her gaze jumped between his bright green eyes and the computer screen. "So?"

"Well, let's just say I don't think he's ever been shot down like that before." His throaty chuckle came out, and she let a smirk loose.

"Guys who act like that drive me crazy. It takes much more than a smile."

Focused on the screen, it took her a minute to realize Sullivan was standing next to her. He moved to sit on the edge of her desk, facing her.

Her jaw clenched. "Problem?"

"Nope."

"Then what's with invading my space?"

Nicer. Rick said she needed to be nicer.

"What does it take?"

"For what?" She furrowed her brows and leaned back in her chair.

His hands clasped in front of him, the beginnings of a smile on his face and more than a shadow across his chin, she felt admiration rise. Man, Agent Sullivan was attractive. It wasn't that she hadn't noticed before, but in her anger and annoyance, it just hadn't crossed her mind.

"What's it take, then? The guy you were with the other night was very similar to Dwight."

"Thomas never flashed his smile to get his way."

"Really? I don't think I believe that."

"Why not?"

He shrugged. "I'm a guy."

Shaking her head, she tried to hide the smile that was suddenly coming out.

"A smile? Really? Two within twenty-four hours, I must be lucky."

Shifting her eyes, she felt the heat rising from her neck and onto her cheeks. When had she smiled at him before?

Changing the subject was necessary, especially since he was looking down on her with those bright green eyes and a smile on his lips.

"Now that you have your ID, did you get yourself set up in a hotel?" Her gaze shifted to the computer screen at the email that popped up.

"I will—if you guys keep the case."

She nodded. Opening the email from Dr. Shaver, she bit the inside of her cheek again.

"That's your thinking face. What's up?"

Her eyes snapped to his. There was no way he knew that.

"Just got an email from Dr. Shaver. Apparently only one of the dental films matched. The other is without a name."

"What? I didn't even know she got them all out." He stood to look at the screen, looking over her shoulder. "She was there when I arrived this morning, then left early."

Ignoring the smell of his cologne and the tingling sensation working through her neck as he leaned in, she tried to focus on the screen.

"She told me earlier she couldn't sleep, so she was up at dawn. She and her intern got to work. These bodies were intertwined like the others. It took her less time to get them up since everything was ready. Plus, having the films probably helped," she added. "Gabby Brown matched, but the other is an unknown male."

"That doesn't make sense."

A clatter caught her attention. She looked up as the FBI agents leaving the Captain's office with scowls on their faces.

"Problem?" She leaned against her desk with a grin as they paused.

Sullivan's friend glared, then shifted his gaze to Sullivan.

"I need a word."

"That bad?" Sullivan sounded amused, which made her smile bigger.

"Gage."

He followed with a chuckle, but not before he turned and gave her a wink over his shoulder.

Hmm. The man she knew today was completely different from the man she met yesterday. She wondered if that was her fault or his. Although, to be fair, after a shootout and the fact he was facing down the remains of his sister, she really should cut him some slack.

"Hey."

She turned her attention to Rick. "So, what's the verdict?"

"Well, we've got the case. Should it lean into active cartel members, we have to clear it with the FBI. And if it intercedes with their investigation, we might have to drop it."

"Of course. At least Mansfield went to bat for us."

Rick took his chair and leaned forward on his desk. "Greer, you realize this case can easily stay cold. After all, a lot of the players are probably already incarcerated, dead, or long gone."

"Yes, I realize that. But think of Sullivan and his family. They deserve us to do everything we can to bring Rachel's killer to justice."

Rick nodded. "You playing nice out here?"

She turned back to her computer. "Actually, I was updating Sullivan on the good doctor's findings."

"Which are?"

"Only one of the dental sets matched. We have one unknown male."

"How did he take that?" Rick stood to come look at the email.

She shrugged. "He was surprised. I was about to get into detail when his buddies came out."

"So, he did know them, huh?" Rick let out a chuckle.

She nodded. Chewing the inside of her cheek, she found herself wondering about Gage. She liked that name. It fit him well.

"How did Ga—I mean, Sullivan determine who besides his sister would be in that grave?"

Rick's eyebrow rose a fraction as a smile came across his face. "I don't know. Maybe you should ask him."

She rolled her eyes. Good grief, Rick was going overboard about a man neither of them knew. And the fact he used to be FBI, used to work with the jerk she had just met—she was not too interested in the character of Gage Sullivan.

He did, however, have a nice name. And he smelled nice. Tapping her pen on the desk she sighed. And he did have really strong-looking arms ...

"Something you want to share?"

She glared at Rick and his smile. "No, would you like to share?"

Rick only shook his head.

It was going to be a long day.

12

"A little heads-up about the captain would've been nice, man." Dwight was red-faced and fuming by the time they got outside.

Gage chuckled. "Look, I've never even seen the captain or talked to him. I was more interested in the little conversation you had with Bennett."

Dwight glared up as he paused. "You knew, huh?"

"I knew she wouldn't fall for your smile and the usual demeanor you have when a pretty woman is in the room."

Dwight shook his head. "Well, we're out. Boss said she doesn't want us wasting our time on cold cases right now. If it strays into cartel territory, and there's enough evidence to take a run at someone, then we'll team up."

"Team up, yeah. That I would like to see." He grinned as Dwight sized him up.

"So, how long you two been friendly?"

He pulled his wrist up and glanced at his watch. "About ten minutes."

Dwight laughed as he slapped his shoulder. "Oh sorry, man. Wrong shoulder."

"Very funny. It's good. I told you that wasn't why."

"You shouldn't have left. We could use you."

"Not my thing anymore." He shook his head. "I needed slower, I need time. How much free time you have Dwight? Ross?"

The two men shrugged.

"Exactly. After Rachel disappeared, then I was injured, my entire perspective changed. And now, I'm good."

Dwight's eyes narrowed. "You are different, I'll give you that." Dwight slapped his arm again, waking up to his SUV. "I'll see you later. Call me the next time you're up in Indy, maybe we can catch up."

He nodded as the two men made their way across the parking lot. Looking back at the building, he rubbed his neck and took a breath. The case, yeah. He needed to focus on the case. Although that smile of hers was more than appealing.

"Nah." He ascended the steps to the building.

Thinking there was more there than a simple smile and friendly conversation was ridiculous. After all, she probably smiled at everyone she talked to. He'd just brought out her irritation during almost all their other conversations.

Letting out a deep breath, he saw Bennett tapping her pen on the desk and staring at the computer screen.

"Already stuck?"

She jumped and turned, the start of a smile on her lips before she regained focus.

Man. He was in trouble.

"How did you get the names?"

"What names?"

"The four you believed to be buried?"

He took the file folder from her desk that he had given her yesterday.

"I already went through that. Rachel is the only one that tracks."

Pulling out a set of pages, he sat them in front of her and leaned over the desk.

"When I started digging and found out about the trucks—"

"Which is a story for another time."

Gage looked up to Rick. "Yeah, okay." He sighed. "Rachel wasn't alone. She was the only mole, but she told me she had a good friend on the inside she trusted."

"Really? That seems like a bad idea," Bennett said. She peered up at him with a grimace. "Sorry."

"No, I said the same thing. But apparently, she trusted her completely. I dug around and discovered she was the younger sister of Bolstero's right-hand man."

"When did you dig around?"

He straightened a moment to look at Rick. "About a year or so before they disappeared. I worked hard to keep her identity safe. I made sure."

"But the woman's name you gave us was Brown. Your notes ..." She took the folder from him and started flipping pages.

The fact she had studied his case file and knew the players made him smile.

"Richard Maxwell. How are they brother and sister?"

"She changed her last name. Maxwell was good with it. Said it would protect her from his enemies."

"So, she obviously knew what her brother was up to."

He nodded at Bennett. "Anyway, she was on the outside of the business and talked often to Rachel. The last time I spoke with her, she mentioned Maxwell and Bolstero having a falling out." He pulled the transcript on the second page. "I documented it."

Pointing to it, Bennett leaned in and the scent of whatever perfume she used wafted around him. He took a step back, trying to keep from grinning like an idiot.

"Oh, I thought I went through this." She took the pages and leafed through them.

"So, things were going downhill?"

He turned his attention to Rick as Bennett read the pages. "Yeah. When Rachel disappeared, Gabby was the first person I went to, but she was missing too."

"And Havier Martinez?"

"He was documented as missing the week before Rachel disappeared. He was set to testify against Richard Maxwell. The police had him in protective custody, but he somehow slipped through."

Bennett leaned back in her chair. "Okay. So, how did Gabby disappear?"

Shoving his hands in his pockets, he leaned against Bennett's desk so he could see both detectives. "Apparently, Martinez was a good friend of Bolstero. They had known each other for a long time and had a history. Martinez wasn't there to prosecute Bolstero, just Maxwell. So, Bolstero was angry Maxwell had put his friend in that position."

Bennett's eyebrows furrowed as her mind worked. A smile crossed his face. She sure looked cute when she was deep in thought.

"So Gabby was retaliation? Bolstero making his point by killing the guy's sister?"

Gage nodded at Bennett.

"And the last name? The only one that didn't match?"

He turned to Rick. "Marlon Jones. He was one of Maxwell's hit men. When things go bad, he's usually the one Maxwell got to clean up the mess. I assumed he would be there since he's missing too."

"Dr. Shaver said the unknown remains are a Caucasian male, six three and broad, probably Norwegian descent."

He stood to look at the email on her computer screen and nodded. "No one matching that description is on Bolstero's crew. No one in Maxwell's pocket either—at least, that I know of."

"Myers? The lawyer wants to talk."

"Who's lawyer?"

"We hauled in Niko Manos. He's not talking." Rick stood and headed toward the hallway.

"Manos says he was threatened by the previous landowners to get the cops off the land or they would kill his family."

"What?"

She shrugged. "Rick's been trying to convince him that he's in too deep to keep the names a secret."

"But the bank owned the land."

"I know."

He sighed and stood. "I'm starved. You eat yet?"

"No, I'll wait on Rick. You go ahead."

"I can wait till he gets done." He stepped around to Rick's desk and sat down.

"You still think Bolstero is behind all this?"

He found her amber eyes watching him intently from across the desk. "I do. But proving it? I'm not so sure we'll get that lucky."

Her gaze bored into his, and he didn't want to look away. The anger and frustration he had seen the past day in her eyes seemed to be gone, and something else sat there.

"I hate to tell you this, but I don't want you to find out later."

He leaned into the desk.

"Dr. Shaver says cause of death for Rachel was blunt force trauma. I just wanted you to be prepared."

He nodded, then leaned back. At least he could imagine it being quick, painless.

God, please let it have been.

"We'll do our best, Sullivan. I think we can nail him if we can get that one bit of evidence we need."

"Thanks."

Being on this side of the glass was humbling. Bennett dropped her gaze and went back to her computer.

"Need help?"

She shook her head. "I'm going to search for Marlon Jones as well as missing persons with the details Dr. Shaver gave us. Maybe we'll get lucky."

He wasn't counting on it.

Leaning back in the chair, he closed his eyes and stifled a yawn. Sleep was little last night since he was on watch.

"You know, if you had gone to a hotel last night, you could've gotten some sleep."

He chuckled. "Maybe. But then who would've been watching your house?"

"I told you. I don't need a babysitter. I'm fine."

Opening his eyes with a sigh, he found her glare. So much for that easy look she gave him earlier.

"You need to be careful, Bennett. Seriously, targeting like that—it leads to something more heinous."

She clenched her jaw and focused back on her computer screen. He watched her work and wondered what it would take to get her attention. It was the question she avoided earlier, and suddenly it was a question to which he really wanted an answer.

IT WAS ALMOST noon by the time Rick came out of interrogation.

"Lawyer said he's not interested in a deal. So, I'm charging him with attempted murder of a county official and federal officer. Maybe once the charges get set, it'll be enough to make him think about talking."

Greer nodded. She noticed Sullivan was suddenly awake from his nap. "Ready to eat?"

Rick grabbed his jacket, and Sullivan stood. She put on her pullover and strapped on her gun as she grabbed her purse.

"So, what're we eating?"

She chuckled. "Hungry, Sullivan?"

He looked her over with surprise and a bright smile. He had a great smile.

"Let's do Chinese. The buffet probably just opened."

She nodded at Rick. "Sounds great."

As they crossed the street, she glanced back to see Sullivan stiffen, his head on a swivel as he narrowed his gaze.

"Relax. Seriously, you've got a big worry gene."

"It's not a worry gene—it's experience."

She paused as he put his hand on his weapon. A shot echoed over her right shoulder. The sudden pressure and weight of Sullivan's body knocked the wind out of her as they fell to the ground in a heap.

13

"**D**own!"

The weight of Sullivan's body crushed, stifling her breath for a moment. Shifting to her right side, Greer called out for Rick.

"Rick? Rick answer me!" She pushed and shoved at Sullivan's unmovable body. "Get off. I need to check on Rick."

"Cut it out, Bennett. You have to stay put," Sullivan growled as she craned her head to get a look at Rick.

He was unmoving, his leg pushed back behind him and still as he lay on the ground.

"Rick? Get off me, Sullivan. I have to check on him."

Rick's leg moved slightly.

"Rick?"

"Greer." The low rumble made her turn to see Sullivan's face inches from hers. "Look at me. You're the target. If I roll off, you run to the cruiser, and I'll take care of Rick."

"But I ..." Her gaze shifted overhead to Rick when the feeling of her chin being pulled brought her back.

"Greer. Trust me here." Sullivan's green eyes and calm tone settled her mind. "I'll roll off. There's a black car parked in front of the gas station, that's where the shot came from. Let me take care of Rick, and you cover me."

She managed to nod as she closed her eyes and took a breath. "Yeah. Got it."

"Ready?"

Her eyes opened to see him watching. "Yes."

"Go."

His weight shifted, and she pushed to stand, her gun aimed across the street toward the gas station as she rushed to her right and behind the cruiser. The car was gone as she searched the area.

"Bennett?"

A few officers were running from the station on the other side of the street.

"Shooter across the street. Need an ambulance for Myers. Check the gas station and the cameras, now!" She kept her aim and glanced down at Rick, the sound of sirens already approaching from the hospital a mile away.

Sullivan had his hand against Rick's shoulder as Rick lay still, the other hand on his gun. Officers flooded the perimeter, and she rushed to Rick's side.

"Greer."

"We've got back up. Let me look." She ignored Sullivan's stern voice as she pushed at Rick's shoulder.

"*Arrgh!*" His scream echoed in her ears.

"Easy, Rick. You're fine. Stop being a wuss," she said, trying to take his mind off the pain.

"Wuss?" Rick groaned as she pushed her free hand behind his shoulder.

The bullet was embedded, and she gritted her teeth as blood soaked through the jacket and ran onto the pavement.

"Greer?"

She closed her eyes and breathed out at the sound of Thomas's voice.

"GSW to the shoulder, it's embedded. He's lost a lot of blood." She swallowed hard as Thomas and the others gathered around her.

"Bennett, let's go." A tug on her shoulder made her clench her jaw as she pulled forward and away.

"He's my partner," she blurted.

He was more than that—he was her family. There was no way she could leave him.

"We need to move, now." Thomas started to push her when an arm wrapped around her middle and lifted her from her position next to Rick.

"Put me down." She fumed as Sullivan relented, then stepped between her and Rick.

"They need access, and you're in the way." He held up his hands when she tried to get around him, blocking her. "Don't, Greer. They need to take care of him."

As the EMTs rushed past with the gurney, she followed.

"We've got to get him stable. There's no room." Thomas frowned as the doors slammed and the ambulance drove away.

Her mouth dropped as she watched the ambulance leave. Her body tensed, and her mind tried to engage. Her heavy breath sat in her chest. She fisted her hands, her wet, bloody hands.

"Come on, I'll drive."

A tug on her elbow brought her out. She saw Sullivan waiting.

He motioned toward the vehicle, and she nodded, grabbing her bag from the scene before she jumped into the passenger seat.

Taking wipes from her purse, she scrubbed her hands. Rick's blood stained her palms, and she winced at the scrapes on her right hand.

"You can clean up later."

"No, Paige ..." Her heart dropped. Pulling out her phone, she called Paige's number.

"Greer?" Her friend's high-pitched voice proved she had already been informed.

"Listen."

"He's ... he's been shot?"

"Paige. Listen to me, he'll be fine. It's a shot to the shoulder —critical, but not life-threatening. They're probably already headed to surgery. He'll make it, okay?"

"Not life-threatening?"

She hung her head and closed her eyes. There was so much blood.

"No. He lost some blood, but he'll be okay. Don't freak out. Do some breathing, okay?"

"Yeah, okay. I—they just said he was shot."

"I know, but I was there. He'll be fine."

"Fine, yeah okay. I'm on my way. Lisa is going to drive me."

She nodded. "Great. See you there."

Shoving the phone back in her purse, she pulled out another wipe.

"Greer, he lost a lot of blood."

She swallowed the bile burning the back of her throat. "I know that. But you know his wife was already admitted to the hospital due to issues with her pregnancy. If what I tell her will keep her calm and her and the baby safe, I'm doing it."

"And if you're wrong?"

She clenched her fists and saw the red on his face, the set jaw as he glanced at her.

"Is there a reason you have to say it?" she whispered.

He shook his head. Silence settled between them. She went back to work on her hands throwing the blood-soaked wipes on the floor. She yanked off the pullover, now stained in blood, shoving it to the backseat.

As soon as he pulled up to the ER, she jumped out the door

and rushed inside, showing her badge. A stretcher appeared in the hallway outside the room she was told Rick had been admitted to. She sprinted to catch up.

"Wait."

The doctor turned, and Rick's pale face appeared on the gurney.

"I'm his partner."

"He's going to surgery. The bullet nicked and artery and it needs to be plugged."

She nodded as they left, the doors slamming shut behind them. Leaning against the hospital wall, she closed her eyes and slid to the floor. Her knees bent to her chest, her arms hanging down. She tried to figure out what happened. That bullet was meant for her, and now Rick ... She couldn't even finish her thought.

He was going to be a dad. Announcing they were pregnant had been the proudest moment of his life. And now, he was in trouble. This wasn't happening.

"Hey."

She held up her hand, not wanting to deal with Sullivan's verbal sparring. Not now, it was just too much.

The smell of his cologne overwhelmed her. His body pushed against hers on the ground.

"It's a shot to the shoulder. It's going to hurt, and it'll take months to recover. But he'll be up and ready to leave here in a day or two."

She shook her head. "Doc said it nicked the artery. He could bleed out." She wiped her face.

"Greer."

"Don't." She leaned away, but he leaned closer. "It's my fault and ... How did you know?"

He sighed. "I was a Marine sniper for five years. I developed a sense for being watched, targeted. I just knew."

Her jaw dropped as she stared. "Why didn't you say something sooner?"

"Look."

"No." She stood, backing away as he jumped up and tried to approach her. "You could've just told me that. As law enforcement we all have that sense, but yours—and your experience—is much more."

He only shoved his hands in his pockets. She couldn't even look at him. If she had known his previous skill set, the fact she was being targeted might've meant more. Right?

Turning, she rushed down the hallway. Paige was sitting in the waiting area, her face pale and tear-stained.

With a breath, Greer forced out a smile. "Hey."

Paige's eyes went wide as she looked her up and down. "Is that Rick's?"

Forgetting about her pants and the blood that seeped through the pullover, she moved in to sit in the seat to her right. Wrapping her arm around her shoulders, she squeezed. "Look, he's going to be fine. He just needs some blood and some rest."

Paige nodded and cried into Greer's chest.

"He'll be fine," she murmured, trying to convince herself just as much as Paige.

He *had* to be fine. If something happened to Rick because she was the target and hadn't taken it seriously, she would never be able to forgive herself.

14

Hours later, the doctor appeared in the doorway.

"Myers?"

Greer helped Paige stand as the doctor entered.

"He's doing well. The surgery went perfectly. The nick to his artery was small. He'll need some more blood tonight, and we'll have to keep him for a few days, but I expect a full recovery. You can go in a few at a time, but let's limit the amount of time you're there. He needs rest."

"Thanks." She nodded as Paige started to cry again. "I need to speak to him really quick, okay?"

Paige nodded. Greer handed her over to her parents and hobbled out of the room on shaky legs. She hadn't been able to take a deep breath since she sat down, and now the weight of it all pushed on her chest.

Leaned against the wall, she breathed in and out heavily and held her head a moment, trying to get her bearings.

"You want to stay?"

She jumped at Sullivan's voice and found him in front of her, leaning against the opposite wall.

"I need to see him."

He nodded, and she pushed off the wall, hurrying down the hallway.

"I need to see Detective Myers." She flashed her badge. The nurse escorted her to his room.

As she walked in, her breath hitched. His body appeared lifeless—pale and unmoving in the bed. She gripped his hand and squeezed.

"G, easy," he murmured.

She chuckled and wiped the tears from her eyes. "I thought you were asleep."

He sighed and fluttered his eyes open. "Paige?"

"She's doing good." Sighing, she felt her emotions welling up. "I'm so sorry, Rick. This is all my fault, and—"

"Hey." He cleared his throat and winced. "How could you have known? The case is the reason we're both targets out there."

She shook her head, feeling the tears falling off her cheeks. "Sullivan knew."

"He had a guess. A good guess, but a guess. There was no evidence to back it up. Drop it."

Wiping her face, she nodded. It was true, but it didn't take away the guilt.

"Get my wife in here, and go catch the guy who did this."

She smiled. "On it. Just don't do anything stupid in here and listen to the doctor and the nurses."

He scoffed. "Like you know me at all."

She leaned down and kissed his forehead. "Don't scare me like that again. You and Paige—you're all I have left."

"We're not going anywhere. Besides, Baby Myers needs an aunt around." He winked.

Walking to the door, she wiped her face clean and opened it, motioning Paige in.

"I've got to go, call me if you need anything."

Paige smiled and pulled Greer in for a tight hug. "Thanks for being here. I wouldn't have made it without you."

Greer hugged back and then released her to the room.

WATCHING Greer head down the hallway, Gage straightened, frustrated at the fact she wouldn't even look up at him.

In silence, he followed her onto the elevator and out to the SUV.

As he went to open the door for her, she yanked it open, slid in, and shut it. Sighing, he walked around and got into the driver's side.

"Back to the office?"

"What was the make and model of the car?"

He started the SUV and backed out. "Pontiac Firebird, black with tinted windows."

Glancing over, she only nodded and pulled out her phone. Her fingers flew over the screen, and he focused back on the road.

She needed to be busy, even though he had already given all the information to the other officers who had come to the hospital right after they arrived. He could handle her lashing out at him. It was all a way to deal with her grief and guilt. But he couldn't handle her deciding the guilt was all hers and this whole thing was her fault.

"They have the gas station footage, but the plates were too distorted to get a read. The car pulled up after your FBI friends left and sat there until we came out."

"That car was there the whole time? And the gas station attendant didn't say anything?"

"She claims she was too busy to notice."

He frowned.

"I've already asked for her to be brought in."

At least they were on the same wavelength.

He heard Greer's slow exhale and glanced to see her leaned against the door. Bloodstained clothes, red stains on her face and neck, and still, it was hard to look away.

"We're missing something here. None of this makes sense."

He cleared his throat and put his focus on the road. "Have you located Bolstero?"

She shook her head. "Mansfield wanted us to get cleared by FBI before we started digging, just in case he was still a person of interest. But now—now he's mine."

Her clenched jaw made him wonder if this case would end well for either of them. Because he wanted Bolstero, and although he didn't want to die, it might just come to that.

"Bolstero won't be easy, Greer. He's evil. We need to be smart if we want to get him."

She nodded as he pulled into the station and parked. Turning in the seat, her glare was already on him, a sheen covering her eyes.

"I shouldn't have blamed you. This was my fault, my place."

"Greer—"

"I'm not done." That stern voice of hers took over. She held up a hand. "This is my case too. I realize it's personal, and I understand." A flash of sadness flooded her eyes, her gaze dropped for a moment. "But this is my case now. I want to trust you here, Sullivan. But I'm not so good with that. I need to know you'll come to me with everything you find, you won't leave anything out."

He nodded, resisting the urge to reach out. Her body trembling and her hands clenched, something else was going on. It wasn't just about Rick now.

"Sullivan?"

His eyes shifted back to hers. "You can trust me. I'm not here to go after him alone. I'm here to convict him."

She studied him a moment, her red-rimmed eyes darting

back and forth between his. Her trust would be hard to gain, between the other FBI situations and whatever happened with that paramedic guy, she was struggling.

"Okay," she whispered before she turned and slid from the seat, her bag in tow.

15

After speaking with Mansfield, Greer fell into her chair, leaning against the arm as she fingered her lip. It just didn't fit.

How did Bolstero hear about the situation so quickly? Mansfield informed her that PR released the information this morning about the grave and the bodies but left out the identities.

So, how could anyone know enough to threaten Manos?

Her gaze flicked to the empty chair across from her desk. It wasn't fair. Rick didn't deserve to get shot like that, a bullet meant for her.

"He'll be fine."

She snapped her head up as Gage stepped up to the desk and leaned against the edge. That soft tone of his filled the space, his green eyes watching.

"I know." She cleared her throat as she straightened. "Um, Mansfield wanted to speak with you before we get to digging. He's already got in touch with the FBI director about Bolstero, and we have permission to interview him."

"Where's he at?" Gage's arms crossed over his chest. All she could think about was how he shielded her, protected her from the shooter. He put his body in harm's way for her, and he deserved much more respect than she had been giving him. "Greer?"

Her eyes flitted to his for a moment until she couldn't look at the concern and worry on his face any longer. "He's in Chicago. Still in business, from what I've heard."

He stood. "We'll get him one way or the other."

She only nodded, working to hold back a wave of emotions that were falling hard on her chest. He gently took her shoulder and squeezed it before walking down the hallway to Mansfield.

Swallowing the need for a total breakdown, she checked for the ballistics from last night and came up empty. The lab hadn't even had time to run the bullet. The search she started before they left was still running, nothing that seemed to be a match for their Norwegian man at the morgue. That left the gas station attendant.

She trudged to the small interrogation room and paused to speak with the officer as he handed her the file.

"Does she know why she's here?"

He nodded. "Yes, ma'am. But she swears she was too busy to notice."

Greer flipped through the pages, noticing the woman's name and how long she'd been employed at the small gas station. The officer opened the door, and she eased through to see a woman sitting in a chair, her leg crossed over her knee.

"Ms. Lawson. How are you today?"

"Um, fine. Is that blood?"

Greer nodded, picking up her chair and setting it in front of the woman, barely a foot away. Sitting down, Greer flipped through the notes, letting the mood sink in as Ms. Lawson shifted in her seat.

"Ms. Lawson, you're here because there was a shooting earlier. Are you aware of what happened?"

Lawson nodded. "I mean, I heard the gunshot and yelling. Someone told me when they came in to pay that someone had been shot. Then your officers basically shut down the store. I gave them the footage they asked for."

She nodded. "You've worked there for almost two years?"

"Yes. It's a part-time job."

"What do you do when you're not there?"

"I also have a waitressing job. With a son at home and no—I mean, his father is gone—I work as much as I can."

Sitting back, Greer studied the woman. Early twenties, long blonde hair up in a ponytail, clean clothes that didn't reek of cigarettes or alcohol. It didn't seem like she would be a woman in such a bind she would take money to look the other way. Then again, Greer had been surprised before.

"This is the thing. My partner is the one who got shot. Had to have surgery. This is his blood." She narrowed her gaze, seeing the nervousness creep into the woman's paling face. "The shooter parked at that pump, waited at least an hour, but you told the officers you never noticed. How?"

Lawson twisted her fingers together as her leg fell down. She leaned closer. "I swear, I didn't see him or the car. I not only have to run the pumps and work the counter, but I make the sandwiches for the lunch rush. The woman who usually handles the food canceled today, and my boss wouldn't call in anyone else. So, I had to do her job too."

The woman was shaking but appeared to be telling the truth.

"Do you get a lot of regulars?"

She nodded. "There are always the same officers, of course, but at lunch time, we get a lot of repeat business."

"Anyone new stand out? A white male with a beard or freshly shaven face?"

Lawson chewed on her lip for a moment, her eyebrows furrowed as she thought. "I did notice a man with a black hoodie on come in. He grabbed a piece of candy, and that was all. I thought it was odd, he just kept staring out the window but didn't get a drink or gas."

"If you were as busy as you claim, how do you know he didn't get gas?" Greer leaned in.

"Well, the diesel pumps are working fine, but the four other pumps have a glitch. You have to come inside to pay. That just started today. My boss said he would get it fixed before tonight. I didn't think to mention it earlier. I thought maybe he was just with someone who already paid for gas."

"Did he talk to anyone else?"

Lawson shook her head, her ponytail swinging side to side.

"Okay, I'm going to get a sketch artist in here and have you describe him. Can you do that?"

Lawson nodded. "Is your partner ... is he all right?"

Greer gave a nod before, not willing to let emotions loose in the interrogation room.

"I need a sketch artist in here now. Call it in from state if you have to. We might have a shot of our killer or maybe his driver. She's free to go after she ID's the man on the video and speaks to the sketch artist."

The officer nodded as Greer went back to her desk. Searching the file for the gas station's owner—Pete Sanchez— she put in a call to the number listed. It went straight to voicemail.

"This is Detective Bennett with the Lexington PD. I need to speak with you about earlier events. Please call me back at this number."

Tapping her pen on the desk, she sighed and stood. Grabbing her phone and gun, she headed for the changing room. She needed a workout.

"YOU WANTED TO SPEAK WITH ME?" Gage knocked on the open door and stepped inside as Mansfield motioned him in.

"Yeah. Have a seat."

Gage sat down and studied the man across the desk. Bald with a full beard and mustache, Mansfield was much younger than he anticipated—especially for the way Dwight spoke about him.

"I've been updated about Rick. It's a good thing you were there to cover Bennett."

"I should've convinced her to be more careful." He narrowed his focus. "Sir, I know it seems off-topic, but she's being threatened. The note, the man who shot at her earlier, and now this. There's something else going down."

Mansfield leaned forward on his desk, eyeing him a moment, as if he were choosing his words carefully.

"I discussed that with her. She seems to think it's simply the case and once she gets on the trail, the guy will bolt."

Gage frowned. That didn't sit right.

"I feel the same way." Mansfield leaned back and studied him a moment. "How long?"

"How long what?"

"You served. How long did you serve?" He pointed to the tat on his forearm that was now showing after rolling up his sleeves in the hospital.

"Eight years. Five as a Marine Sniper."

Mansfield nodded. "Recon for six after a five-year tour of duty. I retired ten years ago and moved out here to enjoy a little quieter atmosphere. We're not without crime, but we're certainly a long way away from the big cities up north. And from the sounds of war."

Gage nodded, clenching his jaw. "What's the plan here, sir?"

Mansfield leaned in again. "I want you on this case. I trust your instincts, and as much as I want Bennett to step back, I'm not even going to try. She deserves a shot here. She's worked much bigger cases than this, and, well, she's too smart to sit this out."

It wasn't that he didn't think her smart—Greer was obviously very intelligent—but there was something he was missing.

"I have a feeling I'm not getting the full picture."

Mansfield chuckled. "With her? No, you aren't. And unless you find a way to play nice, you never will. I've talked to the director of the FBI, and she agreed to reinstate you for the time being. As long as you work with Bennett and let her handle the aspects of the case that apply to your sister."

He gritted his teeth but nodded. "That, I can do."

"We have to be above board on this. Although you have a connection to one of the victims, you know the case, the players, the people still involved. As far as skill, I think you're the best option besides handing it over to the FBI. The director has been clear, she's not wasting time on a cold case."

"So, does that mean I'm cleared from the shooting yesterday?"

Mansfield nodded and sat his gun on the desk. "I have a feeling the FBI helped push that one through. With the fact the Sheriff was shot and the doctor at risk, it was cleared quickly."

He stood and grabbed his weapon. "We're leaving for Chicago then?"

Mansfield sighed. "Yeah. Expense that to the Bureau, will ya?"

Gage chuckled as Mansfield stood. "I know a guy."

"Great. Take care of my detective and report back to me. I want to be kept in the loop."

He shook the captain's hand with a nod. "Will do."

Making his way back to the pit, Greer's desk sat empty. Searching the room, he noticed her talking to someone in the hallway.

He walked up behind her, enjoying the sight. In leggings

and tight tank-top that showed off her toned arms, she was obviously ready for a workout. Greer wasn't what he would consider a petite woman. She was at least five seven, maybe one-fifty with curves and muscle to back it up. He smiled a moment before realizing he was staring.

"Give me twenty."

His gaze shifted to her, and he nodded, watching her walk away. As long as she was working out, he would get one in too. After sitting for nearly two days, he needed to work out his arms and back before he stiffened up.

Good grief, was he really that old he had to worry about being stiff? Thirty-six is old?

He grunted and hustled downstairs to his truck, pulling out his bag and heading to the men's locker room.

16

After a quick workout, Gage found Greer upstairs, busy typing away at her computer. He tossed his duffle behind the desk next to the wall and moved Rick's chair to the side of her desk. Her perfume caught his attention.

She had on a long-sleeve polo with the sleeves already pushed up and her hair tied up in some kind of knot. The strands were still glossy wet, and he fought the urge to smile.

It seemed the more he noticed about his new partner, the more he had to hide a smile and push away thoughts inappropriate in the workplace.

He cleared his throat. "So, did Mansfield fill you in?"

She nodded, her focus never drifting from the screen. Her right hand was covered in gauze, a new addition he hadn't noticed earlier.

"Your hand okay?"

"Yeah." She turned the screen to him. "Is this Marlon Jones?"

He leaned over, recognizing the face. "Yep, did you find him?"

She sighed. "No. He fell off the face of the planet. I've had a friend looking through his financial past and as of seven years ago, nothing's been opened in his name—no accounts, credit cards, bills, nothing. But there's no missing persons report on him either."

"He worked for Bolstero. Those guys aren't usually the family type."

She nodded, turning back the screen. "I mean, he could just as easily be in some other hole somewhere. But something still doesn't sit right with me."

He watched her chew on her cheek before looking over at him.

"Bolstero is in Chicago—hours away and a different state. PR just released the information about the grave and finding human remains. No names are mentioned, and so far, it's been localized coverage."

"So, how did he hear about it a couple of states away?"

She shrugged. "I guess he could have a contact. Maybe whoever is threatening Manos? But after that long, I mean, does that track?"

He narrowed his eyes. Something told him she wasn't really asking.

"Where did you work before you came here?"

She rested her hands in her lap, intertwining her long fingers as she eyed him. "Why? That's pretty off-topic."

"I just wondered if you've worked in a larger city before, somewhere the crime was a bit heavier than here."

Her jaw clenched. "I don't think that's the reason you're asking, Gage."

He could barely keep his smile in. Something about hearing her say his first name felt ... appealing.

She leaned forward in her chair. "When you decide to start telling me the truth, telling me why you really want to know, then we'll talk." She stood and grabbed her coffee mug and left.

Well, once again, that went terribly.

Pulling out his phone, he sighed. It had been years since he'd visited Chicago. During his previous job with the FBI, he'd resided all over the country, wherever his skills and information about cartels were needed. But when Rachel disappeared, he had spent months there off and on, trying to find out more about Bolstero, even though he had been based in Indianapolis. Since they had a few cartel cases in that area, he had been given some leeway to work them through the field office there.

Although his parents lived just outside the city, it wasn't a place he had wanted to visit, especially after Rachel's case went cold.

And now, the thought of diving back into that violent world, with Greer in tow, wasn't something he really wanted to do.

But Rachel deserved more.

Greer came back and sat down, pulling herself into the desk and focusing once again on the computer screen. There was too much he didn't know about her, and it was clearly taking away his focus.

"We've got a flight out for seven-ten in the morning."

"Great."

"Look, I wanted to know about your background, okay? We're working together now, and I was hoping you'd dish out a little trust after earlier."

"Don't try and guilt me into it. Some trust, yes, I trust you to have my back. But I'm definitely not interested in getting into my past or where I came from. Can you handle that?" She looked over her shoulder, those bright amber eyes pulsing into his.

He nodded. "I can."

She turned back to the screen. "Thanks, by the way."

He grinned. "For what?"

"Having my back."

Man, her thanks were worse than her apologies. But it was at least conversation.

"Did you speak to the attendant at the gas station?"

"Yeah. She's working with a sketch artist. Says she remembers some guy coming in just to buy a candy bar, who kept looking out the window and didn't buy any gas."

"You think that's all she knows?"

She nodded. "Were you there when they interviewed Bolstero?"

"No. I was otherwise occupied."

Her eyes jutted to his for only a second before going back to the computer.

"Why?"

"I wondered about the wife. It says she was in the hospital for an appendix rupture during the interview. That seems, convenient."

He shrugged. "I know the agent who interviewed both of them. He's a dependable guy."

A phone call took her attention.

"Yes, Mr. Sanchez. I need to confirm some information about your gas station and its staff."

He half-listened to the conversation as he pulled out his phone and started making his own calls to prepare for the trip north.

THE CLOCK TICKED and moved closer to six. Gage had called the family of Gabby Brown. Speaking with Gabby's mother, the woman still remembered him coming by to check on her daughter. It made him wonder if he messed up by being around too much, which could've gotten her killed.

He set up a meeting with them, hoping they might

remember something about what happened the day she disappeared.

"Of course," Greer said.

As he hung up the phone with Gabby Brown's mother, he glanced up. "Find something?"

"Maxwell. He's in prison. Went in about three years ago. I guess the FBI finally caught up with him."

"I remember that. It was a technicality that caught him. Some racketeering charge that was a shot in the dark and then led to embezzlement."

She sighed.

"What's up with the gas station attendant?"

"Kim Lawson was telling the truth. She was short-handed today. The cook who prepares the food for the lunch crowd called in, and she was stuck working the counter and the food. The pumps were on the fritz as well. Everyone who wanted gas had to come inside and pay, plus she had to manually start the pumps."

He nodded. "Did you get a hit on the sketch yet?"

She sighed and set it down on the desk in front of him. "Chris down in the tech department says it's not gonna happen. He ran it against anything we might have on file, but it's too basic to run against our face recognition protocols."

"Does it look familiar?"

She shrugged. "She said he was wearing a dark hoodie, which tracks with the guy who attacked me. But other than that, I couldn't say it's the same."

"Detective Bennett?"

An officer approached her.

"Yes, Davis?"

"Ms. Lawson has gone through the video and pointed out the man. We have it pulled up."

They followed Officer Davis to the tech room, a small closet that held a wall of computers, monitors, and wires. The two of them packed inside, the smell of her perfume once again hitting his senses. It was like a rose scent, but woodsy.

"Agent Sullivan, this is Chris Fenster, our tech guy."

He came out of his stupor and shook the man's hand. Chris was skinny—very skinny—and young, maybe right out of college.

"So, here's the frame where the guy comes in."

The image quality wasn't great, but a man in a black hoodie stood at the counter, his focus out the window while he paid for a single candy bar.

"Does he look up at the camera at all?" Greer's voice was aching, and it took great restraint to keep from wrapping an arm around her.

Good grief. He shoved his hands in his pockets.

"No, and with all the traffic, there's no way we'll get a print off the door."

He followed Greer back out to the desk where she sat down and groaned.

"Let me send everything to a buddy at the FBI. They have a little more advanced software. Might get lucky."

She nodded, stifling a yawn and rubbing her eyes.

Frowning, he pulled out his phone. Once he got this sent in, he was getting her home. A smile crossed his face before he could stop it. That wasn't exactly what he had meant.

"Hey, Jason."

"Hey, man. Heard a rumor about you."

He leaned back, his eyes fixed on Greer staring at the computer screen. "Yeah, well, don't believe everything you hear."

"This one was you were coming back."

He chuckled. "Well, I'm back for a case, then it's on to Homeland once again."

"Sure, we'll see. What can I do for you?"

"Well, I have a sketch and some video footage of a possible

suspect in an officer-involved shooting. We got nothing here, hoped you might take a look and run it through your search engines."

"Man, sure. The officer all right?"

"Hit to the shoulder. He'll live."

Jason said, "Well, that's a relief. Yeah, send it over. You still have my email?"

"Yeah, somewhere. Thanks. I appreciate it."

"Hey, anything for a friend. I'll text you my email just in case you forgot it. You coming to Indy?"

"Nope. Chicago. Keep me updated."

"No problem."

He chuckled again and hung up, looking down at his phone and waiting for the text. "Jason said he'd take a look at the video and the sketch."

Greer was unresponsive, her chin sitting in her hand and her eyes closed.

Quietly standing, he slid in next to her and gently took her free hand. She woke, her eyes jutting to his. Her face flushed as she yanked away.

"Oh, I guess I took a nap." She straightened.

He set his phone in front of her with Jason's email address. "Send the video and the sketch here. He's a buddy at the FBI, and he's offered to take a look at everything and run it through their search."

She nodded, wiping her eyes as she pulled up her email.

He walked around the table, heaving his bag to his good shoulder.

"Where are you headed?"

"We have an early flight in the morning, and you're exhausted. I'm sure you want to go by and see Rick, and we haven't eaten all day, so let's leave now."

She sat back, pinning him with a glare. "What do you mean, *we*?"

He grabbed up his phone. "You're being targeted, whether or not you want to admit it. You're not going anywhere without protection."

"I can protect myself." She swallowed hard as she stood, her arms crossed. There was some doubt there, something holding her back.

"And I can help with that. I already told you, Bolstero is evil and has a lot of money and influence. When we go talk to him, we have to be ready. And that means getting some rest."

She eyed him for a moment before relenting. Without a word, she grabbed her gun, bag, and phone, then shut down her computer. Walking silently toward the elevator, he followed.

17

I t was six o'clock and Greer struggled to stay awake in the SUV. Falling asleep at her desk when it wasn't two in the morning wasn't normal.

Pulling out her phone, she called Paige.

"Hey, Greer."

"How's he doing?"

"Good so far. He's had some Jell-O, even though he complained it's not the kind he likes."

She chuckled. "Sounds like he's feeling better. I'm headed that way. You want something to eat?"

"No, I'm fine. Thanks anyway."

"Good. I'll see you in a few."

Her energy bottoming out, she slid the phone in her purse and leaned back, hoping to get some rest.

"Rick okay?"

"Yeah."

She sighed and turned to face Gage. His features stood out even under the beginnings of the beard he was sporting. A strong jaw, pointed nose, and bright red lips. She must really be tired, allowing her mind to go where it didn't need to wander.

With a yawn, she settled on the console, looking out the window. Her eyelids felt heavy as she closed her eyes and drifted away. The feeling of relaxation moved her to sleep.

A TUG on her fingertips awakened Greer. She quickly sat up from on top of the console where she had fallen asleep.

Parked at the hospital parking garage, she swung her gaze to Gage, who was watching with a smirk on his face.

"Why is it so dark out?"

"I let you sleep a little when we got here."

"A little?" She ignored his chuckle and gathered her phone from her purse. "It's after seven. Why does it smell like a taco truck in here?"

He smiled and handed her a bag of Mexican food. "I stopped and grabbed dinner. Hopefully there's something you'll like."

"At this point, I'll eat pretty much anything." She took the bag then reached for the door handle.

His hand took hold of her arm.

"Let me get the door. We're still not sure who's shooting and—"

"Look, the bodies have already been identified, and everyone knows. Besides, I'm not interested in another person getting shot with a bullet that's meant for me."

"You wearing your vest?"

She frowned.

"Then I'm covering you."

Before she could respond, Gage left the SUV and came around, opening her door. Trying to be appreciative of what he was doing instead of insulted, she followed and even allowed him to wrap his arm around her as the cold wind settled in. At least that part helped to keep her warm.

The silence lasted in the elevator and then on to Rick's room.

She knocked on the door and made her way inside. "Hey, you."

Rick was sitting up and watching TV. Although his eyes were still droopy, he had his color back.

"Hey. You two get lost?"

"I fell asleep." She gave him a hug. "Where's Paige?" Greer settled at the small table in the corner and pulled out the food.

"Her mother came and got her. They ran to the store or something." He waved his working arm then turned back to the screen. "So, any leads?"

"We have a possible suspect, but the sketch is generic and the video doesn't show us a face." She gave a shrug and stuffed her face with the chicken burrito.

Rick peered past her shoulder. "Sullivan, I assume things are going well?"

She watched Gage with his back to the wall, looking much more on guard than here to visit.

"Yep."

"Mansfield cleared it with the FBI. He's officially on the case."

"Oh? Well, that sounds interesting. And the fact he's related to one of the victims?"

"That's for them to work out. I'm just following orders. How about you?"

"What does that mean?"

She swallowed the bite of burrito in her mouth before wiping her lips. "I know you. Are you doing what the doctor says?"

He yawned and focused once again on the game on the screen. "Can't do anything until tomorrow. PT will come in and do a consult. Then I'll start trying to move it around. It's pretty miserable, though."

"Gage seemed to think it would be easy." She glanced over and caught his glare.

"Oh? How so?"

Gage stepped farther into the room. "Got shot about three years ago, same shoulder. You'll be back to normal in a few months. If you do what you're supposed to."

Trying to cover her surprise, she turned back to her food. He had been shot? Must've slipped his mind when he discussed Rick's recovery earlier.

"That's good news for me, I guess."

A quick rap on the door and a nurse entered. "I just wanted to check on your pain levels, hun."

Greer wiped her face and stood to throw away the bag, bumping into Gage who stood fixed in his spot, unmoving while she reached for the trash can.

"Trying to start something, Greer?" he whispered into her ear.

Fighting the urge to shiver, she clenched her jaw. "You never told me you were shot. You just said he'd be fine," she hissed, facing him.

"You didn't ask."

"I guess I didn't realize I had to ask if you have experience with everything. Just like with the shooter. You could've given up that part about being a sniper sooner."

His eyes darkened again. "I don't talk about it."

"Then why are you pushing me to talk about my past?"

A chuckle caught her attention. Rick and the nurse were watching the argument.

"That was, um, interesting."

Her irritation flared. "You seem to be doing fine. I'm heading out. Tell Paige I'll call her."

"Come on, G."

She ignored Rick's calls and pushed through the door toward the elevators.

Man, her mind wasn't working tonight.

Gage was her partner right now, for better or worse, and it seemed, more often than not, worse weighted the scales. That had to change. If she couldn't get her head in the game, this case would drive her crazy. Well, probably Gage Sullivan much more than the case.

She let out a groan. Yeah, he would be enough to drive her crazy.

GAGE SIGHED AS GREER, then the nurse, left the room.

"She's tired."

"Yeah, I know," he replied and headed for the door.

"Hey, Gage?"

He paused to see Rick's paling face drop.

"Look, I'm trusting you here. She needs protection, and I'm hoping, even though she's a handful, you'll watch her back."

He nodded. Rick looked ready to spill something, so he stepped back into the room.

"You were a sniper?"

"Yeah. Marines."

"Impressive. I bet she didn't appreciate that knowledge after the fact."

He shook his head.

"She's untrusting, okay? Her past isn't great. But give her some time to get used to breaking in someone new. That's why she moved here. She knew me and didn't want to break in a new partner."

New partner? Did that have to do with the case the FBI took?

"Nashville?"

Rick's eyebrow went up. "I'm not getting into details."

"Just how well do you two know each other?"

Rick chuckled. "Greer and Paige became friends the moment she moved here in tenth grade. We hung out all the time and kept in touch after graduation. She's like a sister to Paige and me."

Gage nodded and turned again.

"Sorry about your sister, Gage. I never got to say that."

He paused. "Thanks."

Finding Greer at the elevator talking with Paige, he shoved his hands in his pockets as he approached. At least she didn't go outside without him.

"Thanks. I've got to go. Call if you need anything."

She hugged Paige and followed him into the elevator. Her body stiff, she crossed her arms and leaned against her left shoulder. This time when they crossed the parking lot, she pulled from his arm. It was a harder hit to his ego than expected.

Once in the SUV, the tension pushed into his chest, hanging in the air.

"We need to be able to work together, Greer."

She cleared her throat. "I can't talk right now. Tomorrow will be better," she barely whispered.

Pushed against the door, her body trembled as she wiped her face. With his terrible track record, silence seemed the best option. She had been through the ringer today, and now, she was falling behind. It was a prime moment for him to say something stupid, so clenching his jaw, he focused on the road.

Once at her home, he pulled into the driveway and got out, refraining from making a comment that she got out by herself without waiting for him to clear the area. He followed her up the steps as she unlocked her door and stepped inside.

"Go get a hotel room. Like you said, we both need our rest."

The door slammed in his face, and he stood there a minute, shoving his hands in his pockets. He had no idea how to approach this, and for the life of him, he couldn't figure out why he was still there. But he couldn't make himself move.

A familiar sound softly drifted through the door and he stepped forward to listen. His heart dropped.

18

C ollapsed on her couch, Greer sobbed into the pillow, her body aching, emotions raw.

The visions of Rick lying on the ground looking lifeless, the blood, worrying that he would bleed out—it was her fault. All of it was her fault. She should've taken Gage's comments seriously, been more alert.

"God, please let Rick make a full recovery." She worked herself to sitting, groaning at the pain in her arm and shoulder.

Gage tackling her to the ground had left bruises on her right side and shoulder from taking the brunt of the weight. The skin on top of her knuckles had torn from the rough asphalt. But right now, the emotional weight of yet another low place in her life had her wondering.

"Is this another way to get me to change direction, do something different?"

The same emotional upheaval had put her on a career change and effectively ended her forensic studies. He had put her in a better place, a great career with people she cared for and trusted. But if her actions led to Rick's injury, or worse ...

Swallowing the bile filling her throat, she slowly stood. He would be okay. The doctor said he would be okay.

With a turn, she grabbed a throw blanket and headed for the kitchen. After gathering a glass of water, she stepped outside to the back porch.

The swing beckoned.

Wrapping the blanket snuggly around her body, she sat gingerly, pushing the swing into motion as she set the glass on table.

Wiping at random tears, she took a deep breath, attempting to ease the pounding of her heart. Through blurry vision she stared at the yard, the trees, the darkness edging all around.

If God had led her back here, then why would she need to change direction once again?

A creak to the left snagged her attention. Dropping the blanket and pulling her weapon, she aimed center mass at the man standing against the gate.

"What? Why're you here?"

Gage shrugged, unlatched the gate and walked through. "You can put that up now." He ascended the steps.

Lowering the weapon, she kept it in her palm, glaring at his presence. "I didn't say you could come here. Go find a hotel room."

"I thought we should talk."

"Tomorrow."

"Tonight would be better."

Her jaw clenched. Just what did he think he was doing?

"If you think you're going to stay here, you're wrong."

He waved her off with a shake of his head. "Didn't even cross my mind. It's not like that. You've had a bad day. Talk it out."

"Don't need to." She set the gun down.

It took way too much effort to pull her attention away as he leaned up against the porch beam, the moonlight flooding his features. Focusing on the trees swaying in the breeze, she ignored his prying gaze.

"I'm trying to help. You see that, right?"

Her anger flared. She closed her eyes and inhaled deeply.

God, I'm not sure I can handle this. He's too... too much. Pushy, that's the word, he's too pushy.

"Look, I realize you think you're helping. But it just makes me mad when people push. Didn't we already have this conversation? You don't want to talk about your time as a sniper, I get that. So why can't you understand I don't want to talk right now?"

He sighed and took two steps to the Adirondack chair, easing into a recline.

"What're you doing?"

"Sitting." He leaned back, his long legs stretched out as he put his arms carefully behind his head.

The cool air sent a shiver through her body, and she pulled up the blanket.

"You know, you should go inside. You sure don't want to get sick." His eyes closed, jaw relaxed, his chest rose slightly as he took a breath.

"I'll be fine, thanks." She let her gaze go back to the yard.

Breathing in the night air, the fall breeze smelled wonderful. She loved the evenings here. The orange moon hung in the distance, the sounds of the leaves rushing against the wind soothed that ache to be at home. This was home.

Why had she ever left?

His deep breath disturbed her inner thoughts.

"Where were you and Dwight located?"

"Indianapolis."

"How long did you work there?"

"About nine years."

She glanced over, his eyes still shut. "Is that how you're supposed to protect me? With closed eyes?"

"You know, sixth sense and all that." He waved a hand.

She chuckled and shook her head.

"Where did you come from, Greer?"

She chewed on her lip a moment. As long as he was giving up confidences ...

"I moved here from Little Rock Arkansas, when I was fourteen."

"College?"

"Knoxville. University of Tennessee."

"I assume you graduated with honors."

"*Humph.* You could say that. But why would you?"

From the corner of her eye, his movement proved he was now sitting up straight, his elbows resting on bent knees.

"Your boss mentioned your insight."

"And from that, you got honors graduate?"

He shrugged and stood, taking a few steps to lean against the rail across from her again. Gripping the railing, his gaze fixed on hers.

"Fine." She licked her lips and pulled the blanket tighter across her shoulders. "I hold a BA in Forensic Anthropology."

"And now you're a detective?"

Her jaw clenched and she took a breath. "I changed paths."

Taking hold of the blanket, she stood and grabbed her gun, shoving it into her holster. She reached for her water glass, twisting and losing her balance as the blanket tightened around her legs.

Letting out a yelp, she fell forward. His arms engulfed her.

"Hey," he chuckled.

She sighed and shook her head. "I got tangled."

He bent down, grinning as he gathered the blanket for her. She loosened her legs and took the mass from his hands.

"Gage, I'm good here. Please go get some rest. Sleeping in your car isn't going to cut it, not with everything we have to do tomorrow."

His jaw clenched, and his grin disappeared. "I can't do that."

That easy tone echoed in the night, something silently moving between them. His bright green eyes watched her intently, jutting between her eyes and lips. This wasn't happening, not right now and not with him.

With a huff she pulled away and hurried inside, leaving the back door open. There was no way she was okay with him sleeping in her home, but with everything going on and their interview with Bolstero tomorrow, he needed his rest as well. And that wasn't going to happen if he was sitting in his SUV watching her home for the second night in a row.

Tossing the glass in the sink, she shoved the throw on the couch. The sound of the screen door echoed as she went down the hallway and dug out a pillow and blanket from the closet for him.

"Fine, take the couch. I'll be up at five."

She set the things down and pushed past him for the hallway, keeping her head down and her eyes from his. No need to make things more, well ... whatever they were right now.

Shutting and locking her bedroom door, she collapsed on the small loveseat in the corner and held her head.

"God, please let us both sleep well so we can do the right thing tomorrow, so we can catch the killer. Please give me some patience and grace as I find a way to work with Gage."

She stood and grabbed some clothes to sleep in, then headed for her shower.

GAGE STARED DOWN THE HALLWAY, shocked and surprised.

"Okay." He closed and locked the back door.

Stepping through the front of the house to his SUV, he

grabbed his duffle and headed back inside, locking the door behind him.

Never in a million years did he expect her to let him stay here—it wasn't even a thought on his mind. Now, maybe angling for something on the back porch a second ago, that thought rushed like a wave and still made him pause.

She was in his arms, not free to push or back away and looking up at him like that …

He sighed and grabbed some clothes and his charger from his bag. After hooking up his phone, he headed down the hallway to the small bathroom and turned on the shower. Even though he'd just showered at the gym, he needed another.

Tonight was going to be a long night.

19

The shrill of Greer's alarm went off, slicing through her head as she patted around the nightstand, attempting to find the right button to make the noise stop.

Rolling over, the smell of coffee filled the room. Had she really let Gage stay the night on her couch? The sound of water running reaffirmed the reality, and she pushed the pillow over her head.

What was I thinking?

Struggling to wake, a knock on the door sent a jump through her chest.

She rolled off the bed and yanked on a sweatshirt, then tried to smooth her hair down. Pulling it open, she did her best to reign in the shock of seeing Gage clean-shaven, smelling amazing, and fully dressed in a suit.

"That surprising, huh?"

Her eyes finally met his. He grinned.

"Didn't expect the suit. And you shaved. I don't think I've seen you clean-shaven."

"I've got coffee. You don't have much to eat. You want to grab something on the way?"

She sighed, rubbing her forehead. "Yeah, groceries, I didn't think about that. Okay, give me thirty."

Slamming the door, she headed to her closet. Her normal work attire was the plan, after all, she wasn't FBI. Pulling out her navy dress jacket, she grabbed the pinstriped shirt and pants that matched, then headed to plug in her curling iron.

After dressing and fighting a losing battle with her hair, she finished her makeup and grabbed an overnight bag, just in case. Packing a couple of days' worth of clothes and shoes, she slipped on her dress boots and checked the mirror.

Since Bolstero was cooperate, the formal dress jacket and slacks would perhaps gain a better advantage during the interview. Besides, Gage had planned on meeting with Gabby Brown's family as well, and they deserved the respect of being professional.

She shoved some makeup and personal items in the bag before zipping it and heading down the hallway.

"Wow." Gage had a smirk on his lips, the coffee mug raised to his chin.

"Am I over-dressed? With all the meetings and everything ..." She felt her face flush as his gaze lingered, a smile forming. He shook his head.

"Let me get my coat."

She rushed to her room and dug in her closet for her heavy dress coat, hat, and gloves. Her heart pounding and face hot, she paused and took in a breath.

"Good grief," she muttered.

She closed her eyes. Was she really this worked up about that smile of his? The fact he gave her a compliment? Her mind raced all over the place about a man who infuriated her, argued nonstop, and was annoying and pushy. Why did any of this even matter right now?

Grabbing her tablet and charger from the nightstand, she

rushed back to the room and stuffed everything except the coat in the carry-on suitcase.

"Your sidearm?"

"I'll check it." She pushed her left arm though her coat sleeve.

He held the right side, and she mumbled a thanks as she slid it on, grabbed the bag, her purse, and keys, and followed him out. After locking the door, she stepped off the porch to find him waiting to walk her to the already-started SUV.

"You that cold?" He nodded to the heavy coat.

"No, but I'm guessing in Chicago, I'm going to need it." She pointed at the lightweight black coat he was wearing. "You don't think you'll get cold?"

He chuckled as he opened her door, then took the small suitcase from her shoulder. "I'm always warm." With a wink, he shut her in and then put her bag in the back seat.

She sighed and leaned back. "God, give me some grace today," she whispered.

With his quick wit, she would need strength to keep things civil and friendly. However, with the way he was looking at her last night and the smile on his face this morning, being friendly was the one thing she might have to reconsider.

After tossing her bag in the back seat, Gage took his time walking around to the front. Seeing her dressed up, hair curled and hanging down her shoulders, he realized staying focused would be a challenge.

He needed to stay focused for the sake of Rachel's memory, and even though not knowing much about Greer left him wondering, he had to drop it. If only she would open up to him, it might ease his curiosity.

"Good one, you hypocrite," he muttered to himself.

They pulled through the same bakery with the donuts and coffee she had bought him the other day, and he ordered the same fare, filling up on the way to the airport.

Going through security and getting their tickets, they had forty-five minutes to spare. She stepped up to the window, viewing the sun rising.

As if he needed another reminder of how amazing she looked, the red and gold sunrise highlighted her perfectly.

He ambled up next to her.

"You want to go over the case you have?"

He shook his head. She winced and pulled the bag off her right shoulder.

"Let's wait till we're in the air. How's the shoulder?"

Her gaze flew to his for a moment before shifting back to the sunrise. "I'm fine."

He sat down to wait, and she took a seat two down from him. Resting his arm on the back of the seats, he faced her.

"You gonna fill me in?"

"About what?" She pulled out her phone and started texting.

"Why your shoulder's sore? It didn't seem like it was bothering you the other day."

She ignored him until he pulled at her hair from behind. She sighed and met his eyes.

"I'm fine. I told you." She went back to her phone.

Talking wasn't her forte this morning. He leaned back. Silence would be good for him too. Focus, he needed to find that focus. He had been a Marine sniper, after all. He was trained to maintain integrity and focus. He could do this.

Once on the plane, she raised her arms to stow her small suitcase in the overhead bin. He took it from her and pushed it into the storage area.

After take-off, she unbuckled and slipped off her shoes, pulling her feet underneath her. She covered her legs with her coat. He grinned as she leaned on the armrest they shared.

"Now, what do you have for me?"

Pulling up his binder, he flipped the table down, opened it, and handed her the file on Bolstero. She took it eagerly and moved her table down to go through the pages. He took the four file folders he had on the deceased—well, three, now that one didn't match—and set them out.

"So, what did Rachel do? What was her cover?"

He shifted in the seat, trying to spread out his legs in the small space. "She was the nanny."

She nodded. "It says the kids were ten and twelve when she disappeared. How long did she work for him?"

"Since the oldest was eight."

"Hmm ... Now I understand."

"Understand, what?".

"I've been thinking about Rachel and why she stayed. Nothing she gave the DEA seemed to be working to nail the guy, yet she was putting herself in danger by staying on and being around him. So, what was the pull? But now, it all makes sense. She wanted to protect the children."

He shook his head. "She never mentioned anything about them. Just told me she couldn't leave, not yet."

"When was the last time you spoke with her?" Her voice was soft, gentle.

Clearing his throat, he took a breath. It was a conversation he didn't want to remember.

"She argued with me, told me she couldn't just leave. I told her she meant too much to all of us to risk her life. At that," he sighed, "she said the same thing about me. It didn't end well, she hung up on me."

Her hand gripped his arm.

"She knew you loved her, Gage. Why else would you try so hard to get her to leave?"

His jaw clenched, and he shook his head.

"Do you have a pen?"

Pulling the pen out of his binder, he handed it over as she circled a few items on the page.

"Did you happen to set up an appointment with her DEA handler?"

That would be one of his burned bridges. "Not worth the effort. He won't talk to me."

"That bad, huh?"

Glancing at her smirk he scoffed. "Worse than what you can imagine."

"I'll call when we land. I want to talk to him."

"Don't tell him you're with me."

She chuckled.

During the rest of the flight, she worked on the pages as he zoned in and out, trying to find a thread to pull that would link Bolstero to the crimes he'd orchestrated. But that was the problem—the man was too clever to have any link to whoever actually carried out his orders. Everything so far on him had been hearsay, and that wasn't even enough for a warrant.

Gage leaned his seat back a little, then turned to watch Greer. Pen in hand, she went through the pages, methodically circling, underlining, and jotting down notes in the margins.

A degree in forensic anthropology must come in handy as a detective. It made him wonder if after digging up so many people, she decided the crime itself needed her attention, not just the body.

Was that the connection? What turned her from anthropologist to detective? His heart clenched a moment.

She had yet to mention family of any kind. She was living alone, and not even Rick had mentioned a worry for her family. So that could mean ... He hoped he was wrong. To lose even one member of your family like he had, was overwhelming. If tragedy had happened to her with one or more members, that would bring up all sorts of emotions and issues just stepping into the case.

It was time to make a better effort, to ease the fighting, at least on his end. God seemed to have put everything on this strange timeframe and as thankful he was that Rachel had been found, it came so late. The evidence was dated, their witnesses gone, and memories faded. They could only hope for a miracle to link everything together.

God, You've got this right? I know You do, but this is harder than I thought it would be.

Glancing at Greer again, he clenched his jaw.

Give her some kind of peace. I can see it all over her face. She's holding on to so much. What's it going to take for her to let it go, to let me in?

Because that was the plan, right? Why else would this situation link up like it did? Her move during the past year, his as well. It seemed much more than a coincidence.

20

After landing at the airport, Greer called the DEA. The file Gage had given her held the lead agent's name.

"I need to speak with Agent Buchannan."

"Name?"

"Detective Greer Bennett."

Her call was put on hold, and Gage took her suitcase, heading outside while she waited in the airport lobby.

"Detective Bennett, what can I do for you?"

"I'm in Chicago and would like to speak with you about Bolstero and the case."

"Oh? Mind telling me why?"

Watching Gage slide into the rented SUV, she frowned. "Rachel Sullivan. Does that name ring a bell?"

The silence confirmed her suspicions.

"You have Sullivan with you, huh?"

"He is."

A deep sigh moved through the line. "You can promise he won't overreact?"

"Seeing how he just discovered the murdered remains of his

sister, who was last seen working for you as a mole for a high-end criminal like Bolstero? Not a chance."

"Fine. See you here at the office at one."

"We'll be there."

She ended the call as Gage rolled down the passenger window, motioning her out. Pushing through the airport door, she gripped her coat and slid into the seat. "Should've grabbed my hat and gloves." She buckled in and aimed the heat vent directly toward her.

The snow scattered, and the wind blew the flakes into the windshield as they drove down the street.

"You get a meeting set up?"

She nodded. "One o'clock. I'm assuming that will give us enough time to see Bolstero and Gabby Brown's family."

He only nodded, growing quiet since their talk on the plane.

"I know this is a hard case."

His eyebrow rose as their car stopped at a red light. "Really?"

When did he become so intuitive? Or was she just that transparent?

"Yeah, but now's not the time."

Turning back to the window, his hand wrapped around hers. Maybe he needed to cling to something as much as she did right now. She hung on and blew out a deep breath, on edge and confused. The case was bringing up feelings she had been doing well to keep pushed down for years.

God please, I need to focus on the case. That's why we're here.

"Are you going to set up a meeting with Bolstero?"

She nodded. When he let go, the comfort left too. So much for her focus.

"I want to be there."

"Gage, you know that's not a good idea. Based on the reports, he knows exactly who you are, and you're supposed to stay away from anything that links to Rachel. We can visit Gabby Brown's family, look into that together, but your sister's part of the case needs to be just me."

His jaw clenched as he focused on the road in silence. Pulling out her phone, she called Rick.

"How's it in Chicago?"

"Cold." She smiled at Rick's chuckle. "You sound well."

"Feeling pretty good. The meds are helping."

"Good. Have you called in to the station?"

Another chuckle came out. "How did you know?"

"I know you too well, Rick."

"Mansfield put a rush on the bullets, the one from your shooting and my shoulder. He expects a call by this afternoon. Dr. Shaver called, looking for you."

"Oh? I don't have a missed call."

She gazed down at her hand buried under her leg. Gage's arm rested back on the console, his hand hanging over on her side.

What changed him so quickly? Even last night she thought he was pushing for more on the porch and now...

"G?"

"Oh, yeah, sorry. I guess I zoned out." She shifted her gaze to the window. "What'd you say?"

"She said she's comfortable dating the grave with seven years."

"Did she find anything useful in the dirt?"

"All she would say was a few abnormalities but wouldn't go into detail. I have a feeling she might be onto something. I just don't know why she wouldn't tell me what."

She grinned. "She's not into speculation, Rick. That's not her thing."

"What do you have planned today?"

"Lots of meetings, including the DEA."

"That sounds, ominous. How is Gage going to handle it?"

"He's a big boy. Pretty sure he can handle it."

She chewed on her cheek, her skin pricking to feel Gage's stare.

"Oh, by the way, Mansfield mentioned the Manus case."

"Did Manus decide to give something up?"

"A little. He said Manus finally came to his senses and gave up the shooter. He's a hired guy from up north, but they've already got a line on him. With the distance he's already traveled, he couldn't have been the one to shoot me."

"What about the landowner?"

"I don't know, that's all Manus would give."

She sighed. "Well, maybe that's one down."

"All right, I'll let you go. I'll keep you updated if I find anything else."

"Thanks. Sounds like Mansfield has it under control at the office, but you need to take care of yourself."

"Nah, I'm good. Besides, while you're out with the special agent, someone has to take care of things around here."

"I'll talk to you later, Rick," she responded, refusing to take the bait.

"Okay, bye."

She hung up.

"I take it Rick is feeling good?"

She nodded and kept her gaze out the window and away from those great eyes of his. "Yeah. He's been doing some follow-ups. I need to call Dr. Shaver at some point."

"She found something?"

"Well, she dated the grave at seven years, but Rick seemed to think she had something else she wasn't ready to discuss yet. Maybe she'll talk to me."

"We've got ten 'til we get to Gabby's parents' home."

She shook her head. "I'll need more time." She glanced over to see Gage fully focused on the road. "You sure it's going to be okay visiting them? Are they still in touch with Maxwell?"

He shook his head. "I asked when I called yesterday. They're still estranged."

"Since he's here in the state pen, want to set up a visit?"

"Why? He'll simply blame Bolstero and deny anything about Martinez."

She nodded. "Well, I would like to see if there's anything else he might be willing to give up."

He sighed. "Look, Maxwell—he's not that kind of man. He won't give up anything on Bolstero. That would kill him. He knows prison isn't far enough away to escape Bolstero's reach."

She clenched her jaw, committed to doing what she needed to do to solve this case and restraining herself as much as possible to keep from arguing. But in her investigations, she spoke with everyone who had any contact or reason for the victim to die. All three victims deserved justice, and the very fact Martinez had been in police protection because he'd been due to incriminate Maxwell was motive enough.

"I'll make a few calls, but I think I should be the one to interview him."

"You have got to be kidding me."

"Greer."

"No, you're not in protection mode here. Remember, this is an investigation—that thing you used to do with the FBI? I'm assuming you don't do it anymore with Homeland the way you're acting. I'm investigating this case, and I'm going with you. If you want to lead out the questions, we can see how that goes. But I will be there."

His neck went red and his jaw clenched.

So much for playing nice.

21

L etting the silence settle, Gage directed the car up a private drive in a gated community.

They needed conversation, something they wouldn't argue about, something case-related.

Greer cleared her throat. "What do the parents do?"

"Nothing. They're retired."

"So, what did they *used* to do?"

He glanced over with a frown and she nodded. Even if they disapproved of their son's actions and were estranged, they obviously didn't mind the monetary gifts he undoubtedly gave them.

Gage parked in the driveway. Greer glanced up at the large front door before sliding from the seat. Buttoning up her coat, she stepped carefully in her heeled boots on the icy asphalt. Coming around the front of the car, Gage took her elbow and guided her up the steps.

He rang the bell as they waited. Shoving her hands in her pockets, she blew out a shiver.

"I'm cold," she muttered. Gage's arm went around her waist, and he moved in closer.

Looking up at him in surprise, he kept his focus on the door as if nothing had changed.

Okay ...

The door finally opened. A lovely looking woman greeted them with a smile. "Please, come inside."

He led Greer in as the door closed behind them.

"Agent Sullivan, so nice to see you again." The woman was of Asian descent, beautiful brown eyes, styled hair, and dressed impeccably.

"I'm sorry it's under such terrible circumstances."

"Nonsense. You've found her, just like you always said you would. For that, we are grateful."

The woman, whom Greer assumed was Gabby's mother, held her hand out for them to follow, and Greer fell in step behind her.

Stepping into a sunroom, the heat made her smile. She unbuttoned her coat.

"Where are my manners? My name is Natasha Maxwell." She extended her jewel-clad hand, and Greer shook it gently.

"Detective Bennett."

"The detective who found her?"

Her eyes widened a moment. "Well, my partner and I assisted in the case."

"The news reports messed it all up. I told you." A throaty voice came from the recliner to her left and a large, bald man stood.

His gut hung over his pants, and the oversized shirt barely contained the rest of him.

"Detective, this is my husband, Garland Maxwell."

The man lifted brow, a smile forming on his face. "Nice to meet you, miss."

She reluctantly shook the man's outstretched hand, pulling back as quickly as possible. Gage stepped in closer at her shoulder.

"So, she was buried? With Rachel, I'm guessing?" The man's gaze swung to Gage for a moment before returning to hers.

"Yes." Gage's guttural response echoed in the room.

"You think it was the boss? Because if it was, I'll kill him myself." Garland Maxwell's voice rose as he angrily waved his hand and jabbed a stocky finger into his chest.

"We're here to re-open the case."

"Won't do you no good." Mr. Maxwell narrowed his eyes, staring over Greer's shoulder at Gage. "You know, I remember you promising me something there, agent. But now, to look at you, I'm guessing things have changed."

She turned enough to see the stern glare coming off Gage, the closed-off stance with his arms crossed over his chest and his face turning crimson.

"Regardless of what the two of you discussed seven years ago, the case is re-opened, and we wanted to come by and give our condolences."

"*Humph*," grunted Maxwell. He collapsed his large frame back into the recliner.

"I'm just so relieved you found her. We never got to bury her, put her to rest."

Turning to face Mrs. Maxwell, Greer nodded. "I am so very sorry for your loss, ma'am."

"When can we have her back?"

"That's yet to be determined. We have to wait for the ME to release the bodies."

The woman's gaze swung to Gage. "And Rachel?"

Gage nodded. Mrs. Maxwell wiped her eyes, her face turning red.

"She was an amazing woman. So dedicated."

Greer led Mrs. Maxwell to the large kitchen table and sat next to her. "Tell me about Rachel and Gabby."

Mrs. Maxwell beamed. "Our son's secrets were obviously not very well hidden. We knew early on that things were not as they seemed, but we tried to encourage him on the right path. Gabby, though, was an amazing woman, bright and talented. She graduated top of her class in college."

"What did she major in?"

"Physics. She loved numbers and equations. It was an addiction, really. She took a job as an engineer at a local company. When she first brought Rachel by, we were skeptical, considering her employer. But she was the sweetest woman. She and Rachel were the same age and would go out for coffee, movies, things like that."

Greer smiled, getting a picture into the women's lives made them much more than the files on her desk.

"Gabby told me one night that Rachel would do anything to protect the children of that man—even from him, if necessary."

"Did you have any reason to think they were in danger?"

Mrs. Maxwell glanced over her shoulder at Gage, then back to her. "Well, no. Gabby never said anything of the sort. But a few weeks before they disappeared, she did mention that Rachel was worried about something at work. Gabby asked if we could have her brother meet her somewhere."

"Did you set up the meeting?"

"I did, but I urged her to reconsider. My son is no saint. His business was ... unsettling. I didn't want her to put in the middle." Mrs. Maxwell took out a napkin to wipe her face.

Greer reached across the table and took Mrs. Maxwell's wrist in her hand and squeezed as the woman wiped away her tears.

"She said it was urgent, that as much as Rachel said she was fine, she said it didn't seem right."

"What didn't seem right?" Greer asked softly.

"Something about her job. She wouldn't go into detail."

She nodded. "How did Gabby seem after the meeting?"

"Angry. She said he was the same old Richard, never willing to do the right thing."

Another interesting insight.

"Gabby dropped the subject after that."

"I know this is a hard thing to process, ma'am."

"We've had seven years to accept she was gone. We always knew, and now, we're just glad to have her back."

She nodded. "I wondered if I could look at her room?"

Mrs. Maxwell straightened. "I ... I guess you could. Besides some dusting and vacuuming, I've left it the same."

Greer assumed as much. Standing, she followed Mrs. Maxwell up the stairs, shedding her heavy coat and cradling it in her arms as they ascended.

Opening the door at the top left of the stairs, Mrs. Maxwell sighed.

"I don't mind you looking, the police did so years ago and found nothing. But please, if you could, keep things as they are."

"Of course." She nodded as she stepped past the woman into the room.

The walls were painted a pale yellow. Bright white trim edged the windows, where yellow and white trellis curtains framed the view outside. The room had a high ceiling, and the windows and doors extended to accentuate the extra space.

A large, king-sized bed sat facing the window while a white armoire and matching desk lined the walls. Setting down her purse with her coat, Greer pulled out some gloves and noticed Mrs. Maxwell was already gone.

"Something you want to share?"

She shrugged at Gage as she scanned the desk. "I just figured, if Gabby was so concerned, there had to be some form of evidence that confirmed her worry."

"We went through the room seven years ago. Wiped it clean and took her laptop, calendar, and everything else that had journaling or anything that could be important into evidence. I'm sure it's still there."

"I'm sure you were thorough." She glared a moment before going back to her search. "The thing is, you aren't a woman."

He chuckled. "Glad you noticed."

She grinned, sweeping her gaze across the room and opening up the armoire. "What I mean is, she knew her parents would always be connected to her brother, her life would intersect with him and his deeds. If she was that concerned for Rachel, and she did have some kind of proof, she wouldn't put it where anyone would easily look."

"Why do you think there was proof? Knowing Rachel's boss is scum is proof enough."

She shrugged. "Well, I could easily be wrong. But we're here, and I want to look, okay?" Putting her hand on her hip, he grinned. "Why are you smiling?"

"Just found your comments, interesting."

"Why?"

He shrugged. "You just admitted you can be wrong."

"Of course. What? You think me that magnanimous that I would assume I was always right?"

He chuckled. "That's a big word and yes."

It hit a little harder than she thought it would. Shaking her head, she turned back to the room.

"Greer."

She waved him off. "I'm okay up here, you can go speak with the parents."

Keeping her eyes on the room, she ignored the irritation working its way up her spine as the door opened and closed once more. He didn't know her very well, obviously. Unless of course, she really did act that badly around him and was really a know-it-all when it came to their interactions.

"Great, just great." Another personality issue she'd have to overcome.

Standing at the foot of the bed, the pillow on the right

appeared flattened. If this was her side of the bed, maybe there was something missed.

She sat down and pilfered through the nightstand, coming up empty. Running her hand under the mattress and behind the stand turned up empty too. Maybe she was going to strike out as well.

Sitting back down on the edge of the bed, she studied the room. The window was directly in front with a desk to the right. What appeared to be a closet sat on the left side of the bed. Her brows furrowed.

Why did the molding look so, odd? There was a cut in the middle instead of one long piece that should stretch across the top.

She grabbed the chair from the desk and pulled it to the closet. Standing on top, she felt around the molding. After shimmying it back a forth a few times, it loosened, pulling away from the wall. With a hard yank, it came off in her hands. A narrow space appeared. Stepping down, she sat the trim on top of the desk.

"Hey, I'm ... What're you doing?"

Ignoring Gage, she stepped back on the chair and used her phone's light to look inside the narrow crevice. A purple book sat in the space. She carefully pulled it out.

"How did you find that?"

"It was just my magnanimous attitude, I guess." She stepped down, Gage's hand on her elbow.

At the bed, she opened the book and found pictures—lots of pictures of Gabby and a man.

"You know who this is?"

Gage peered over her shoulder. "No, I haven't seen him before."

Pulling the book closer, she took in a breath. One picture had Gabby and the man standing next to her car.

"I'm guessing you have?"

She shook her head. "He's tall, guessing around six three based on the car? Blond hair, blue eyes."

"You're kidding."

Chewing on the inside of her cheek, she sat the book down. "We need to see if Mrs. Maxwell will let us take this and at least make copies."

"You might be looking at a fight."

"Technically, you're FBI again, Gage. It's evidence."

He sighed.

Looking over her shoulder, she saw Gage's irritated expression. She returned her focus to the book, flipping another few pages. Pictures and scribbles lined each section.

His quick inhale made her pause as a picture of Rachel stared back up at them. The picture in the file he gave her was her license picture, proving the beauty of Gage's sister. But in this one, she was laughing, holding onto Gabby as they shared in their laughter.

"Gage, she's beautiful."

He nodded.

The words *Coffee with my bestie* were scrawled across the back.

"Are you—oh."

They both turned to see Mrs. Maxwell at the door.

"I see you found something that was missed?" She walked up as Gage stepped back for her to see. Her eyes teared. "I've never seen this."

"Ma'am, could we take this and make some copies? I assure you I would get it back to you."

"I ... I don't know."

"Mrs. Maxwell, we need some time to look through this. I don't want to have to bring a warrant."

"No, no. It's fine. Take it"

Greer turned a few pages. "Ma'am, do you know who this is with Gabby?"

Mrs. Maxwell stared down at the book. "I-I have no idea. Who is he? Was she seeing someone?"

"We don't know, but we'll find out."

Mrs. Maxwell wiped her eyes and nodded as she left the room.

"Gage, would you double-check the hole? I can't see in the back."

He nodded, silent once again as he picked the chair up. "You need to look. That chair isn't sturdy enough for me."

She sat the book down. He took her elbow once more as she pushed on her tiptoes and shined the light.

"I think, there's something else." Her flashlight picked up a glossy reflection. "There wouldn't be anything like vents behind this wall, right?"

"No."

She pushed her arm into the space. "I can't reach."

Her body was lifted and she gripped Gage's shoulder as he held her legs, lifting her up. With the elevation, she was able to get her arm farther back, taking hold of the cold plastic.

"I've got it."

Gage walked her back to the chair, then slowly lowered her back down. As she stepped off the chair, she dropped her gaze to the bag and froze.

"A Glock."

22

"We need some evidence bags. I don't have any in my purse and we need one big enough for the molding too. All of this needs to go into our custody and dusted for prints."

Gage pulled out his phone and dialed. "You on your way? ... We need some evidence bags out here. No, no lights. Plain car, no uniform. I'll meet you out front."

Opening the bag, she pulled out the gun by the trigger guard and smelled the barrel.

"I realize it's been seven years, but I smell gunpowder."

He took a whiff and nodded. "If it's been in that bag the entire time, that means something else happened seven years ago."

She pushed it back into the bag and sealed it, then set it next to the book. "I don't suppose you know of a place we could set up, go through the book and everything?"

"FBI office. I just called a buddy of mine, he's bringing the bags and will follow us back."

She nodded as his gruff voice grumbled, that stern

expression back in place. She had to admit, she missed the smiling and playful Gage who had been around yesterday.

With a sigh, she turned back to the book and flipped through the pages.

"I'll be outside if you need me," he said as he left the room.

Feeling sick for him, she opened to the page that held Rachel's picture.

I'm worried. He won't stop until he gets what he wants. How do you tell your best friend that they're wrong?

Feeling as if those comments created more questions than answers, she turned back to the pages of Gabby and the mystery man, hoping to find a name.

"What'd you find?"

Mr. Maxwell stood in the doorway, filling the space.

"Seems your daughter had a journal hidden. I think it'll help."

He glared between her and book. Her nerves kicked into gear as his face reddened.

"You can't have it," he growled and stepped closer.

Freeing her hands, she unhooked her weapon. "Sir, I suggest you take a step back."

He laughed. "You're going to threaten me in my own home?"

"We already have permission from your wife to take the book. Either way, it's coming with us."

His eyes widened.

"Where is your wife, Mr. Maxwell?"

His gaze shifted back and forth, his jaw clenched. "You can't take it. I won't let you."

"Sir."

All at once, he rushed forward, shoving a beefy fist toward her body. Dodging the punch, she punched his face, following through with her elbow. He wrapped her up, and she hit his ears with her open hands, then yanked until his grip lessened.

As she pushed off, she kicked his chest and then hit him over the head with her fists. He fell to his knees.

"Greer!" Gage appeared, tackling the man to the ground.

Maxwell pushed Gage off, coming up to his knees as Gage punched him in the face, then yanked his arm behind his back. Maxwell fell to his stomach on the floor.

She pulled her weapon. "Stop resisting, Mr. Maxwell."

"My arm. He broke my arm," Maxwell yowled as Gage cuffed him.

"Problem?"

She aimed at the stranger until he flashed his badge. With a nod, she lowered her weapon.

"You okay?" Gage pushed into her space.

Stepping back, she nodded. "I'm fine." She worked to ease her breathing from the adrenaline rush.

He nodded released her arms.

"He needs an ambulance." She nodded to the large man groaning on the floor.

"Already called it in. They were in the area." The officer from the door knelt next to the man.

"Where's his wife?"

The officer peered up at her, then Gage. "No one was around when we came through."

Taking the bags sticking out of Gage's coat pocket and ignoring his stare, she loaded the gun and the book in separate bags then sealed them. Pushing the large piece of molding into the longer bag, the voices of paramedics entering the house drifted to the room.

"Up here."

Stepping around a writhing Mr. Maxwell, she shoved the bags into Gage's chest and pushed past him, descended the steps and bypassing the paramedics.

"Mrs. Maxwell?"

She searched through the entry and the sunroom, the odor of gunpowder hung in the air as she hit the hallway. Pulling her weapon, she looked past the kitchen and down the narrow corridor.

"Gage?"

"I'm here."

She jumped a little at the fact he was right behind her, gun drawn.

"You have to stop sneaking up on me," she snapped.

Opening the doors as they went, she found various broom closets, a bathroom and laundry room, but the odor became stronger as they went further down. Gage tracked in front of her to the door at the end. She nodded as he counted down.

Busting open the door, her heart leaped in her throat to see Mrs. Maxwell slumped on a chair, her face upward. The small bullet hole in her forehead proved there was a reason she hadn't come running. Gage stepped into the room and checked her as a formality, then sheathed his weapon.

"I can't believe this. Why now?" Greer shoved her gun into the holster and ambled into the workshop. The smell of gunpowder and blood overwhelmed the space.

"Mr. Maxwell knew we found something. Just because they didn't approve of their son's activities on the outside doesn't mean he wasn't in on it."

She stared at Gage a moment. "But was it him or did someone follow me here?"

Gage stepped forward, and she held up her hand.

"Don't."

Turning her back on the room and Gage, she headed to the sunroom. The officer from earlier came down the stairs.

"Agent Ari Munoz."

She shook his hand. "Detective Greer Bennett. We found Mrs. Maxwell."

"Oh?"

She pointed down the hallway, and he nodded. Pacing the space, she groaned as nausea burned through her stomach.

How could that man kill his wife in cold blood? Had they missed something? As uncomfortable as the guy made her, she didn't expect him to be a killer. Or did someone else show up and kill Mrs. Maxwell while they were looking for her?

"Ari's going to take care of the crime scene so we can get moving." Gage appeared with the evidence bags in hand.

"Where did you put those?"

He shrugged. "The linen closet."

She followed him out the door where the ambulance was moving slowly down the winding driveway.

"So, you think he did it?"

"I don't know." He opened the car door, then set the evidence bags in the seat behind her.

"Oh, my coat and bag."

He opened her door and eased her inside. "Get in and lock the doors, I'll get them." He slammed the door after tossing the keys in her lap.

With a sigh, she started the car, locking the doors and turning up the heat. In her shock, she didn't even think about the cold and her coat ...

Closing her eyes, she leaned her head back. Mr. Maxwell had unnerved her, but he was just an obtuse, large man who used his size to intimidate. Even after the attack, she didn't think he was trying to kill her, just take away that book.

A knock made her jump. Gage stood outside the driver's side door. She hit the unlock button.

He climbed in and handed her the coat and purse. Wrapping the coat around her legs, she shivered.

"So, FBI?"

He nodded, jaw clenching.

"Gage?"

He ignored her, his hands clenching the wheel so tight his knuckles turned white. Holding her arms, she sighed and put her focus outside, trying to push away the image of Mr. Maxwell lunging at her and Mrs. Maxwell's lifeless body slumped in the chair. This case was stacking up even more bodies, and the only connection they had was Bolstero.

"I shouldn't have left."

She shrugged. "Wouldn't have changed much."

"He wouldn't have attacked you." Gage protested.

"You handled yourself well. You do a lot of hand-to-hand combat in sniper school?"

His jaw clenched as he shook his head. "Not the time, Greer."

She nodded and turned back to the window, leaning her arm on the middle console. He let out a heavy sigh and pushed his hand around her elbow, taking hold.

"I'm sorry for leaving. Seeing that picture just surprised me." He cleared his throat. "It's like I'm reliving all this again. Seven years ago, and I'm right back in the middle with no answers."

She took his hand in both of hers.

"The last time I saw her was New Year's at my parent's house, seven years ago. We had dinner, watched the fireworks. Things were good. I hoped she had planned to leave. She seemed relaxed and happy."

He pulled into the underground garage, releasing her hand to get a parking ticket and driving through the rows until he found a parking spot. Pushing the car in park, he turned and pulled her hand back in his.

"He wouldn't have gotten to you." His bright green eyes stared into hers.

"I was trying to lighten the mood by making that comment. You know, getting you out of your head? I can take care of myself. You do see that, right? I'm not your responsibility."

"You are. You're my partner." He clenched his jaw a moment. "Although I do believe you can take care of yourself, tell me you won't depend on hand-to-hand with the next man who comes at you like that." He leaned closer as she felt herself leaning back.

"I can handle myself. I have your back, too, Gage," she whispered.

He nodded, squeezing her hand tightly as his thumb moved across her fingers. "Glad to hear it." His gaze moved across her face, drifting to her lips more than once.

Clearing her throat, she made herself speak, "We should go inside."

He nodded again, taking his time before finally letting go of her hand. He slipped out of the SUV.

She shook her head. "Good grief."

The tension between them heightened, but mostly because he kept pushing something she didn't understand. After all the arguing, fighting, and disagreements, it was obvious they had different personalities, different points of view.

Why was he pushing still? Holding onto her all the time, looking at her like that?

Her door opened, and she slid out, gripping her purse as she pushed her coat on with a grimace. Taking two of the evidence bags from his arms, she followed to the elevator that would lead to the upper level of the FBI building.

Silence spread as they rode up and then stepped through the open doors. Signing in, they both checked their weapons, then Greer followed Gage to another elevator. He guided her down the hallway, his hand on her back once again. They paused a few times as he nodded to the greetings from people who apparently still remembered him.

The conference room had his name on the door. Setting down the evidence bags, she released her purse and unbuttoned her coat.

"I need to check on some things. Can you wait here?"

She nodded and sat on the top of the desk. "I'll be fine. I want to look through the book."

"We don't have much time. We need to head to see Bolstero, catch him off guard before he learns we're here."

She nodded and stood, pulling out a chair that faced the door. "Then get to work, Gage." She winked as he nodded, the sternness on his face barely changing as he stepped out and slammed the door.

She sighed and bowed her head.

"Lord, please give Gage some peace and grace. He needs You, and I pray that You can guide us both to find the killer of his sister and Gabby."

Taking a seat, she pulled the book closer, studying the pictures. Bolstero sat in the back of her mind. If he was really behind all of this, she needed more information about him and his position. Digging through the files on the table, she pulled out Gage's case file and scanned the interview with Bolstero after Rachel disappeared.

The officer described the man as emotional, upset at the loss of Rachel. He had no idea of what could've happened. The children were too young to be interviewed. Bolstero's lawyer made sure of that.

What about Bolstero's wife?

Flipping through the pages, the cold case was followed up, but Mrs. Bolsero was never interviewed, even the year after Rachel's disappearance.

"Why didn't she give a statement?" Pulling out her phone, she put in a call to Captain Mansfield.

If she was about to go head-to-head with Bolstero, she wanted much more information.

23

Hustling into the men's locker rooms, Gage leaned against the wall and blew out a heavy breath. He had left her, left her in that room without protection, and she'd almost paid the price.

The image of Maxwell inches from Greer, the massive man lunging at her, pricked his skin. He punched the wall.

"Get a grip man."

How did Greer figure out the molding was the door to the hiding place? How had they missed it? He and the FBI both searched that room and only found a few items that had nothing to give.

He grunted and went to the sink to rinse his hand.

But to see Rachel in that picture, to see her happy, laughing like she did. It was a full-body laugh, her hands clasped or clapping, her wonderful laugh echoing through the room.

He missed that. He missed her.

Drying off, he pushed through the doors and headed back to the conference room. Taking a deep breath, he stepped in front of the glass door and saw Ari's back to him as he sat on the desk, talking to a smiling Greer. His jealousy jumped as he opened the door.

Ari stood and turned, a smirk on his face. Greer hid her smile from behind her hand.

"Problem?"

She shook her head as Ari stood there, smiling like an idiot.

"What did you tell her?"

"You really dove off a bridge after an Olympic swimmer?"

He groaned as Ari let out a laugh. "It wasn't like that."

"So, you didn't jump off the bridge?" She leaned forward, a wide grin on her face that eased his irritation, if only slightly.

"We got a call about a jumper, and since we were the closest, we headed over there. Ari approached and tried to talk her down."

"But she didn't understand a word I said."

Greer's eyes bounced between them. "Was she dressed in a bathing suit?"

"No, of course not. It was some kind of leggings and a long-sleeved shirt. She went in with a smile, and I took off after her. She was fifty feet ahead of me by the time I came back up. Neither of us knew she was German and didn't speak English."

Greer let out a chuckle and stood, grabbing her purse and digging out some bills. "I'm hitting the vending machine, you want something?"

"I'll get it." He turned to the door when she stepped in front.

"I think I can manage."

Instead of arguing, he simply nodded. "Coke."

"Got it." She narrowed her eyes a moment before letting the door slam behind her.

"Man, you are in so deep." Ari had a wide grin on his face.

"We work together."

"Don't even. I saw your face after getting that guy down. You were more than concerned. You're in trouble."

As he started his rebuttal, Ari shook his head, holding up his hand.

"She's tough, headstrong, and can take out a man three times her size. The marks on the guy's chest prove it."

"What marks?"

"She kicked him hard enough to leave a bruise from her heel and toe. A woman who can do a kick like that in heels? You better watch yourself."

"She kicked him too?"

Ari shrugged. "I just got her statement." He slapped him on the arm. "Word of advice—I wouldn't let her walk around here unescorted."

"I think she can handle it," Gage remarked.

Ari only shook his head as he went for the door. "You know how some of these guys get when they see a drop-dead gorgeous woman walking around with no ring."

Gage's jaw clenched as Ari opened the door, a smile once again on his face as he held it open. Greer walked through, thanking Ari and shoving the bottle into his chest. Ari only shrugged as he let the door shut.

"So, nice chat?" Greer perched on top of the table, drinking her Coke and eating a bag of cookies.

"Yeah. Ari's a good guy."

She narrowed her gaze again. "You miss it?"

Opening the bottle, he took a sip. "The FBI?"

She nodded.

He shrugged. "Sometimes, I guess. But the move to Homeland has been ... therapeutic."

She almost choked as she covered her mouth. "What?"

He chuckled and sat down beside her in one of the chairs. "I was busy—really busy—when I worked here. Had no social life, well, not much of one anyway. Rarely got to see my family. And then when Rachel disappeared, I couldn't deal with it. My parents, my brother struggled, and I just ... ignored it. When I got shot, all the chaos suddenly didn't work anymore."

She slid down into the chair next to him, chewing on the cookies as she gazed at the wall.

Shaking his head, he stared at her profile. Bright lips, hair falling around her face, he'd not be able to focus the rest of the day if they stayed alone in this room together.

"You moved to Homeland to not be so busy?"

"Basically. It took me a while to get back up one hundred percent after getting shot, then getting cleared to work. When that day came, I wasn't as eager to get back into it. Started looking at other options, and this job fit."

"So, you lived for the chaos, huh?"

"Yeah, chaos, adrenaline, drama, it was addicting. I was always an adrenaline junky. When I got out of the Marines, the FBI just seemed to call to all those addictive qualities I thought I needed."

Brushing off her fingers, she paused. "What do you do in Homeland?"

"I work the terrorist board, translation."

Her eyebrows went up. "I guess I didn't expect that."

He chuckled. "You said you didn't think I ran investigations anymore. You're almost right."

"So, you do?"

He shrugged as he finished his drink. "On occasion, when something strays into my realm of expertise."

"Which is?"

He enjoyed the toying sound in her voice. That was something new.

"Europe."

She nodded as she set the bag down and took a drink. He leaned forward, grabbing the empty bag with a frown.

"You couldn't leave me one?"

She eased into his space. "You didn't ask." She smirked and stood, pulling on her jacket.

He watched her try and hide the same grimace from earlier as she slipped her arms into the sleeves, then buttoned up her coat.

She took her bag and then turned, motioning to the evidence. "This will be good?"

"I'll get it locked up and have someone posted."

"You know, you could stay here instead."

His jaw jumped.

"I think the interview with Bolstero would go better if you weren't around."

"You're not going alone."

"What about with your friend? He could go."

Heart pounding, he took a beat before responding. "Greer, walking into that building is the last thing I want you to do."

"But you being there will make it worse. He won't give me anything. I know you know I'm right." Her head tilted. "Let me do my job."

"You can do it with me there. I'll stay out of your way."

She turned and pushed out of the office.

"Lord, if this is Your plan, I need some help here."

Because the thought of her being in the same building, the same room as Bolstero, made him sick and angry. The man was evil, and they were about to walk into his territory.

"Give us protection, Lord," he prayed as he trailed down the hallway after Greer.

24

Back in the car, Greer's phone went off.

"Hey, Rick. What's up?"

"I got some info on the woman you called about."

"I called Mansfield to look into it. How do you have it?"

"I'm going nuts here. All I do is eat and sleep. I need something to keep me busy. You should've just called me."

"I'm trying to let you rest. You should take it easy."

"I'm good, G. You want to hear what I found or not?"

"Yes, of course."

"Mrs. Bolstero is at a rehab facility in the Caymans."

She glanced at Gage. "Rehab for what?"

"I can't tell. It doesn't give me anything, and we won't find out. The patient-client thing. I can't even tell how long she's been there. The only reason I know is because the cold case detective followed up four years ago and made Bolstero give up the information when he couldn't speak to the wife."

She chewed on the inside of her cheek. "That's interesting. When interviewed about the disappearance of Rachel, she was in the hospital, then she ends up in a rehab facility out of the country where no one can talk to her? Seems odd."

"Yeah. Watch your back, Greer. I don't want to hear about you getting attacked there too."

She grimaced. "Okay, bye." She hung up with a groan. That wouldn't be a good conversation. "Rick says the wife is at some kind of rehab, out of the country."

Gage nodded.

"Hey, what's going on?"

No response.

"He may not even let us in. You know that, right?"

"He will. Just to spite the entire situation, he will," Gage grumbled.

"Well if you go in there, he'll find a way to get you all worked up. I'm not even going to pretend you can deal if you're this mad and we're not even there yet."

His silence lasted as they pulled into a parking lot. The building was three stories tall, all glass across the front.

"This is his office?"

"Not what you were expecting?"

She shook her head. "Not at all."

He had a firm grip on the steering wheel as he stared at the building. Leaning on the console, she tried to find another way to distract him, and the only thing that came to mind was definitely not happening.

But it did cross her mind.

"If you have to go in, let me do the talking. Just be my backup and don't talk."

"I think I can handle myself."

"It's not that. I want to see how Bolstero's going to play this off, and I need his focus on me. Just trust me."

He shook his head, his jaw shifting.

"Oh, so you need me to trust you, but it doesn't go both ways?"

"It's not the same."

"Yes, actually, it is."

Sliding from the vehicle, she rushed to the front steps, smirking and hoping it would at least buy her a little time—enough for her to get him to see her plan.

With a smile, she made her way to the front desk. "Hello, I need to see Mr. Bolstero."

"Name?"

"Detective Greer Bennett."

"Do you have an appointment?"

Greer winced. "It's about a cold case I'm working. I was hoping Mr. Bolstero would be willing to take a few moments. You can tell him it's about Rachel."

"Let me check." The woman nodded and picked up the phone.

She could feel Gage behind her, the smell of his cologne wafting through the air.

"He's agreed to see you. Please, come this way."

She smiled and followed the young woman to the elevators. "I love that sweater, it's beautiful."

"Oh, thanks. It was a Christmas gift from Mr. Bolstero."

They made their way into the elevator, and the woman looked Gage up and down.

"Never mind him. He's an associate of mine. Kinda grumpy." Greer smiled and tried to get the woman's focus again as she felt Gage's hand rest on her lower back. "Your boss bought you a sweater? That's really nice. I don't think any of my supervisors have ever bought me anything for Christmas."

"Oh, he's a wonderful boss. Last year, he pulled out all the stops for the Christmas party. Live band, drinks, amazing food, and everyone received a hundred-dollar gift card."

She felt the pull on her coat before his hand dropped. He had noticed the cameras in the elevator as well.

"How awesome. I think I'm in the wrong profession."

The woman laughed as they left the elevator and proceeded to open two large glass doors leading into an impressive room.

"Thank you so much." Greer smiled as the woman left.

A large flat-screen TV sat on the wall in front of her, along with couches and wet bar. The L-shaped room led to a desk sitting in front of a panoramic scene. Behind the desk, sat Mr. Bolstero.

"Detective Bennett. So nice to meet you."

She put on another smile and hustled forward to shake his hand. "Thank you for taking the time to speak with me, sir."

"No problem. Anything for the police." His gaze shifted behind her. "Special Agent Sullivan, I presume." Bolstero immediately went stern, his arms crossed and he glared.

"Um, sir?" She stepped in front of the man's gaze. "Is there any way *we* can have this discussion? The only reason he's here is because of what we found. I was ordered to bring him," she whispered.

Mr. Bolsero dropped his gaze from Gage, then nodded, giving her an eerie smile. "That's fine with me. Please, have a seat."

"Thanks."

She took her time unbuttoning her coat and draping it over the chair with her purse. Glancing over her shoulder, she motioned Gage to step back before taking out her phone and tablet and sitting with an exaggerated sigh.

"Okay, may I record this? I'm terrible at shorthand." She made a face and Bolstero chuckled.

"Of course. I have nothing to hide."

"Of course not, sir." She turned on the recorder and set it on the desk. "Now, the reason I'm here is because we discovered human remains. One has been identified as Rachel Sullivan."

Bolstero's face fell, and he leaned on the desk. "Yes, I could only assume that's why she would disappear. I told the FBI when she disappeared that foul play was to blame. She was like a second mother to my children."

"Oh? How long did she work for you?"

Bolstero's gaze cut between her and Gage. "I'm surprised you're not aware of those things."

"Honestly," she scooted forward. "He hasn't said much about his sister, and I'm afraid to ask. I was only given the case recently, told to come talk to you and cinch up any lose ends."

Bolstero did a bad job of stifling his grin. "Well, she came to work for me when Johnny turned eight. So, four years."

Greer wrote it down. "And how did she come to work for you?"

"She was my nephew's first-grade teacher. I heard wonderful things about her and asked my brother-in-law if he could find out if she would be interested in a career change."

She nodded. "So, she taught your son and took care of him during the day?"

He shrugged. "Well, mostly. She also had my daughter, she's a few years younger than Johnny."

That was odd. Leaving out the fact he even had a daughter? Perhaps that might be a good pressure point.

"And there were no problems?"

"No, she was amazing. Johnny loved her dearly."

"Yes, you mentioned like another mother. Since she was a nanny, I'm guessing your wife was very busy?" She tilted her head with a smile, and he smiled back.

"Yes, she had her engagements and meetings that took precedence. For the most part, she was actually at home. But Rachel made the children happy, took them on outings, and I never had to worry about anything."

"As her employer, I'm sorry I have to question you, but the missing person's report mentioned you saw her early in the morning on the day she disappeared, and when you came home, she was already gone?"

He nodded. "Yes. That was common. She worked from seven-thirty in the morning to three-thirty or four in the afternoon. If they were on a trip, sometimes it would be later.

But I never saw her during the day and rarely saw her in the evenings when I got home."

She nodded. "Did she have an outing planned that day?"

He shook his head.

"The missing person's file mentioned your wife being there. Would it be better for me to question her instead?"

Bolstero went stern. "She's not in the country, so no."

"Oh, okay then." She shrugged. "The report mentioned your wife saw her at lunch and then at four. But after that, she couldn't remember seeing her around the house. Did Rachel usually announce when she was leaving?"

"Of course."

Greer nodded and made a note. "Is there anyone else we could speak to? I haven't found anyone else who seemed close, besides family, I mean." She made another face, and Bolstero nodded.

"She had a woman she was close with, an associate of mine's sister. Gabby, I think? You'd have to speak with Richard Maxwell, for certain."

"Oh, that would be wonderful. Do you have a number for him?"

Bolstero chuckled. "State pen. He was arrested several years ago. It shocked me."

Her jaw dropped. "How close were you?" She leaned in, looking at him in bewilderment.

He leaned forward on the desk, his eyes darting from behind her. "He was a close associate. Maxwell worked for me for a period of time, did some good things with my company. I was just starting out and needed someone to help me delegate.

"But things went bad when he tried to implicate me in some kind of deviance he was being charged with. I told him I wouldn't have someone in my company I couldn't trust and fired him."

"Oh." She nodded and bit her lip. "Well, I think that's all the questions I have." She stood and reached out her hand across the desk.

He stood and shook it with a smile that made her want to yank back and wipe off her hand. "If you have any other questions, please let me know."

"Thanks for all your help." She turned off her phone and gathered her things in her arms, awkwardly handling her purse and her coat.

Bolstero chuckled. "Do you need some help?"

"Oh," she stepped back from the chair and then Gage, "no, I'm fine, thanks. Have a nice day."

Gage opened the door and followed her to the elevator. As they stood in silence, she could feel his irritation coming off in waves, but he kept silent.

"Thank you again." Greer nodded at the woman at the desk, who rushed forward.

"You mentioned a Rachel, but do you know of anything about Mrs. Bolstero?" she whispered with wide eyes.

"No, but I really do need to speak with her. Do you have a number for her? I can't find one."

The woman made a face and took her elbow, pulling her away from Gage. "She's been gone for years. The word is she's at some kind of medical retreat."

Greer widened her eyes. "Really? That's odd. Was she in bad health?"

"I don't think so. I only met her once when I first started here."

"When was that?"

"About eight years ago. But she was unnerving. Always looking me up and down." The woman shuddered.

"She doesn't come to the Christmas parties?"

The woman shook her head. "Nope, and I heard she's been in the center for at least seven years. So, it must be something serious. It's awful, but I'm kinda hoping things are south with them." The woman raised her eyebrows and smirked.

Greer shrugged. "Oh, well, I don't know. If I hear anything, I'll call, okay? What's your name?"

"Tisha Johnson. I would appreciate a heads up." She winked.

"Of course."

Watching the woman walk back took all Greer's effort to keep from making a comment about the fact she was going after a married man, a deviant married man. Gage walked up, and she pushed her bag and tablet into his chest, then put on her coat before grabbing them up again.

Once outside, they crossed the parking lot, and he opened her door. "We need to talk."

"Easy, just wait." She slid in and he slammed the door with a little too much gusto.

Great, this was going to be fun.

25

G age barely kept his mouth shut before he got in and drove away from the office.

"I can't believe you did that. You didn't even let me say a word. Next time you want to play a game, let me know beforehand, so we can discuss it."

"Excuse me? You're the one who's sitting in the car, unable to hide your hate and anger for the man. How on earth would you be able to interview him? He wouldn't give you one bit of information."

"And you think you got so much? Because I didn't hear anything new."

"Then you weren't listening." She shifted to glare at him. "Besides, I just found out the wife disappeared seven years ago. That seems strange, doesn't it?"

"We knew she was out of the picture," he said.

"But now we have a timeline. I need to get back to that journal, see if what Mrs. Maxwell was talking about has something to do with the wife."

He clenched his jaw till it ached. The problem was, she had

been amazing. Bolstero had practically fallen over himself to speak to her, and she had played her hand perfectly.

"It's not that I don't think it worked. But next time, I need to know."

"I think you standing in the back brooding helped to sell it."

"I can't believe you did that."

"Did what?" She had her eyebrow cocked, lips pursed.

"You played a pretty good part."

She chuckled. "It worked. But man, he creeps me out."

Gage couldn't believe she could dispel his anger so quickly. He was ready to rip her apart when they left the office. Standing there, watching Bolstero stare at her, leering like he did, was almost too much.

"I really want to speak with his daughter."

"Even with your performance, I don't think that'll happen." He glanced over to see her staring out the window and chewing on the inside of her cheek. "Why?"

"He was uneasy about her. He blew her off, basically tacking her on as a sidenote to the conversation."

His phone rang, and he hit the Bluetooth.

"Sullivan."

"Hey, man. We need to talk." Ari's voice sounded upset. Not a good sign.

"I'm here on speaker with Greer."

"Oh." He paused. "The thing is, I'm not sure it was Maxwell who shot his wife."

"What?" Greer's voice dropped.

"No gunpowder residue on his clothes at all. The security system was turned off, so anyone could've entered from the back, and we never would've seen them."

"Someone else was there?"

"Then, then why did he lunge at me for the book?" Greer blinked and turned to face the front.

"Have you finished going through that book yet?" Ari's voice turned terse.

"Not all of it, we're going to finish as soon as we get there. We're about ten minutes out."

"Boss wants a word when you do get here."

His jaw clenched. "Okay, anything else you need to tell me?"

"No, just remember, this is a cold case. I have a feeling she wants to remind you of that."

He sighed. "Thanks. See you in a few." He hit the button and shook his head.

"I think I might let you do that interview on your own," she said.

Leaning against the door, she held her head. Her finger rubbed back and forth on her bottom lip.

"Why?"

"I need to study that book, and we're running out of time."

"We can stay an extra day if we need to. You said Mansfield was running the bullets and following up with Manos, right?"

She nodded.

"Then we have all the time in the world."

"Sure," she muttered. "Tell that to my boss."

"You've already made a lot of progress." He paused, glancing at her flushed face. "I don't think it's the time you're worried about."

Her lips pulled to the side.

"What's on your mind?"

"Nothing's adding up. If someone was in that house looking for me, why shoot Mrs. Maxwell? If they aren't there for me, why shoot her at all?"

"Maybe someone tried to sneak in, and she caught them. It's probably one of Bolstero's guys trying to keep them in check. The Maxwells might know a lot more than what they've given up so far. There's nothing that says this is about you, Greer."

With a shake of her head, she shut down, staring out the window.

As Gage went to speak to Executive Director Torrance, Greer set up in the small conference room.

With a notepad at her side, she flipped through the pages of the journal, documenting the dates and order of events.

Gabby's pages of her mystery man intrigued her. Could this be the man in the trench?

Pulling out her phone, she put it on speaker and dialed Dr. Shaver.

"Detective, good to hear from you."

"Yes, I'm sorry I missed your call this morning. I must've been on the plane."

"Plane?"

"We're out of state following up some leads." Greer leaned back and rotated her head. "I wondered if you could give me any more specifics on the mystery man we have in that grave."

"I can. He has a healed left radius, probably injured at a young age. He was around thirty, perhaps a few years older based on the bone density."

She added the information to her notes. "And cause of death?"

"There is evidence of a projectile, possibly a gunshot. The scoring on the rib is similar to other cases I've worked."

"That should help me out. I appreciate the assist on this one."

"Anything to find an identity. Have you found anything new?"

That was an odd question coming from a forensic scientist.

"Actually, I was going to ask you the same thing."

Dr. Shaver chuckled. "Well, I've got a bit of a mystery."

"Oh?" She sat up as the door opened, and Gage came in. She held her finger to her lips and pointed at the phone. "What's that?"

"A finger."

She paused. "As in, you have an extra digit that doesn't belong?"

"That's correct."

"I would say that is definitely a mystery. Are we looking at another body buried deeper?"

"There's a lot of speculation here, detective. I've requested some ground-penetrating radar equipment. I plan to go over the scene when it gets delivered."

She glanced to Gage. "Thanks for the information. I appreciate you keeping me posted."

"Have a good trip."

The call ended, and she leaned back. "Have you noticed any nine-fingered men? It's a slim chance, but it could be the killer's."

Gage collapsed in the chair next to her. "No, I think I would've noticed that." His gaze dropped to the book.

"Did you check with ballistics on the gun we found? See if it hits anywhere?"

He shook his head. "I'll give them a call." He took out his phone.

Returning her focus to the book, she flipped back to where she had ended before Mr. Maxwell interrupted her earlier.

"They're running it now. Once it comes through, I'm afraid that's all the assistance we're going to get here."

Gage stood and paced the room.

"What does that mean?"

"Executive Directive Torrance doesn't want any of her teams working on a cold case when they have so many others on the table. She's adamant."

"Okay, but we're not her people. I get the techs or something, but so far, ballistics is all we've asked for."

He continued to pace.

"Gage, what're you not telling me? You seem awfully worked up when we have a great lead."

His stern façade was different now, like he was wrestling with something more. But silence filled the room.

With a huff, she went back to the book, not interested in whatever he was keeping to himself. Hitting her phone, she pushed the button to call Rick.

"Hey, got something?"

"Actually, I do. A picture of a man with Gabby, looks like she had a boyfriend no one knew about."

"Really? That's quite a jump."

"Well, I found a book that was missed by the FBI." She grinned up at Gage, who only pulled out his phone and left.

So much for diffusing that situation. Reading him was getting harder and harder.

"What book?"

"Oh, it's got some pictures. I'm hoping it will give us a better timeline. I actually called to see if you could run a search for me. I think we have our mystery body figured out, we just need to find his name. I'll email the picture and the details Dr. Shaver gave me."

"Glad you called her. What did she say?"

"There's an extra finger in the trench."

"What?"

She chuckled. "Yeah, it could be the killer's, it could mean there's another body somewhere. There's a lot of speculation, and she doesn't do speculation. She's calling in ground-penetrating radar to scan the area, so be sure Mansfield keeps protection around her. I've got a nagging feeling about her being out there alone."

"Security detail is still set up, and I'll make sure she has someone escort her to and from the lab and the scene."

"Thanks. Bullets?"

"Nope, not yet. I'll call."

"Take it easy, Rick. Seriously. Mansfield can do most of this, let him."

"G?"

She sighed. "Yeah?"

"You good?"

"We just visited with Bolstero. Gage wasn't too happy about it."

"I can imagine. Just cut him some slack. Whatever he's dealing with, he doesn't strike me as the open-and-share kind of guy. He's just processing."

"I know. I'll talk to you later."

"Bye."

She took a couple of pictures of the book and sent them to Rick. Knowing she could trust him to be thorough and find the man gave her the ability to focus on the journal.

Looking up at the glass door, she let out another sigh. So much for her focus.

"You came to find me to discuss the Maxwell case?" Ari leaned back in his chair with a smirk. "Nothing's changed. I would've called you."

Gage nodded and shoved his hands in his pockets. "I've got a problem."

Ari's chuckle was more than irritating. "Man, more than one."

"Why didn't you tell me?"

"Tell you what?"

He paused and glared at his friend. "Torrance. She's divorced?"

Ari's jaw dropped. "She ... no way."

His jaw clenched.

"I'm guessing Bennett wasn't in the room with you?"

"No."

"I mean, I didn't even think about it. It's been years since you two hit it off."

Executive Director Torrance used to be a field agent like him. His time in and around Chicago after Rachel's disappearance created an on again, off again affair with the then-single woman. When he decided he had to stop visiting, he ended things for good. She got married, and he hadn't thought twice about it.

"I just didn't think it was an issue." He shook his head.

"So, problem is, you want Bennett, not her." Ari grinned big again as he groaned.

"This isn't funny."

Ari laughed. "I have to disagree. I knew that little fling would come back to bite you one day."

Her advances led to him brushing her off, which would lead to more vindictive actions the longer he was here.

"We need to get on that plane."

"You done with everything?"

He shook his head. "Not even close. We meet with the DEA at one, and she wants at least one of us to interview Maxwell in prison. I even suggested we stay another day so we wouldn't be rushed."

"Well, Torrance isn't a field agent anymore. She's the Executive Director. Her actions are being closely followed. Lashing out won't work."

"After the look she gave me when I left, I wouldn't be surprised."

"My advice? Tell Bennett before she finds out the hard way."

"We're not dating. We're not even close. To bring it up would assume something else entirely. Something I'm not working on until after the case."

Ari leaned back. "Look, just casually—"

"How do I casually say, 'Oh, by the way, the Executive Director is a former girlfriend who I just turned down and is going to kick us out of her building'?"

Ari shrugged. "Guess you'll have to be creative."

"You're absolutely no help. Let me know when you have the killer." He stormed out, heading back to the room where he'd left Greer.

Flushed, embarrassed, and annoyed, he couldn't imagine what was going to happen if Blair decided to ... He stopped dead in his tracks to see Executive Director Blair Torrance in the room with Greer.

Oh, man.

26

G reer noticed Gage's red face on the other side of the door, past Director Torrence's shoulder.

"If you need anything, please let me know."

She shifted her focus. "I do appreciate your help, ma'am. This case is far-reaching. We were hoping to finish up today, but we might be here an extra day."

Torrance shrugged, stiffly. "No problem. You said you needed some finger-print analysis here?" She pointed to the molding.

"Yes, that and the book. But I've been so busy going through it, it's already helped us out, and I have a lot more to go through."

The woman nodded. Taller than Greer, with jet-black hair, the director was gorgeous. Definitely a woman used to getting what she wanted. That would explain her rise to the top at such a young age.

"I'll tell Gage to get them downstairs. He knows the way."

She nodded as Gage entered the room.

Why was he acting so odd?

"Agent Sullivan, glad for you to join us." Torrance's stern candor echoed in the room.

"Ma'am." He narrowed his eyes.

"Detective Bennett was just informing me your trip might extend to tomorrow."

His eyes jetted to hers and then back. "Not sure yet."

The tension in the room went icy.

Torrance turned back to Greer. "If you need anything else, please let me know. We like to extend help to fellow agencies whenever possible."

Greer nodded as the woman left, noticing the close brush as she practically pushed right into Gage before heading out the door.

Greer's eyes went wide. "That was uncomfortable."

Sullivan just nodded, his jaw tightening.

Tuning back to the book, "She said you would know where to take the molding for fingerprinting."

"What?"

She looked up at his strained tone and wide eyes and shrugged. "What? She said you would know where to go to take the evidence."

His jaw dropped.

"Okay, spill. What's going on?" She stood, pushing herself into his field of vision. "Since we got back you've got this look on your face. Obviously, there's something going on."

"Nothing's going on. That's the thing," he said as he paced. "If I tell you, you can't—" He shook his head.

"Oh, good grief. Just spill it."

She crossed her arms and leaned up against the wall, not really sure what to expect here. The way he was acting, the world could be coming to an end.

"Eight years ago, I spent a lot of my time here. We had some cartel issues and with Bolstero. Then I did what I could here after Rachel left." He didn't even look up, just kept pacing. "Back then, Torrance wasn't the Executive Director."

"Oh, so you two were ... That explains the tension." She smirked.

He sighed. "Well, apparently, she and her husband split a few months back." His neck and face were turning a bright crimson.

Suddenly, it felt like her heart was going to pound out of her chest.

"With her attention and me stepping back, I think we need to be careful—"

"What does that mean, careful? We're here to do a job." She eased her voice as much as she could despite the anxiety building.

Why was she so upset anyway? It's not like they were, there wasn't anything really happening ... She couldn't even lie to herself. There was most definitely something going on between them. She just didn't want to know what.

"The evidence—we used to meet when I would take evidence. I'd drop it off, and we'd meet up." He paused, but still didn't make eye contact. "We didn't work the same cases, we were at the same level, so rank wasn't an issue. But we just wanted to make sure our relationship wasn't noticed. Several people knew about it, but we kept things quiet. And now—"

"Now what? You really think she'll kick us out because you're not going to meet up with her? Or *are* you?"

His eyes hit hers that time, a frown on his face. "No. That's not happening."

Greer nodded, biting back any comments as she sat down and slipped on some gloves to go back to work on the book.

"Greer?"

"Look, if you're that concerned, I'm going to get as much done as I can here. Why don't you go interview Maxwell?"

She didn't really know what else to do or say. They were treading on thin ice as it was, everything between them going hot then cold. She felt like a ping-pong ball, bouncing between the two.

But it didn't really matter.

He wasn't hers.

"You hungry?"

No, she most definitely was not hungry. But seeing how it was almost noon, and she hadn't eaten since breakfast, she needed to eat.

"Sure."

He sighed and left the room.

AFTER STEPPING out of the room to call in some food to be delivered, Gage decided to blow off everything but the case at hand. He needed to focus.

The situation with Blair, finding Rachel, Greer being attacked—everything was hammering into his mind and stressing him out.

The case needed to become the focus, and Greer had been doing all the work. Just because it had been a while, didn't mean he was that rusty when it came to investigating.

His phone rang. "Sullivan."

"You on your way?" Torrance's smooth voice came over the line.

He clenched his jaw. "Not happening."

"'Cause of her?"

"No, because that's over. It was a long time ago, and I'm not interested in going back. I've changed more than you would probably like anyway." He felt his face heat.

"Look, Gage, I can take a hint. But don't lie to me. You haven't changed that much."

Peering into the room, he saw Greer sitting at the desk, holding her head and working through the book.

"Trust me, I've changed a lot after seven years. Why do you think I moved?"

She sighed. "Maybe I've changed too."

"No, no I don't think you have. Let me do my work, then I'm gone."

"Now that sounds like the old Gage."

He bit back a retort. There was no way he would let her get to him like she used to. "I've got to go. I have work to do." He hung up and stepped back into the room. Sliding on a pair of latex gloves, he sat down next to her. "What do you have so far?"

She glanced up with a raised eyebrow.

"What?"

"You're suddenly checking in, huh?"

"Sorry, this case has been distracting on one too many levels. I need to be working more, get out of my head."

"Okay. Well, this might put you back in your head."

She turned a few pages and pulled out the picture of Rachel and Gabby. "Gabby mentions Rachel being in danger. She worries about the situation and says there has to be more she can do." She flipped a few pages.

"This is dated a week before they both disappeared. 'If only she had said something sooner. She's terrified and now, I am too. Hopefully Harris can get us through this because if not, we're all dead. I've never thought much about Rachel's God until now, and now, I think I would like to get to know Him.'"

His face heated.

"I've had Rick on the boyfriend, and I just sent him the name Harris to see if it matches."

Gage cleared his throat and tried to keep his focus on her, not the picture of his sister. "So, basically, it looks like Rachel found out something and told Gabby. Gabby tells her boyfriend, and he tries to find a way to protect the two of them, only it fails miserably."

She shrugged. "I just confirmed cause of death for our mystery man was a probable gunshot wound as was for Gabby. But why was it different for Rachel?"

He stood and paced, his body weary of the action. "It could still be a gunshot is the cause of death, there's just no evidence. If she was shot," he took a breath, "then fell, it could account for the blunt force trauma."

"I'm sorry, Gage."

His eyes jumped to hers. "Why? I'm the one out of my mind lately, I can't seem to stay on topic, on focus. My past—"

"Isn't relevant. Look, I know this case is hard for you, and I've been strong-arming you into sitting back and letting me do it. That's my fault, and I'm sorry."

He smirked. "Strong-arming me, huh?"

She chuckled. "Well, as close to it as I imagine it could get."

He collapsed in the chair. "I need to be in this, not just fuming around the edges. It's been a while since I've allowed my anger and frustration out at the fact Rachel's gone. But I'm good, as good as I'm going to be." He picked up her picture. "I just want this over. I want to know why, and I want to know who."

She patted his arm. "We'll get there."

He watched her eyes leave his, traveling over the book as her jaw jumped. Setting down the picture, he leaned in. "You good?"

She nodded. "We need to get everything figured out. We have the meeting with the DEA in an hour, and then we still need to meet with Maxwell. What time's our flight?"

"Seven."

"Well, that's cutting it close."

A knock on the door turned his attention to the officer standing there with boxes of food.

"Thanks, man." He set down the Tai food, hoping she would enjoy it. He had no idea what kind of food she liked. "But first, let's eat."

She stood, leaning over the boxes. "Smells good."

"It's one of the best places in this area."

Unpacking the food, he did his best to calm the pounding in his chest. Not meeting up with Blair, realizing he didn't want that kind of relationship and seeing all too clearly the woman in front of him, was compounding quickly.

Knowing God had put this together, he needed to just sit back and let God do whatever He had planned. 'Cause so far, he'd done nothing but mess it all up.

27

Food and a phone call into the state pen to make an appointment with Maxwell made the hour fly by as they headed to the DEA. Gage readied himself for a battle, knowing the attitude of Agent Buchannan and his arrogance.

Instead of warning Greer, he decided to allow her to work her magic, perhaps she would have luck where he had always failed.

"Detective Bennett, nice to meet you."

She shook Buchannan's hand, a formal smile on her face. "I didn't realize you were anticipating our visit so much."

Buchannan shrugged and grinned, ignoring Gage completely. But since he'd slugged the guy the last time they met, he would give him that.

"Please, have a seat." Buchannan motioned to a chair,

Stepping in behind her, Gage helped her pull off the coat.

"So, you've found Rachel?" The agent's gaze was still on Greer.

"Yes, as well as three other missing persons." She sat down and pulled out her tablet. "I'm sure you'll recognize the names Gabby Brown and Havier Martinez."

Buchannan nodded. "I thought you said three more?"

"We're waiting on confirmation on the fourth victim."

"Well, I don't see how I can help you." Buchannan leaned back in his chair, sheer arrogance coming off him in waves.

Greer opened her tablet. "For starters, you can tell me why Rachel Sullivan was approached as a mole to begin with."

"Look, it doesn't matter why. Bolstero got to her before we could pull her out."

Gage fisted his hands. "There's much more to that story, Buchannan, and you know it."

Buchannan flashed his gaze to Gage for only a second. "I'm not allowed to go into detail."

"No, that's not how this works." Greer leaned in, her tone icy. "This case is alive, no longer cold. I go to your boss and tell him or her what's going on, we'll get the details, and they'll be annoyed we had to go over your head. Now, tell us what happened."

Gage took the seat next to Greer, the tightness in his chest easing. Just getting in here to see Buchannan was a miracle. Greer seemed to be working a different approach, and he appreciated her intensity.

"She was approached by Simon Masters, brother-in-law to Bolstero. We had eyes on the family. After she had a meeting with Bolstero, we brought her in. She agreed to work with us."

"And what happened to all the information she retained on Bolstero? It wasn't enough to make a case stick?" Greer asked.

Buchannan shook his head with a glare. "No. Everything she found was circumstantial."

"From his home, his property, inside his company? It was all circumstantial?"

"His lawyers were good, and our lawyers weren't interested in making a case without a slam dunk. Things weren't as they seemed. She had a hard time getting into any of his business accounts or plans. She was there as a nanny, not in the company. Her information was trivial."

"So, why keep her on?" Greer questioned.

That was the question that had bothered Gage for years. If nothing ever worked, why did they keep her in that position?

"She was in a good position to make things work." Buchannan narrowed his gaze and Gage gripped the arm of the chair.

"You mean, Rachel volunteered to become involved with Bolstero with his wife in the picture?" Greer asked.

"No way."

Buchannan sighed. "Look, she simply made it clear she was available, and he worked things from there. As far as I know, nothing ever came of it. But we did see it as a promising lead."

Gage stood behind Greer, pacing.

"I must congratulate you on keeping your cool this time, Sullivan."

He ignored the comment to keep from jumping across the table and killing the man. His sister would never think to interfere in a marriage, not even to convict a scum like Bolstero.

"We have intel that Rachel was in danger and scared. This was a few days prior to her disappearance."

Buchannan's face dropped. "What?"

Greer leaned forward in her chair. "Look, I want all of it, not just the tidbits you think are enough to give us. What happened a few weeks prior? You had the family under watch, correct?"

He nodded.

"Then what about Maxwell?"

"He was being watched too." With a sigh, Buchannan stood and shoved his hands in his pockets. "Maxwell had a meeting with his sister a few days before. It didn't go well. We only heard bits and pieces about something between him and Bolstero, and his sister had a fit. When she left, she mentioned convincing Rachel to go to the police."

"And you didn't think it was relevant to tell me that seven years ago?" Gage glared at the agent, who only stared right back.

"It was need-to-know at the time. We were trying to figure out why Rachel would go to the police instead of simply coming to us."

"We've yet to determine that, but we do have new information. Is there anything else you want to inform us before we do your job for you?" Greer's tone dropped, her shoulders taught.

"I did my job. You have to do yours. I believe you know your way out." Buchannan glared down at Greer.

Standing, Greer pulled her bag to her shoulder. "If I were you, I would seriously rethink holding out during murder investigations. Surviving family members tend to get upset when they learn evidence or materials that could've been used to assist their deceased loved one gets left out of the picture."

"Is that a warning, Detective Bennett?"

Gage took a step forward as she grabbed his arm, stopping him.

"Not a warning, just a word of advice. In one day, we've already found more evidence than you did during the entire case. If we get Bolstero, and you don't, it's going to look very bad for you."

She turned and pulled at Gage's arm, making him back up to open the door.

Walking down the hallway, he watched her switch sides once again with her bag, then pull her coat up in her arms. His hand to her back, he guided her in silence to the elevators and then the lobby.

Receiving their weapons, they headed to the parking lot.

"You good?"

She nodded.

He opened the door for her, and she slid in. He followed to stand in the space.

"What's up with your shoulder?"

"Sore." She clenched her jaw as she wrapped the coat around her legs. "Let's get out of here."

With a sigh, he closed the door, went around to his side, and started the vehicle. "Let's go to the state pen and see Maxwell. It's a little early, but they should let us in."

She only nodded, her gaze focused out the window.

"Thanks for being hard on him. As much as I wanted to step in, I figured it wouldn't do any good. Last time I saw him, I busted his jaw pretty good."

"What?" She stared with wide eyes.

"Yeah, it was a rough few days when we couldn't find her," he murmured.

The pain had been horrific. He knew Bolstero had done something, but there was nothing he could do to prove it. He was ordered to keep from interfering with the investigation and was livid.

"It wasn't just that we couldn't find her, but that Buchannan didn't seem concerned. That's what got me."

"I can't imagine," she muttered under her breath.

The thing was, he really believed that maybe she could.

Letting the subject go, he called ahead to make sure they were good to see Maxwell.

"Do we have word on how his father is doing?"

He hit the Bluetooth button on the steering wheel and called Ari.

"Hey, man. Good talk?"

"Um, I'm with Greer, we just met with the DEA."

A pause of silence.

"Oh, yeah? I bet that went well."

"Better than expected. Do you have word about Maxwell? We're headed to see Richard."

"Well, he's alive. He went into cardiac arrest in the ambulance, and they stabilized him. His arm is still in bad shape but until he wakes up, they can't do much. We have a guard posted until we can charge him for attacking Bennett. The case with his wife is tricky."

"How so?" Greer chimed in.

"We found the suspected murder weapon about a mile away in a ditch. It'd been wiped clean."

"Have you matched the bullet yet?"

"Still running tests. I've got the tech room scanning local surveillance cameras for anything out of the ordinary. No hits yet."

"Does Richard know?"

Ari sighed. "Honestly, I have no idea. If he doesn't, I'd wait until you have all the information you need before telling him. He's got a long burning temper and will blame both of you for everything."

"Thanks for the heads-up."

"You staying an extra day?"

He glanced over at Greer, her focus out her window. "Not sure. I'll let you know when we get back."

"Well, good luck."

"Thanks." He ended the call.

After silence enveloping the cab for a while, Greer finally spoke.

"Have you spoken with Maxwell before?"

"I was there for the interview after Rachel disappeared. I wasn't allowed to ask questions."

"Maybe you should lead off then," she suggested.

Her focus still outside, he shifted in his seat.

"It's not your fault."

Her shoulders dropped.

"Killing Mrs. Maxwell could've just been a message. Bolstero reminding Richard to keep quiet."

He reached over and squeezed her wrist before she pulled it away. As much as they had been there for each other this trip, why did she suddenly not want his comfort?

Was it because of Torrance?

He rolled his eyes and gripped the wheel with both hands. Of course it was. Why else would she go from holding his hand to pulling away?

The state pen came into view as they rounded the corner, and his focus shifted.

"You sure you want to go in?"

"You think I haven't been anywhere else as bad?"

He let the comment go and parked. Letting Greer go in was going to be hard enough. She was too good to be in a place so awful. Those men were animals, and he didn't want her to be leered at.

He opened her door and waited until she had her coat on and buttoned before taking her elbow and slamming the door shut.

"I'm fine."

"Not negotiable, not here," he stated as he escorted her to the gate.

It was Greer's turn to pace as they waited for Maxwell to be brought out.

According to the warden, they had not received any phone calls or word about his family. At least they might be able to get something out of him.

Gage stood in the corner, his arms crossed and looking even more stern than before. If he was that upset because she wanted to be in on the interview, he would just have to stay mad.

The clanging of the door made her turn to see Richard Maxwell brought into the room in chains.

"Well, hello." His smile widened and she saw the same slimy look his father had given her.

Ugh.

"Have a seat, Maxwell." Gage pointed to the chair and the guard moved him toward it. "Thanks."

The guard nodded and went back out the door.

"I was hoping she would be the one here with questions." He leered again, and she rolled her eyes, situating herself in the corner with her arms crossed.

"Not likely."

"You look familiar." Maxwell leaned forward, his handcuffs clinking against the metal. "When Gabs disappeared, right?"

Gage nodded. "My sister also disappeared."

"Oh, right. Rachel. Man, you two are brother and sister?"

"Their bodies have been found."

Maxwell's face dropped as he sat back in the chair. "Have you ... do you know what happened?"

"You don't know?"

"Of course not. She was my sister," he hissed loudly from across the table.

She waved off the guard who turned.

"Mine too. I want to take out the man responsible."

"Who?"

"I have an idea, but no proof."

"You won't get it," Maxwell said. "Look, I don't have nothing to link them. If I knew how, I would tell you. My mom deserves to know what happened."

A lump swelled in her throat.

"But he's too sneaky, slimy. You won't get him."

Gage leaned back. "Tell me about your fight with Mr. Bolstero."

Maxwell went pale and shrugged. "He was my boss, we got into lots of arguments."

"Okay, what about your fight with Gabby right before she disappeared?"

"Mom called and wanted me to meet with her, calm her down. She was all worked up about something." Maxwell shook his head. "I had no idea they were that close, her and your sister. But she just kept saying I knew what was going on with Rachel and I should do something. I had no idea what she was talking about."

Gage must've given him the stink-eye the way Maxwell sat up.

"Look, I swear. Just that she would convince her to take it to the police, and then I'd be in trouble too."

"Did you mention your chat to your boss?"

He shook his head. "I wasn't crazy enough to give him a reason."

"Did you know about her boyfriend?"

Maxwell swung his gaze to her. "Yeah, seemed legit. Did a search on him."

"What's his name?"

"Harrison Dodson. He was some kind of accountant or something. Dusty checked him out for me."

She sat down. "Who's Dusty?"

"After Gabby changed her name, she tried to disown me, said she couldn't be seen with me. I was fine with it, it gave her some protection. But she was run off the road once, even after she'd changed her name. That's why she moved home.

"My mom got scared, begged her to move back in. After that, I hired a guy to keep an eye on her. Just in the evenings when things get harsh. He took a few pics, showed me the guy, and I had him check him out."

"Where's Dusty now?"

Maxwell shrugged. "Don't know, don't care. He never came

back once Gabby disappeared. Probably thought I would drop him for letting Gabby get hurt. He'd be right."

"Dusty have a last name?"

"Not really into that. Wasn't necessary to know a last name."

Gage glanced over his shoulder, and she nodded. He turned back.

"We visited your parents, told them we found Gabby."

"Good. My mom, it's been her thing, to finally bury her."

"While we were there, we were upstairs looking through Gabby's room. We found a Glock tucked into a secret hiding space."

His brows furrowed. "What? She hates guns, wouldn't even take lessons."

"We also found a book, had a lot of pictures and comments. Said Rachel was scared, worried about something." She leaned back in her chair.

Maxwell's gaze went to her. "When she talked to me, she was erratic. I couldn't even calm her down. The only thing I got was that she would convince Rachel to go to the cops. I mean, that and the fact I would be in trouble."

Her gut said he was telling the truth.

"Is there anyone who would still want to get to you?"

Maxwell narrowed his eyes, glaring at Gage. "Why?"

"When we were upstairs, your mother was shot and killed."

"What?" Maxwell bolted from the chair as Gage waved off the guard, standing slowly.

"We thought it might've been your dad."

Maxwell's face went stern. "Did you arrest him?"

"You think he did it?"

Maxwell shrugged. "Probably. I don't speak with him."

"He attacked me. Wouldn't let me take Gabby's book. Does he have contact with anyone?"

Maxwell shook his head. "This isn't nothin' you guys can fix, trust me. I'm ready to go."

"If there's something you can tell us—"

"No." Maxwell cut her off as he turned to the guard and was taken out of the room.

She sighed and leaned back in the chair. "So much for information."

"Let's get back. We've got more questions now, I think."

He took hold of her elbow to assist her up. She pulled away, feeling defeated. The case seemed to be pointing to a dead end, one where Hermann Bolstero sat with a smile.

28

As Gage pulled out of the parking lot, he let go of his question. "Okay, what's with the side? I've let you have your space, but now, I need to know." He was tired of seeing her wince and shift, pull away from him when he wrapped his arm around her right side.

"It's sore, that's all."

"From?"

"You tackled me, Gage."

When he went to protect her from the shooting, he had hoped he took the brunt of the hit as he rolled on his side. But getting her down must've been enough to injure her.

"Sorry."

"I said it's fine. Just a little sore. It's not as bad as this morning."

Just a little? That was probably a lie.

"I'll see if Rick can start a search on Harrison Dodson and search for a Dusty. Maybe we'll get one of them to match our extra man in the trench. It might be what we need to finally nail Bolstero."

"I told you, we may never know what happened."

Her phone rang as she typed.

"Huh?"

"What?"

"It's Bolstero."

His heart picked up the pace as she answered.

"Yes, sir?" She gritted her teeth and a forced chuckle. "That sounds great. Can you text me the address?"

Address? This better not be what it sounded like.

"Thanks so much for calling. Anything you can tell me will be helpful." She brushed her hair from her face. "Yes, okay see you then. Bye." She hung up with a shudder. "That guy."

"What does he want?"

"He says he has a few things he wanted me to know."

"So, you're going on a date with him?" His tone came out a lot more heated than he intended.

"What? Don't be absurd. He wants to meet and discuss things, without you there glaring at him."

"Not happening." He could feel her icy stare as he tried his best to focus on the road.

"Excuse me?"

"He's evil, Greer. I told you that. This is a bad idea."

She scoffed as her phone sounded. "The address is La Café Desporito."

He groaned.

"Look, a meeting in a public place with a detective, you really think he'll try anything?"

"That's his restaurant. That's where he does his business," he explained. "My guess is there won't be anyone else there but you, him, and all his bodyguards."

"You're being way too overprotective."

"I'll be there."

"No, you won't. That's the thing, he wants to talk to me, and he'll talk more freely if you're not there." Her voice rose, and he gripped the steering wheel tighter. "Besides, we need a break, and he might let something slip."

"He's probably going to bust you. Don't think he hasn't looked you up. He'll know you're brilliant and a great detective. He won't buy the act anymore."

The tension-filled silence drifted on, and he worked to ease his mind. She was a detective, a smart woman he assumed could take care of herself. But this was Bolstero, and she probably had no idea what he was capable of. A mastermind criminal, killer, and cold-blooded like she had never seen.

The sound of her typing broke the silence.

"What're you doing?"

"I'm looking for hotel rooms. The meeting is at six, didn't you say our flight was at seven?"

He squeezed the wheel. "Greer."

"Cut it out. I'm not discussing it anymore."

He swerved to the right, pulling into a parking lot and slamming the SUV in park. He turned to see her gripping the door and her phone, glaring at him.

"What're you doing?"

"You're not getting it. He's not someone you can outwit. He's already five steps ahead of you. Greer, he's a killer."

"This is my job. Why are you fighting me on this?"

"I'm not going to lose you to him too."

It came out before he could stop it and her eyes went wide as she turned to face the front. Heat flooded his face, and he could barely stop himself from reaching out.

It was like a nightmare, losing Rachel for seven years, having a hole he didn't know how to fill. And now, Greer was headed down the same path.

"I'm not your sister, and you're most definitely not responsible for me," she argued. "This is my job—a job I do well—and you cannot sit there and treat me as if I have no idea what I'm doing. You don't know me well enough to make that kind of assumption."

He stared out the window a moment before stepping outside the car and slamming the door, letting the cold air wash over him. It wasn't his place, even if they were in a relationship. It wasn't his place to give her orders. But he was her partner, and he knew things about Bolstero she didn't.

Walking around to her side, he opened her door, blocking the wind as she gaped up at him.

"I don't know you very well, but you are my partner. I intend on keeping you safe even if you don't believe you need it."

"If Rick tried to scare you—"

"Do I look worried about Rick or anyone else?"

She turned away, a red flush on her cheeks even with the cool air flowing through the cab. He sighed. Reaching across her body, he unbuckled her seat belt and took her hands in his, pulling her out of the vehicle. She stood next to him, her coat on the floor of the SUV, and her perfume swirling around him despite the effort of the wind. He pulled her arms, bringing her closer.

"There is something, though. Something we're both pushing at, and that makes this, complicated."

She cleared her throat, stepping back and crossing her arms as her focus dropped. "Nothing is complicated. I'm just doing my job."

It was another kick to the gut. First, she pulled away, and now this. Shoving his hands in his pockets, her eyes danced away from his. She was trying hard to blow it off, and he hated her for it.

"You can say that all you want, but it doesn't change anything. If you intend on going tonight, you have to clear it with your boss. You will have an earpiece, and I will be outside in a car waiting on you. That's non-negotiable."

She licked her lips, still focused elsewhere as his gaze

landed on those lips. It took more than his human restraint to keep from proving there was much more moving between them.

"Fine." She stepped back and slid into the seat.

He shut the door, returned his side, and got in. She was already on her phone.

Glancing up at him, she put it on speaker.

"Mansfield."

"We have an update."

"Good news?"

"Well, a few things. We found a notebook that was missed on the initial search of one of the victim's homes, I'm still going through it. We also found a gun in the same hiding spot, bagged and smelling of gunpowder residue."

"You getting a match?"

"It's running." She paused a moment. "After our interview with Bolstero, he's asked if I can meet with him tonight. He says he wants to be able to speak plainly without Sullivan around."

Mansfield was quiet for a moment.

"But you will have backup, correct?"

"It's not necessary, sir. It's a public restaurant."

"No, you will have backup."

She clenched her jaw. "Sullivan has already mentioned it."

A chuckle made him smirk. At least Mansfield gets it.

"Take another day, give me an update first thing in the morning about the meeting. I expect you to take every precaution, Bennett. This guy is more than a little bad news, nothing like the Madrid bust. Bolstero is twice the evil."

His head snapped around. Did he say Madrid?

"Yes, sir," she said as she hung up.

"You were in on the Madrid bust?"

She only nodded, not offering anything else about the huge bust a little over a year ago.

The case had made national headlines, and the FBI got a

pretty big slap on the back for the accomplishment. Madrid was a code name for a high-profile drug ring, a heinous group that had been on the FBI's radar for a long time.

Was that the case Rick told him about? Where someone she knew was killed?

The look on her face proved she wasn't interested in talking about it. But it all lined up. He did remember a police officer dying on the scene.

"Your partner?"

She gave a quick nod.

"I'll get the equipment from Ari. You'll have a com, and we'll record everything. I'll be outside and will come in if I feel it's warranted."

He glanced over to see her jaw twitch. He was stepping on her toes, but he didn't care. This meet was dangerous, and the second she understood that, the better.

As they drove back to the FBI, he realized his parents at least deserved a phone call. And if they had to stay another night, he might as well see if they could stay with them. It was an hour out of the city, but less he'd have to haggle for with his buddy in financial resources.

Besides, since his move to Homeland, he hadn't made an effort to visit.

"If we're staying, we can stay at my parents' house."

"No. I think we should stay at a hotel," she mumbled.

"Your boss isn't keen on paying for more than he has to."

"I'll pay."

He pulled into the FBI parking lot, taking hold of her wrist to keep her from bolting out of the car.

"Greer. What's up?"

Her flushed face turned to him. "I just think, professionally, we should stay at a hotel. What if Bolstero has us followed?"

He shrugged. "I don't really care. Bolstero has already figured you out. Your scam won't work tonight."

"Still."

"Look, my parents' place is safer than a hotel. You're still a target."

"I'm not in Lexington. I'm fine."

She pulled her arm free.

"We're staying with them. It'll be safe, and we'll both get sleep."

She shook her head, grabbing her coat and bag then scooting off the seat. Chasing after her, he caught up at the elevators. He let her have her silence and space until back in the conference room.

As the door shut, he crossed his arms and waited.

"Okay, what's up?"

She dropped her bag and coat, hanging her hands on her hips as she glared. "Look, I'm not okay staying with family. It's nothing personal. I just don't think it's professional." She swallowed as her neck turned red.

He pushed in front of her, sitting on top of the table and watching that red flush move across her face. "Nothing personal? Because it feels that way."

She crossed her arms. "This," she motioned between them, "isn't going to get easier if we're staying with your family. You're pushing much more than I thought you would." Her eyes danced around his face as he grinned. "Don't be so smug," she muttered as she turned to pace.

He took hold of her elbow. "It's not a big deal. We can work together. But I am glad you finally admitted it." His eyes worked around her face, feeling that tension again. "There is one way to take away all that unmitigated tension we have."

She glared, but he could see the smirk behind it all. "Not funny."

"I wasn't really joking." Standing, he took her elbows and searched her face, landing on her lips more than once.

"Gage, stop. You're just looking for a distraction and ..." Her eyes went wide as her hands pushed against his chest, a pressure that wasn't enough to make him flinch. "I'm sorry. I didn't mean—"

"Hey." He sighed as she grimaced.

"I'm sorry."

"Stop. Just hang on." He squeezed her elbows. "It's okay, I know what you meant. And you're not completely wrong. Yes, this is a distraction, a welcomed distraction. But that doesn't mean it's not more."

"Seriously? You think attraction is all it takes?"

He shrugged. "You think staying at my parents' will make this harder? Because I think it will either push things or end things," he whispered.

"Nothing's going to happen at all. No matter where we stay." Her jaw clenched as she backed into the wall, crossing her arms again.

He sighed. It was in his head now, and he wanted to find out, because the thought of kissing her breathless pushed hard into his brain, and he couldn't let it go.

Settling back on the table, her body eased as he gave her space.

"You never answered my question."

She narrowed her eyes. "What question?"

"You said it takes more than a smile. What does it take?"

Looking past him, she bit her lip, making him groan internally as he shook his head.

"When I figure it out, I'll let you know." She shrugged, a smile playing on her lips.

Man, those lips.

"But right now, we have to focus on the case." She pulled at his arm, trying to make him stand.

That perfume of hers distracted him so easily.

"What perfume do you wear, Greer?"

She straightened in surprise. "What?"

He chuckled, enjoying the sight of her off guard. "I like it."

"Thanks," she whispered as she moved to his side, pulling open the book.

He grinned at her trying to ignore him, move around as if nothing had happened. Even admitting to the attraction didn't seem to ease anything, but it did bring up other things.

Stepping into a lesser role at Homeland was a move to be around family, have a life. But so far, he hadn't been interested in anyone romantically and hadn't visited his family in over a year. So, now what?

God, Greer is amazing, and I feel a connection I've never... he sighed. Connection? Really?

It did seem that way. Besides the girlfriend he saw a couple of times a year during his first five-year deployment, he hadn't had anyone serious in his life. And that hadn't lasted past the second year. Then there was Blair ...

"We have work." She nudged his arm and he stood.

"I'm going to get the equipment ready for tonight and see if Ari is free to back me up."

She only nodded, her focus on the book in front of her.

Good grief. How did they go from fighting, arguing and the distain she had for him to him falling all over himself thinking about her?

The heaviness crept in as he made it outside Ari's office. She was going to meet with Bolstero, and that fear fell on his shoulders. There was no way he would let Bolstero get close to her. No way.

29

Sitting back in the chair, Greer watched Gage leave.

She had never had a guy get under her skin like he did. Overprotective and bossy and ... man, he was hot. She pushed her hair out of her face, twisting it up in a knot on top of her head to cool off.

Looking into those bright green eyes of his, his smile, seeing him reaching out to her and focusing on her lips. It was getting harder to dismiss him.

And now that he laid everything out there, she was more than a little frustrated.

What made him bring it all up? Couldn't he just keep ignoring it like she had been trying to do? If he agreed it was all just a distraction, why did he keep pushing for something more?

Shaking her head, she settled in the chair, calming her heartbeat from their earlier interaction. He was about to kiss her. It was all over his face. And that couldn't happen here. Well, it couldn't happen anywhere, really.

Groaning, she sat up and focused on the book. She had a few hours before the meeting with Bolstero and was determined to find something in all this muttering that pertained to why Rachel was scared and Gabby was scared for her.

Her phone buzzed, making her jump. She sighed as she hit the button and put it on speaker.

"Bennett."

"What's going on Greer?"

She winced at Rick's heated tone. "Um, what're you talking about?"

"Don't make me come up there."

"Look, I have a meeting with Bolstero, and it should give us some more information—"

"I want to talk to Gage."

"Then why didn't you call him?"

"Greer."

She sat back with a groan. "He's not here right now. He went to get surveillance equipment for tonight."

"Oh?" Rick's voice sounded eased. "Okay, well, that's something. I'm surprised he's letting you—"

"*Letting* me?" Her voice rose at the accusation. "I'm not some rookie. I can handle myself. I don't know why everyone is doubting that."

"No one's doubting it." Gage's deep voice echoed in the room, his quiet stealth allowing him to step inside without her even noticing.

"Well, between you and Rick, it's starting to feel that way."

He shook his head.

"Gage, you going to be there?"

"In the parking lot with backup. We'll have eyes inside though."

"What? You have a mole working inside his restaurant?"

"It's *his* restaurant?"

She winced again at Rick's aggravated tone.

"It's been tapped for a while, a court order that allows us

access to their monitors. Too many things have come through that restaurant, and Ari said they've been watching for a while."

"There, you don't have to worry. Now, I have some work to do."

"Yeah, yeah. I wanted to let you know the bullets came back. They were shot from the same gun, a .45 mm. Nothing's come back about other cases, so I'm not sure if it'll link up."

"Have you found anything about Dodson?"

"He's alive and well, living in Florida."

Her mouth dropped. "What?"

"He moved out there six years ago. Works as a manager of a chain of convenience stores."

"Send me his number, I want to call him." She chewed on her cheek a moment. "Did you find a Dusty?"

"Nope, still looking through employment records. Maxwell and Bolstero seem to have a lot of connections, so I'm sifting through them for around that time."

"Thanks, Rick. How's the shoulder?"

"Well, as long as PT stays away, it's good."

"Let 'em do their job. It'll take less time to heal."

She glanced up at Gage, feeling more and more admiration welling inside for the man as he stood there watching her with a smoldering intensity.

"Yeah, yeah."

Forcing her eyes from Gage, she stared down at the phone. "I'll talk to you later."

"Hey, where're you staying?"

"A hotel."

"My parents."

She looked up as they spoke in tandem. Rick's chuckle made her shake her head.

"Good luck with that."

"Bye, Rick." She hung up with Rick and leaned back in the chair. "Seriously, I don't think it's wise. Are you not worried for their safety? I mean, this guy may come looking for us."

"He wouldn't. It would be too easy to tie it to him."

Not that she wanted his family in any danger or trouble, but staying with family was daunting. She was still uncomfortable around Paige's parents, and she had basically lived with them while in high school.

"I don't have to be happy about it." She went back to her book.

"And I don't have to be happy about you meeting Bolstero. Seems we're both dealing."

She chuckled and flipped the page. Her phone buzzed. "That's Dodson's number. Let me call."

Pushing the number and selecting call, she waited as Gage put on some gloves and flipped through the pages.

"Hello?"

"Mr. Dodson?"

"Yeah? Who wants to know?"

"My name is Detective Bennett. I work for the Lexington PD. I have a few questions."

The silence spread for a moment.

"Mr. Dodson?"

"You found Gabby."

"Yes, sir."

He sighed heavily over the line. "I knew it was bad. I tried to tell her to be careful."

She pushed the speaker and set down the phone for Gage to listen. "Be careful about what?"

"She and her friend. They were messing with the wrong person. I told them he knew too much to be pushing things."

"Sir, do you mind backing up a bit. How did you meet Gabby?"

Dodson cleared his throat. "She was in my engineering class. I had to drop it, I couldn't keep up. Besides, Gabby set the curve pretty high," he chuckled. "We hit it off and were pretty close friends. We started dating a few months before ..." He trailed off.

"Mr. Dodson, why was Gabby so upset?"

"I don't want to get involved. Can I tell you off the record? I don't want to end up dead too."

"I can keep your name out of it for now."

Silence spread for a moment.

"Mr. Dodson?"

"Fine. Gabby met with me one day and was upset. She said her friend Rachel was having problems with her job. I said no big deal, get a new one. She said Rachel didn't really have a choice but wouldn't tell me why. Apparently, her boss was hitting on her, made her uncomfortable. He bought her some major jewelry, stuff like that."

"Why was that so bad?" She glanced up to see Gage's stern expression as he crossed his arms over his chest.

"He was married. She was supposed to be watching his kids. Anyway, when she told him she couldn't, he was a married man, he said that wouldn't be an issue if it bothered her that much. Gabby inferred the boss had mentioned taking care of the wife and moving on with Rachel. She was really upset, like majorly upset, but I just didn't get it."

He was holding back, she could hear it in his voice.

"What changed?"

Dodson sighed. "A week later, she called me all frantic. Said Rachel did something bad, she was in trouble. I went to the address she texted me and Rachel was pacing the sidewalk and Gabby was trying to calm her down. Seems the boss's wife didn't appreciate the attention and had tried to kill her."

Her heart leapt to her throat as Gage stood. She grabbed at his hand, pulling at him to sit.

"What happened next?" She pulled at Gage's arm until he sat down and relaxed enough for him to hold her hand.

"Rachel said it was self-defense and she tried to take the gun away. It went off and shot the woman, but she was still alive when she left. She said the police wouldn't do anything, which didn't make sense, but she was terrified.

"I told her to take the gun to the police, it would prove what happened. Gabby put it in a few bags and said she would keep it until Rachel decided what to do. That's when they slipped up and mentioned his name."

"And who was it?"

"Hermann Bolstero. I don't know him personally, but I've seen him on TV and read about him being a cartel guy. It really freaked me out. I had no idea that's what this was all about. And then Gabby started talking about her brother and how he could help them. I promise, I tried to get them to go to the police, but they wouldn't."

She chewed on her cheek a moment to let him calm down. "Do you know what happened after that? Did Gabby get in touch with her brother?"

"She said she called, but no one answered. Gabby decided they would stay at her home, and then they could figure out a plan. I talked to her that night, told her I was worried and she said it would be okay. By the morning, she wasn't answering her phone, and I couldn't find her. I had no idea where she lived. She always just met me somewhere."

"Was that not strange to you?"

"Well, yeah. But she said her parents were different. They wouldn't appreciate her trying to move on with her life. She said her dad wasn't the best guy, he used to hit her and her mother around. It made me mad she would even stay there, but she said she couldn't leave her mother alone."

She shook her head. "I really appreciate your help, Mr. Dodson. Just so you know, Gabby wasn't the only body we recovered. We found three others."

"What?" his voice broke. "What happened?"

"That's what we're trying to figure out. The information you gave us will help a lot. It gives us a timeline and a motive."

"Look, like I said, I don't want to end up like her and apparently three other people that got on the guy's bad side. That's why I moved. I got sick of feeling like I was being followed."

Her gaze shifted to Gage. "You were being followed?"

"I think so. I was paranoid after all that, so maybe not."

"Can you describe the person or the vehicle?"

"Yeah. Guy was a little shorter than me, light brown hair with a full beard, looked muscular. He always drove a black sports car. I'm not good with cars, it was two-door, had some red on the hood, some design."

Her eyes widened. "Like a Firebird?"

"Yeah, maybe."

"Thanks, Mr. Dodson. I need you to keep all this information to yourself and please stay in contact. No one knows we've talked, but I might need you to come in for a statement if we get enough to prosecute."

"Yeah, okay. She deserves it."

The phone call ended and Gage stood to pace.

"Well, that explains why Mr. Maxwell didn't want me to take the book. He probably thought it talked about him beating up on the women in his life." She chewed on the inside of her cheek. "We need to speak with Mrs. Bolstero, if she can speak."

He grunted.

"Gage, that answers a lot of questions."

"I only have one." His face turned red as his body stiffened. "Why didn't she go to Buchannan? He was her handler. He should've been able to help her."

She nodded, empathizing with his anger. "We'll get to that, but right now, we have a few other things we need to get to first. If Rachel shot Bolstero's wife, was he mad enough to kill her? Or did his wife do it?"

He sighed and leaned against the wall, shoving his hands in his pockets. "I'm wondering if he did it at all. Rachel anyway."

She sat back and watched his shoulders fall, defeat on his features.

"If he was willing to give up his wife for Rachel, he was already looking at a way out of the marriage, and his way was not divorce."

"The ruptured appendix." Her eyes went wide as she shook her head. "That's what didn't fit. Mrs. Bolstero was in the hospital during the interview. But, why put her in some kind of rehab place in the Caymans? Why the ruse? He could've just ended things with her."

He shrugged. "Maybe it's like you said, since it wasn't enough to kill her, maybe she was able to go after Rachel again."

She nodded as she chewed on her cheek. It still didn't fit, but she couldn't put her finger on why just yet.

"We know who's trying to kill you now."

"Well, we know the connection. But we haven't seen the car here." Pulling out her tablet, she checked her email. "Nothing on the BOLO. I wonder if Rick can narrow the search enough with the car now that we have a first name and a specific car."

She texted Rick the new information. "If we can get to Dusty, I think we can find out how and why everything happened."

"We're still missing a piece."

"The mystery man in the trench?"

He nodded. "Let's do a search on the driver."

"What driver?"

"The one who drove the bodies out there and dumped them. If Dusty was supposed to be protecting Gabby, he was involved. Maybe he was supposed to be in that trench, maybe he was able to switch places, taking the driver by surprise and put him in that grave."

Grabbing the folder, he flipped through the file and pulled at a piece of paper. "Here." He pointed out the name. "I did a search on all the drivers when I found the trackers. He was the one driving through Tennessee."

"Let me see what I can find. We've given Rick too much as it is."

As she searched the database for the name Alex Smith, hundreds pulled up in the area. But what about Marlon Jones? He was the cleaner, and it was obvious there was stuff to be cleaned up. So, where was he if he wasn't in the trench?

"Did you find something?"

She held up the search. Narrowing the database by age, he was able to narrow the search to fifty.

"Still a lot to look at."

Standing, she paced the room, rotating her neck and stretching out her arms.

"Your shoulder good?"

She nodded without looking at him. "I'm fine. I've just been stressed and sitting all day. I need to move around."

He chuckled. "There are other ways to relieve stress."

"Sparring in the ring? I'm sure they have one here." She grinned as he shook his head, a smile hitching up the side of his lip.

She rolled her eyes. "Cut it out, Sullivan." She felt the heat on her face.

It was like he did it just to get a rise out of her. He couldn't possibly be that forward. She wondered what he would do if she suddenly took him up on the offer. The thought had her heart pounding as she shook her head and took out the knot in her hair.

Drop it, just drop it. There was nothing more than attraction, and that wasn't something she was interested in falling into again. Besides, she could tell Gage had much more bottled up. After finding out about Thomas and his need to hold back, she couldn't trust herself with men that were hiding secrets.

"Hey."

Gage sat with the phone to his ear, a smile on his face.

"Good to hear from you too. Yeah, I'm in town."

His parents, he wouldn't.

His big grin proved he would.

"Actually, I'm here on work, but we're staying an extra day. I wondered if my partner and I could crash there." He grinned even bigger, his whole face lit up.

Man, he was even hotter when he grinned like that. She sighed and paced some more. Staying at his parents' house, learning much more about him and in close quarters like that sure wouldn't help anything.

"Thanks, Mom." He hung up and sat back, obviously proud of himself.

"I can get a hotel room."

He shook his head. "Nope, we're a team, Greer. We're staying close. Besides, if Dusty is our shooter, he might come back and take you out to keep his name from getting back to Maxwell. Especially if he's supposed to be dead."

She collapsed in the chair opposite him. "No pushing. I don't like it."

He smiled again, and she rolled her eyes.

"I'm serious. I'm not here for a relationship. I'm here to work."

He nodded. "Wouldn't even dream of interfering with your work." He leaned forward. "But I do hope I'll be on your mind tonight at the meeting. Take me seriously with this, Greer. Bolstero is dangerous. I won't hesitate to come inside."

"Don't mess anything up." She leaned forward, too, looking into those bright green eyes of his, determined to keep her focus. "This could be our only chance to find some information we can use, and you crashing the party won't help."

"Don't let him fool you and don't let him take you anywhere."

"I don't get fooled. You should get that."

"Why?"

She smirked. "You've got this whole macho I can do everything myself vibe going on and then you try and push something more with me. But the thing is, you have no idea what you want or who you want, and you're clinging to whatever you can find.

"You asked earlier what it takes? It takes being real. I'm tired of games, pretending to be something I'm not. I'm very much a what-you-see-is-what-you-get kind of person. I don't want to try and guess what the guy has planned when he can just tell me. I don't do secrets."

His eyebrow rose as he stared her down, searching her face again. "Interesting. But you're wrong on one point."

She waited.

"I do know what I want and who I want. I don't cling to anyone out of need, I would say I cling only to the people I trust and care about." He sat back, leaning to look over her shoulder as her face heated. "Hey, man."

Sitting back in her seat, she glared at him a moment before whoever came in, spoke up.

"I've got everything ready for tonight. What's the plan?"

She swung her gaze to Ari. "No plan, just backup. Which I won't need." She glared between the two.

"Okay, well, I've got the setup on my laptop, thought you might want to look at it, see where the exits are." Ari cleared his throat as he sat down the computer and pulled up the plans. "There are a few ways out, and usually, there are only three guards when he's here." He pointed to the exit out back. "The other two stay close, but there's always one here for when he's ready to leave."

She nodded and focused her attention on the screen.

"Ari."

Out of the corner of her eye, Gage moved past her to the door, and Ari followed suit.

"Focus," she muttered to herself as she pushed Gage and his annoying ways out of her mind.

Tonight would go well. It would be easy, and Gage would owe her an apology when it was all over and admit he had over-reacted, right?

Straightening, she rotated her head until her neck popped. It would be good, it had to work, she needed it to work. Because admitting he was right seemed a bad idea when he obviously had other plans.

God, please help me to focus, put my work first in my mind so I can solve these murders. I need Your strength.

30

"Wow, talk about tension. What on earth were you two talking about?" Ari shoved his hands in his pockets as he glanced to Greer and back.

"We talked to a witness, told us a little about Rachel." Gage shrugged and tried to blow it off so he could focus on the case.

Much more lingered than what he wanted to say in that moment, but it was too much to admit. Rubbing his eyes, he leaned back into the wall.

"You think she'll be good?"

Gage nodded. "Yeah, she's too smart to be bullied by him. I've warned her enough."

Ari chuckled. "By the way, Torrance came to my office after you two left. She wanted to know your status."

Gage's mouth dropped. "What did you tell her?"

"You were involved. I left it at that, and she didn't push."

"Why did you say that?"

Ari crossed his arms. "So, you want Torrance to come after you again, and you don't like the good detective? Because if that's the case, I'll give Detective Bennett my number."

"Don't," he said as Ari's grin slowly came out. "I'm just surprised, is all. Didn't think you would lie about something to the director."

"I can see it all over your face. You might not be officially together, but you're in. You talk to her yet?"

"We're pretty busy. The case is intense. We've got some leads about Rachel and Gabby's deaths. It's not the time."

"Don't wait too late, man. A woman like that doesn't come around all that often."

Gage chuckled. "That I do know. Let's just say, it's out there."

"She needs convincing?"

Gage's smile vanished as Ari laughed. "Not funny."

"Load up in ten?"

He checked his watch. It was already almost five, and they hadn't even gone to the restaurant to scout. Although, it wasn't the first time he had been in a van listening to the details of the meetings inside. He figured he knew it well enough, not much could change in seven years.

"I'll see where she's at, see if she needs more time to look over everything. We might go later."

"Just give me a call, I'll be in my office."

He nodded as Ari left and his gaze fell to Greer. Still studying the computer screen, he sighed. It could be a mistake to stay at his parents' home, but he wanted to change the dynamic of their situation.

His parents deserved some time, and with Greer tiptoeing the line between them, he honestly hoped the ease of being in a house, a home instead of a hotel, would make her more comfortable. Although, based on her reaction, it didn't look like any of that would matter.

Greer stood from the computer and rotated her head again, rubbing the back of her neck as she moved to her bag. Taking off the dress jacket, he smiled at the button up shirt that sat nicely on her frame. She pulled out a brush and started to brush her hair, then threw it all in her bag and headed to the door.

"Where's Ari?"

"Went to his office. You ready to drive by?"

"Give me a minute." She barely glanced at him as she headed down the hallway and into the ladies' room.

Pushing back into the conference room, he shut down Ari's computer and grabbed her coat. After calling for someone to lock up the room and texting Ari, he sat outside and waited for her to return.

God, watch over her please. Help this night to go well and for Bolstero to give up something about Rachel, anything that could help us with the case.

He swallowed hard at the lump in his throat. It was going to be a grueling night.

As THEY DROVE to the restaurant, Ari followed in an FBI sedan with fake rental plates, just in case Bolstero ran them.

Gage gritted his teeth at the tension in the car. Greer hadn't even spoken since returning from the restroom. As gorgeous as he thought she was, he was a little speechless when she came out with her hair looking great, bright lipstick on, and the tight-fitting shirt unbuttoned, revealing a black tank underneath.

A twinge of anger and jealousy had been sitting on his shoulders since that moment. Why would she want to look good for the likes of someone like Bolstero, but not want anything to do with him? It was more than frustrating.

"You've been here before?"

His head snapped to his right. He nodded. She was staring out the window, obviously oblivious to his other urges.

"Yeah, several times. The guy's a piece of work," he

commented as they pulled up to a stop sign, lingering long enough for her to get a good look.

"Yes. I believe you've mentioned that about twenty times," she grumbled.

He pulled around the block and parked. "As it starts to get busy, if it's even open to the public tonight, we'll pull around closer. But for now, we'll stay here."

She sighed, her fingers twitching in her lap as she scanned the area. He needed to say something, and he needed to say it now.

"You need me in there, just say my name, got it?"

"Don't worry so much."

Her legs bounced as her back was taught, staring out the window. He didn't need to make things worse. But leaving everything like they did ...

"Hey, Gage?"

He took a breath, pulling the radio from the car. "Yeah, Ari?"

"We waiting?"

"Yeah, give us a minute."

"Let me get in the car and get settled. You're making me nervous."

She gathered her bag in her arms and he took her wrist as he leaned over the console. Inches from her face, he paused as her eyes bolted back and forth, searching.

"Please be careful, Greer." His thumb moved across her hand. "I don't want to be right about any of this, I want to be wrong. But I just ... I know him all too well."

She swallowed hard, her lips parting for a second as she peered out the window. He pulled her chin toward him, making her see him.

"Your call. Trust your instincts." He fought the urge to do whatever it took to keep her in the car.

"Thanks for actually believing I have instincts."

"Greer, I already told you I think you're an amazing detective. You're smart and have more skills than I've seen, I'm sure. It's not me doubting your abilities—it's him."

She nodded, dropping her gaze, her lips parting just enough to make him lean forward. Her fingers trailed along his jaw as he ducked his head. Smiling, she patted his cheek.

"See you in a bit." Biting her bottom lip, she opened the door and slid away, leaving him frozen in his place.

"That was just wrong." He straightened, sucking in a huge breath.

Leaning his head back, he closed his eyes, trying to calm the heartbeat pounding in his head. The car door opened and slammed shut.

"Well, looks like you might've made some progress."

He opened his eyes to glare at Ari. "What?"

"She was bright red and grinning. Have a nice goodbye chat?"

He shook his head, a smile forming on his face. For someone who was specific about not playing games, she was working a big one with him.

The sedan drove past and to the next block before she circled.

"This better go well." The ease of her little game left and the fear of what lay ahead landed on his shoulders.

"She's smart. Trust her."

"I'm trying."

Shoving the earwig in his ear, he swallowed the frustration.

Trusting her was new. It seemed unwise to let someone into that part of his heart. And after Rachel, he didn't feel whole, didn't feel as if he could allow himself to go through any kind of hurt again.

With Greer, there was more than attraction. She kept him thinking and on his toes as they worked together. But there was something deeper, something he couldn't put his finger on just yet. They had more than just this case in common, and he wondered what linked them.

If he could just get through the case first. Bolstero had disrupted his life permanently and now, he was hindering whatever could be between him and Greer.

Man. He really hated that guy.

31

Sitting a few blocks away, Greer eased her pounding heartbeat, closing her eyes and doing her breathing exercises to take away the stress.

To move in that close to Gage, see him so concerned for her, so worried and more than willing to move into something deeper took a lot of restraint to play it off. It wasn't that it didn't cross her mind. But they had a job to do, and they were distracted enough. To give in would make it that much worse.

Besides, he needed the levity, and she couldn't handle something so serious right before going through those doors. He couldn't be on her mind if she was going to battle with Bolstero and whatever he had found out about her past.

Bolstero had probably done his research, and since Gage didn't know about her family or why she left school, it would be a surprise if and when it all came out.

But it didn't matter. Embarrassment was nothing right now. She needed answers to the case. That was why they were there, why she was risking this step. Although, after looking at the restaurant blueprints and driving by, she realized it was much more upscale than she imagined.

At five-fifty, she slid in the earwig and put on the necklace with the hidden microphone. It was a delicate chain, similar to the one she had on this morning, so hopefully Bolstero wouldn't notice the switch.

Looking down, she noticed the buttons, and fixing the two that had come undone, she took a breath.

"You hear me all right?"

"Loud and clear." Gage's voice was stiff.

She raked her hand through her hair and started the car. "Here we go."

Silence greeted her as she went through a couple of turns and ended up back at the restaurant. There were several cars there, and people were walking inside.

"It's open for business."

"Great. One hurdle down."

She chuckled at Gage. "Ease up. I'll be fine."

Parking, she grabbed her purse and checked her lipstick in the mirror. Shoving her phone into the bag, she slid from the seat and locked the doors, pushing the keys into her coat pocket.

As she walked inside, the smell of food made her mouth water. She had barely eaten today.

"I'm meeting a friend here. Mr. Bolstero?"

"Yes, Ms. Bennett. So glad to meet you. Please, this way."

She smiled and followed the *maitre d* into the plush dining area. Glancing around, she already noticed a problem with the escape route she had set up. There were more tables than she assumed, and they blocked her planned exit.

"Detective. Glad you could join me."

Her gaze jumped to Mr. Bolstero, and she smiled. "Thank you for the invite. This is nice." She took his offered hand as he stood.

"Please, have a seat." He pulled out her chair, and she

unbuttoned her coat, sliding it from her arms before she sat down.

"Thank you."

He sat directly across from her, facing the door and leaving her exposed. The small table was close to the back wall, leaving her nothing to look at but his smug face.

"I've already ordered for you. I hope you don't mind."

"Mind? No one has ever ordered for me. But how do you know what I like?"

He shrugged. "I'm pretty good at reading people."

She sat back, holding her hands in her lap and watching his smile linger on her. "I'm interested to see what you ordered."

"Careful, G," Gage's voice whispered in her ear.

"I hope your associate didn't mind me singling you out. He seems very attached to you."

"Agent Sullivan is a respectable agent. He does have some concerns about you, though. He wasn't happy I came." She waved him off and took a sip of her water.

Bolstero sat smiling silently.

"What information do you have for me?"

"That's it?"

"What's it?"

He chuckled.

"G."

Ignoring Gage's voice, she leaned into the table, folding her arms across the top.

"I thought I was here because you have something you wanted to share. I told you, anything you can remember will help us."

"None of your other contacts have been helpful?"

She shook her head. "We've got nothing. Everyone around here seems tight-lipped. Do you know why?" She tilted her head with a smile.

She could do this all day, but he could too. Tonight was going to be a bust.

"Actually, detective, or should I call you doctor?"

"I'm not a doctor."

"But you were studying to become one, correct?"

She took another sip of water with a nod. "Yes, but that's not why I'm here"

The waiter arrived and set down a plate of food. The spinach alfredo looked amazing and smelled even better. But Bolstero had her full attention.

He pushed his plate aside and leaned forward. "Detective Bennett, you played an impressive role this morning. I'll admit, I was fooled for a bit. But after learning about you, I know you're not as bumbling as you made yourself out to be."

"I wouldn't say bumbling. I mean, I am terrible at shorthand, and I hate to have people help me with all my things."

"Detective, you are many things, but bumbling, you are not. Even with the suffering that has followed you, you've become an accomplished and intelligent woman. It must have been difficult, losing your father at a young age, moving around and never finding a home. What about your partner from just last year being killed in *your* bust? How unfortunate."

Greer clamped her mouth shut. Her heart pulsed in her ears.

"And now your current partner getting shot? What a terrible thing. A bullet meant for you. Not that I care a bit about this new agent of yours, but does he know everyone around you dies?"

"That's enough," she said, painfully aware Gage had gone silent.

He let out an eerie chuckle. "Detective Bennett, I invited you here to let you know, I know who you are. In detail.

Whatever you think you have on me is a fleeting hope, a vapor that disappears."

She sat back, arms folded and hands fisted. "I'm curious, why do you think I care that you know?"

He glared in silence.

"I don't care one bit about you, who you are, or what power you possess. All I care about is why Rachel Sullivan had to die."

His jaw clenched before he relaxed. A tell?

"That seems to bother you, too, doesn't it, Mr. Bolstero?"

"I think you can go." He waved her off as he pulled the plate in front of him.

"G, get out."

"I'm not done." She stated it to both men. "So, who was it? I know it wasn't you who killed her. Was it your wife?"

His fingers tightened around his fork.

"Or maybe your daughter? She was young at the time but perhaps by accident—"

"Enough!"

The yell caught everyone's attention, and she was quite certain Gage would be here within seconds. A hand gripped her shoulder and she stood, swiftly pulling the man's arm behind his back and putting him on his knees while she pushed the barrel into the man's shoulder.

"I've just been attacked while inside your restaurant. Not good for business."

"Greer, let's go." Gage's stern voice cut through the silence from behind.

She released the man, her focus on Bolstero. "We'll have another chat later. Maybe then you'll be interested in giving me the information you promised."

Grabbing her coat and purse, she turned and marched past the three men behind her with their hands up as Gage and Ari covered her back.

She shoved her gun into the holster, then pulled on her coat as she waited outside.

"Come on," Gage grumbled as he marched past.

"You just upset a cartel kingpin, Greer. Not the best idea."

She shrugged, tossing the car keys to Ari. "I never threatened him. Just his associate. Better check that car first," she called as she rounded the corner.

Once out of sight, she let the tremors move through her body as she paused and leaned up against a wall. Taking a few breaths, she flexed her hand.

"You hurt?"

"Of course not." She hustled past Gage to the SUV.

Once inside, Gage slid in and Ari drove past them. Gage followed as the silence fell between them.

"I'm sorry."

"Why?" She turned. "I expected you to come in."

"Greer. That's not it."

Jaw clamped shut, she stared out the window.

"I am worried that he's going to come after you."

"He won't get a chance. He'll be in jail."

"Explain to me how that works."

"It was his daughter." Feeling his gaze on her neck, she cleared her throat. "He's mad at his wife, but furious with his daughter. As demented as it sounds, I think he actually loved Rachel."

"Don't."

She turned to him. "Gage, I'm serious. His reaction is classic. That's why he won't talk about his daughter, dismissed her in the conversation. She took away the one person he loved."

Gage's jaw tightened.

Sitting back in the seat, she let the silence settle. As mad as he was, she figured they would have an easy night tonight, no more pushing. It should make her happy, but instead, there was a prick of disappointment. Once again, her mind was missing the mark, her focus skewed.

32

Back at the FBI, Greer turned in the necklace and earwig. "You're right."

She glanced up as Ari entered the small room and leaned against the counter.

"He was in love with her."

She nodded. "I hate it for Gage, but that's what I saw."

"You really think it's the daughter?"

Letting out a sigh, she rubbed her forehead. "Look, it's an educated guess. We spoke with a witness who knew about the gun. Mrs. Bolstero tried to kill Rachel. Rachel wrestled it free, but not before it went off and shot Mrs. Bolstero. That's why she was in the hospital when they did the initial interview."

"Okay, so how do you get the daughter?"

"The cause of death has been ruled blunt force trauma. Two others were gunshots and the third torture. It seems odd that Rachel's was so, mundane."

Ari nodded. "A child could've easily pushed her over, knocked her down, and her head hit something by accident, causing her death."

She nodded. "But proving it is—"

"Yeah, that's not going to happen." Ari straightened.

"If we could talk to the daughter, we might get a confession."

He nodded. "But what about Gabby? The others?"

Sighing, she paced the small room. Pausing mid-step, Gage appeared against the doorframe, his arms crossed. Ignoring that glare once again, she turned to Ari.

"Martinez is Maxwell. That's obvious. The cut marks were to punish him for betraying his trust. Gabby, well, I'm not sure the retaliation theory works. Since it was Bolstero's truck that moved her body, it has to be him somehow. Unless it's to get back at Maxwell?"

"Or Bolstero knew she had information about what happened to his wife. He needed her out of the picture, and if Gabby went to the police and told them, a case would be opened up. It wouldn't give him time to get rid of the evidence."

Gage entered the room, leaning back against the counter where Ari stood. His theory worked better than hers.

"We still have the mystery man."

Gage nodded. "That, we may never find out."

"You two, watch your backs the rest of the time you're here. Bolstero isn't stupid, and he is connected."

She nodded as Ari slapped Gage's arm and left them standing in the tech room, feeling more than awkward.

"I don't think we should go to your parents' house."

He shook his head. "They'll be fine. We'll be safer there than anywhere else. They have a state-of-the-art security system."

"Fine, let's go." She turned toward the door.

He grabbed her hand and spun her around, pulling her in for a hug. Tentatively, she wrapped him up, letting herself enjoy the comfort for at least a little while.

"Don't do that again," he whispered into her ear, making her shudder.

"I didn't do anything you wouldn't do. Besides, I knew you were there."

He chuckled. "I'll be there whenever you need me. But antagonizing a guy like that is dangerous."

He pushed into her neck with a sigh, her whole body tingling as he took a few deep breaths. Snapping out of the trance he had her in, she stepped back. Being in Gage Sullivan's strong arms was a dangerous place to be.

"As for your little stunt in the car."

"Now look." She held up her hand as he smirked and took a few steps toward her. "I was trying to lighten the mood. You were all upset and worried—"

"I was. I was very worried." He pushed into her outstretched hands. "That's why I was—"

"Stop. Just stop." She shook her head and tried to ease the smile off her face. "You can't keep doing this."

His smile, however, dropped instantly.

"I enjoy having fun, but it always seems to lead to something else, and I can't. We can't." She focused on his chest as he froze in his spot.

Her hands still resting on his chest, she dropped them and stepped back. Friends she could do, enjoy time with him. But he just kept pushing.

"Okay." He cleared his throat. "Let's get going."

Throwing on her coat, she grabbed her purse and followed him out. Not shoulder to shoulder, not wrapping an arm around her waist, no contact at all. And she hated it.

He opened her door and she slid in, buckling up as he moved around the other side.

God, make this easier.

It wasn't fair. Why couldn't she have met Gage before Thomas? Maybe then the need to protect herself wouldn't be so strong. Then again, the pressure of this case was much more important than a possible relationship.

"We've got an hour drive. You want to get something to eat?"

"No thanks." She leaned against the door, holding her chin in her hand. This was going to be a lousy night. But that's what she had wanted right? No pushing, no pressure, no worry.

Right?

THE SILENT DRIVE gave Gage the distinct impression Greer was either exhausted or she was worried about their friendship. Yeah, that's what this was— friendship. As it was made clear there would be nothing else.

He clenched his jaw and gripped the wheel.

How did he get here?

He wasn't the relationship guy, the one who thought about marriage and a future and all that. How did he end up so messed up in his mind about this woman when all she did was irritate and argue with him?

Chalking up his internal whining to being too tired to think, he pulled up to his parents' gate and entered the code. The driveway was long and narrow. Trees shaded the road and swayed in the evening breeze, welcoming him home.

It had been too long.

"This is where your parents live?"

He nodded, not willing to look over at those eyes of hers.

"What do they do?"

"My mom was a teacher and dad owned a company. He sold it forever ago. That's pretty much what they live on now."

Parking next to the kitchen doors. He paused for a minute.

"Just so you know, they know about Rachel, but they have no details. I'd like to keep it that way." He glanced up to see her nod before she slid from the seat.

Pulling the bags from the back, he heard the door slam shut.

"So nice to meet you, dear."

"Oh, hi. I'm Greer."

"Yes, Gage told me you would be joining him tonight. I hope everything is well with your case."

"Mom." He came around the side of the SUV with the bags. "We don't talk about it, you know that."

His mother nodded as she wiped her eyes. He set down the bags and wrapped her in a hug.

"Thank you for finding her," she whispered as he gave her a squeeze.

"Let's get inside."

She let go and nodded. "Come now, Greer."

He chuckled as his mother took Greer's arm. She threw him a help-me look over her shoulder.

It seemed odd that Greer didn't act comfortable with his mother. She usually excelled at being around people, just like with Mrs. Maxwell.

Taking the bags to the stairs, he smiled to hear their voices echo through the hallway. Walking through the den, he met his dad.

"Hey there, boy. You look a little big around the middle."

He grinned as his dad wrapped an arm around him. "Like father, like son."

His dad chuckled and squeezed his shoulder. "It's good to finally see you."

Gage nodded.

"Now, let's go meet this friend of yours."

He laughed as his dad left him to find Greer and his mom.

Rounding the corner, he leaned against the wall as Greer nervously peered between the two after formal introductions were made.

"Just Janet and Mark, okay?"

"Yes, ma'am." She nodded.

His mother laughed. "You Southern girls are so polite. I love that."

Greer's eyebrow went up as his mom left to go get a tray of food and drinks, no doubt.

"Have a seat, young lady."

Gage grimaced. "Dad, seriously?"

Her gaze drifted to his for only a minute before looking around the room and sitting on the edge of the couch. Her knees were jumping up and down, and she gripped her hands so tightly, her knuckles turned white.

"I'm just out of practice. It's not like you bring over guests, ever." His dad chuckled and sat in his recliner.

"Look, I know Mom is getting some snacks and stuff, but we—"

"Nonsense. Now, Greer, tell me about yourself."

Her eyes went wide. "Oh, there's not much to tell. I'm a detective."

"Well, where are you from?"

"I grew up mostly in Arkansas, before we moved to Tennessee."

His dad nodded as Gage moved in, taking the seat next to her. Her hands were still clenched in her lap, but at least her legs had stopped bouncing.

"Well, what do your parents do?"

"Um, right now my mother is at some kind of retreat. She likes those yoga retreats and things. I don't have a dad."

Getting his father's attention, he shook him off.

"Interesting, yoga retreats, huh? Must be a woman thing, I know Janet has done a few, not sure of the purpose."

"Me either," Greer agreed.

"Here we are. I know you two are tired, but I wanted to make sure you had something to eat and drink before bed."

"Thank you." Greer nodded and took a glass, scooting to the back of the couch as she held it tightly with both hands.

"Thanks, Mom. So, where's Max?"

"Oh, he's out and about. Said he'd come over in the morning. I told him to bring Misti and Martha."

Gage grinned. It had been too long since he laid eyes on his nieces. "I haven't seen them in forever. They probably won't remember me."

"They're eight, Gage. I'm sure they'll remember you."

He sat forward, and they discussed the rest of the family for the next thirty minutes before he finally got a break in the conversation. He stood, and so did everyone else.

"We really need to get some rest. We have to finish everything up tomorrow in order to get back."

"To Lexington, right?"

Gage nodded at his mother. She was thinking about Rachel, and the look in her eyes killed him.

Greer set her drink down and stepped in before he could say anything. "I-I didn't get to say this earlier. I'm so sorry for your loss. I've learned so much about Rachel the past few days. I know she was an amazing woman."

Greer took his mom's hand with both of hers.

"Thank you. That's so kind of you." His mom patted her hand, then wiped her eyes for a second before they let go.

Greer turned and nodded to his father, although not offering up the same sentiments, she was definitely sincere.

"Okay, let's get upstairs." Gage was unsure what else to say as the silence spread.

Greer walked into the hallway, pausing at the bottom of the steps as she grabbed her suitcase from the floor.

"If you need anything, just ask."

She nodded at his mother's comment as he came around the staircase, grabbing his duffle and heading upstairs. He walked past several different rooms, until he reached the end of the hallway.

Opening the room across from his, he turned on the light.

"This is your room. There's an adjoining bathroom, but no one is there, so it's all yours."

"Thanks."

She dropped her bag and peeked through the curtains.

"That window faces the front. I'll be across the hall. I'm sure Mom stocked the mini fridge with water, just grab one."

She barely glanced up at him as she nodded.

"Greer."

"I think we need to get some rest." She crossed her arms, still looking uneasy and nervous.

He nodded. "Yeah, night." He shut her door, then headed across the hall to his room.

Throwing the bag on the floor, he slammed the door shut. She was all he could think about, and for the life of him it made no sense. He barely knew her but leaving her in that room alone was much harder than he imagined.

So much for a good night's sleep.

33

G reer paced the room, uneasy as her stomach churned. Sick, she felt sick. What was she supposed to say when someone asked about her father?

He disappeared when she was six and died mysteriously in an unmarked hole outside Nashville.

Nice, real nice.

Grabbing her overnight bag, she went to the bathroom, pulled her hair back in a bun, and splashed her face with water. The disappointed look on Gage's face pushed into her mind, and she groaned.

Being here was such a bad idea.

Stepping back to the room, she untucked her shirt and took off the belt, tossing it on the desk with her gun and badge. Yanking off her boots, she collapsed onto the king-sized bed and shoved a pillow over her face. The sound of her ringing phone brought her out of her stupor.

Pulling the phone from her pocket, she hit the green button and then speaker.

"Bennett."

"You should've called after you were done."

"I'm done, Rick. Anything else?"

"Why do you sound weird?"

She pulled the pillow off her head. "I was trying to smother myself with a pillow, okay?"

Rick's laugh just made her more irritated. "I assume you ended up at the parents' home?"

"Do you have anything to tell me about the case?" She rolled over on her stomach, wedging the pillow beneath her.

"Actually, yes. It's not a slam dunk, but it's info."

A knock at her door made her pause.

"Yes?"

Gage stuck his head in. "I heard Rick."

"Hey, man. How's things at home?"

She rolled her eyes and laid her forehead down to the pillow as Gage chuckled and stepped into the room.

"I'm good. Seems Greer is feeling a little, I don't know. How are you, Greer?"

She shook her head at the laughter from Gage and Rick. "I'm fine. The case, Rick?"

"Yeah, okay, okay. You know, G? You used to be much more fun when you were the troublemaker."

Her head shot up. "Rick."

"Oh, the troublemaker, huh?" Gage's grin made her heart pound.

"Rick, don't you dare."

"When she played ball,"

She snatched the phone and took it off speaker as Gage lunged across the bed, barely missing her.

"She used to—"

"You're off speaker. Tell me about the case." She turned to see Gage laying across her bed, pushed up on his elbows on her pillow wearing a smirk on his face.

"Come on, Greer. I'm just playing around. Besides, if you don't loosen up, you're going to get miserable."

"Rick."

"Fine, no more secrets."

She hit the speaker button.

"Rick."

"Nope, sorry man. She scares me more than you. Besides, when this case is over, I still have to work with her."

She sat the phone on her night-stand, refusing to look at Gage laying across her bed, that great smile of his on his face. Pulling the chair from the desk, she sat down, pulling her hairtie back out and fluffing her hair.

"So, this is the thing. I've been trying to figure out why we can't find this Dusty guy."

"Did you find him in the employment records?"

"Nah. If he worked for Bolstero or Maxwell, it was off book."

"Or it might not be his real name. It could be a nickname."

She nodded at Gage.

"The car, I've got it on camera, but the plate is distorted, we can't get a number. There was one witness who called in, said he did some work on the car while it was in town."

"So now we know he's for sure not a local." She rubbed her forehead.

"He gave a description of the man, and it matches what we have on the gas station footage. He paid cash of course, no trail. The car you shot out was found this evening as well."

"Oh?"

"Yeah, it was in a pond. A farmer reported the taillights sticking up, and it was pulled out. No fingerprints or other evidence. It was reported stolen a few days ago."

She sighed. "I think this guy is the pin. We find him and get his story, maybe we can figure out where all this tracks. By the way, when you were looking up the wife, did you discover anything about the kids?"

That great smile left Gage's face.

"Let's see. Oh, yeah. The son is a freshman at University of

Chicago, living on campus there. The daughter, well, she fell off the map."

She leaned in on her knees. "What do you mean?"

"She made it through high school, she graduated a year early, then she disappears."

"We need to find her."

"What's the rush?"

"I think she knows something about what happened to Rachel."

Gage pushed up from the bed and stood.

"I'll keep digging."

"Thanks, Rick. How're you feeling?"

"Well, I'm better. Just tired. Having computer work helps keep me busy, so I don't notice it as much. But the pain is there."

"I'm sorry. If this is too much, I'll find someone else to help."

"Don't do that. I need to work. I need to cinch this up. Finding the shooter is my priority, and that seems to be connected to the whole case. I want him."

She nodded. "Okay, thanks."

"Night you two. Try to keep from killing each other."

She hit the button and leaned back in the chair.

"You still think it was her?"

She shrugged at Gage. "The look on his face, it was rage. It wasn't aimed at me or the situation. I just want to check it out, be thorough. We might only have one chance at getting answers."

He nodded as he leaned against the footboard of the bed. "This isn't going where I thought it would."

"It doesn't change who Bolstero is. He's still evil. It's his sin that did the family in."

Gage straightened and turned to face her, his arms crossed again. "So, you got into some trouble back in the day, huh?"

She fought her smirk at seeing that grin cross his face. "Don't even think about it. I have a wealth of information downstairs, and don't think I won't tap into your parents for stories."

He shrugged. "Not so worried." He sat on the edge of the bed facing her. "What's going on with you? You usually are a lot more open with people you don't know."

"Oh? I was open when we first met?"

"Okay, I'll give you that one."

She sighed and leaned back in the chair. "I'm not comfortable around parents and family stuff. This isn't my job. I can do it with my job. But here, it's casual, and I'm out of place."

"Why?"

"You heard. I didn't have a home life, a normal mom and dad. So those questions always come up, and it's uncomfortable." She stood and headed to her bag.

"You could've told me."

She scoffed. "Okay, because that's so much easier."

His hand gripped her elbow and she set down her bag.

"I think—"

"I know, we need to get some rest." He pulled at her until she turned and he wrapped her up.

The feeling of his heartbeat pounding in his chest was enough to make her take a breath and try to calm her own.

"You can always talk to me. Stop acting like we can't talk. Just relax around me, okay?"

"Then stop pushing everything." She wrapped her arms around his waist and sank in.

He chuckled and gave her a squeeze. "I like when you get all upset and flustered about it."

She stepped back as he grinned. "So, you're just pestering me?"

He shrugged and headed for the door. "Night, Greer."

She bit back her grin as he stepped through the door, closing it quietly.

Grabbing her clothes, she headed to the bathroom and planned to shower. The pounding in her heart proved it wasn't going to happen anytime soon.

"Good grief," she mumbled.

Changing into sweats and a tank, she pulled her hair back and slipped on some tennis shoes, grabbed her sweatshirt, then headed downstairs. Easing through the quiet house, she passed by the pictures and antique furniture that lined the halls. Surely there was something she could do around here to get out her energy, a treadmill or exercise bike.

A light shown through a door next to the kitchen and she peeked out the window. Mark was sitting at a workbench in the garage, using a clamp to attach a few boards together. She opened the door, and he glanced up with smile.

"Oh, good. It's you. Close the door."

She closed the door behind her and took a few steps inside. The massive three car garage was empty except the workbench and tools. A basketball goal sat attached above the garage door on the inside and she tilted her head.

"Yes, I know, it seems strange. But the boys were insistent. With the weather here, it snows so much they wanted a way to play basketball all the time."

She grinned. "I didn't know Gage played basketball."

Mark chuckled. "Oh, yes, and football."

Her gaze fell on the bench and what Mark had in his hands. "I didn't mean to interrupt."

"Nonsense. I just didn't want it to be Janet. I'm making something for her."

"Oh, that's so nice. Is it her birthday?"

He shook his head as he sat down the woodwork.

"Your anniversary?"

He grinned and shook his head again.

"I give up."

"I just wanted to make something nice for her." With a wink, he pulled a stool out from the bench and sat it down a few feet away. "Have a seat."

"I don't want to keep you."

"You're not." He smiled as she sat tentatively.

"I guess I'm just surprised you're making something so amazing to give to her, and it's not even a special occasion." She eyed the intricate detail on the woodgrain. "Did you carve that?"

"I did. When I retired, I enjoyed woodworking as a hobby. Janet mentioned needing a shelf in the living room for her tea sets." He held up the wooden shelf containing an etched space for the plates to stand up behind the cups.

"That's amazing."

Mark sat the shelf down, taking a seat himself.

"I'm sorry about your father. Did you ever meet him?"

She chewed on the inside of her cheek a moment. "He left when I was six. I don't really remember him. I have two or three pictures of us together."

That was all she had from her childhood. The only reason she had them was because she found them in a few books as bookmarks. Her mother didn't really believe in keepsakes or memory books like some mothers.

"I assume he passed away?"

She nodded, her fingers twisting at her waist. "My mother remarried several times, so there was usually someone there ..." Trailing off, she gazed at the shelf. "I just think it's wonderful that all she had to do was mention what she needed, and you're actually making it for her."

"Can I say something, Detective?"

"It's Greer." She forced a smile.

"Greer." He smiled. "Marriage is many things to many people. It can make or break a couple if you don't want to give

257

everything you have to that one person—not just for a day or a week, but for your whole life, you will never last. Too many people give up, they become selfish and greedy. One of the main keys to marriage is wanting more for your spouse than you do for yourself."

"And what's the other key?"

He chuckled. "God. I don't know if you believe, but having a wonderful marriage, one that lasts and one that means more than what this world can offer, means having God. He gives you the strength to love when you don't want to, the grace to forgive when you don't want to, and the happiness you need because as much as you love your spouse, they will never be enough."

She nodded, feeling enlightened about something she had never seen work. "I know that God has definitely given me more strength and happiness than I've ever thought possible." Face heating, she glanced up at Mark.

He gave a wink. "Well, I'm sure sitting out here listening to an old man talk isn't what you had in mind is it?"

"Oh. I was just—"

"Come on." He stood and walked to a large bin, pulling out a basketball. "I can see it in your eyes, you're a player."

She smirked as she stood and he passed her the ball.

"Let's play a game of horse. Just take it easy on me."

"Yes, sir." She winked and made a shot, smiling at the swish of the net.

34

T hat sound, that was the second time he heard the sound of laughter.

Gage slid out of bed and pulled on some shorts over his boxers and donned a T-shirt. Stepping into the hall, he noticed the light on in Greer's room. He knocked and the door pushed open, revealing an empty room.

Rushing down the stairs, he heard the bouncing of a basketball coming from the garage. He stood in front of the door, a grin spreading across his face as Greer and his dad played one-on-one in the garage.

After seeing her spin move and shot from under the goal, he decided it was time to step in.

"Well, glad to see you're getting some rest."

She paused, then put up a shot, the net still as the ball slid through.

"Son, glad you're here." His dad had the biggest smile on his red face. "She's too quick for me. I'm already worn out."

"I'll be glad to take your place."

She spun around at that, her arm holding the ball to her hip with a smirk on her face. As his dad passed, he patted his back.

"She's a keeper," he whispered. "Have a nice game. Don't be as easy on him as you were on me."

She winked. "Not happening."

Gage chuckled as his dad left and she tossed him the ball. "You always bring exercise clothes wherever you go?" He tossed back the ball and shoved on some old tennis shoes from the bin at the back door.

"What time is it?"

"Oh, no, you're not getting away that easy. You owe me a game."

She narrowed her eyes. Her sleeves pushed up, hair back, and sweat beading off her face, she looked amazing, and he failed to guide his attention away.

"Who says I owe you?"

"That stunt earlier? In the car?"

She gave a shrug as he pushed into her space and yanked the ball free.

"That was levity in a stressful situation."

He dribbled the ball some, taking a few shots as she stood in silence. "Well, now it's my turn. Your ball." He bounced her the ball.

"I'm not stressed. See, I've had my workout."

He grinned, stepping into her space.

"Gage."

"I'm just testing that stress, Greer," he whispered as he took hold of her waist.

Her smile vanished as her eyes met his, something different stirring in her gaze.

"Greer, right now, you have one of two options." His jaw clenched a moment as he leaned in closer. She didn't turn away, her amber eyes didn't divert. She was fully in, and it made his heart pound. "You can either kiss me or play a game. We both know how you don't like games."

Before he could lean in, her gaze dropped to his chest.

"Wrong game, Gage," she whispered.

"Well, the thing is, I'm stressed. This whole thing has me stressed, and I'm tired of fighting all of it at once. The case and finding out so much about Rachel, the fact someone is trying to kill you, the fact I have much more than an attraction to you, and the fact you won't acknowledge it back—it's killing me."

Taking a breath, he realized he spilled much more than he intended, but he was done. He wanted to see that fun side, everything she was holding back when they were together.

"Gage, I'm sorry the case isn't working out like you thought."

"Don't. That's not the deal here." He squeezed her waist.

Was she making him mad on purpose?

"Fine, one game."

She started to turn, but he couldn't let go. Her eyes finally found his again.

"I can't get into all this," she whispered.

"Why not?"

She stepped back, and he let her, taking the ball as she shoved it in his chest.

"Look, the last time I went through all this, the attraction, the friendliness, it came with a bunch of stuff that was bad and unexpected. I don't like surprises, and since you're about as open as a bank vault, I figure you're just the same."

She grunted and tugged off her sweatshirt, revealing a UT tank underneath. "So, don't keep pushing. After this, no more." She snatched the ball from him and took a few dribbles, then threw it up, making a shot. "That's one. We play to ten."

Fighting the urge to argue, he nodded and retrieved the ball, tossing it back to her to start the game.

FALLING into bed after her quick shower, Greer groaned. Her body ached from thirty minutes of playing one-on-one with Gage. He was too big and strong, she had a hard time keeping him from making a shot inside the key.

They had tied twice, and she gave him the last shot, ready for the game to be over. She didn't even care if he ribbed her about it all day tomorrow, it would hopefully be the only thing they discussed outside the case.

Putting everything out there about what happened in her last relationship, she hoped it would make him back off. But the pit of her stomach said it wouldn't work. He seemed much too determined, a trait she was becoming to think of as appealing.

That was a bad sign.

Huffing, she rolled over and plugged in her phone, then lay on her side, pushing her damp hair from her face. Taking a deep breath, she groaned. The pillow smelled like Gage. It was the one he had pushed up under his chin as he lay here listening to Rick.

Pulling another pillow up under her head, she rolled over, then sighed. Rolling back over, she pulled the pillow to her chest and held it tight, letting her mind rest even though she knew it was a bad idea. Holding on to anything that reminded her of Gage tonight would just push things further.

But she needed sleep, and as exhausted as she was, she needed her mind to shut down too. Taking a deep breath, she calmed her heartbeat.

"God, let us navigate better tomorrow. Protect us and give us answers. Amen."

35

The aroma of bacon and coffee made her eyes pop open. Rolling to her side, Greer let out a groan. Her body was sore, too sore.

"I've got to get in shape." She shoved the pillow on her face.

Her stomach growled and she sat up, throwing off the blankets. Stretching out her shoulder with a wince, she rotated her neck and slid off the bed.

Even with all the stress the day before, she had slept well.

Trudging to the bathroom, she pulled her hair up into a bun, frowning at the sweatshirt on the floor of the bathroom along with her other dirty clothes. Going down in her tank top and pajama pants wasn't happening.

"Greer?" Gage's voice came through the knock on the door.

"Um, hang on."

Pulling another T-shirt out of her suitcase, she pulled it on over her pajama top and opened the door. Gage stood there with a mug of coffee and a big smile.

"Morning."

She forced a grin as he handed her the mug. "Thanks. I was trying to find something to wear to come down."

"You need a sweatshirt?"

She nodded and he turned into the room across from hers, returning with a sweatshirt and tossing it to her.

"Better hurry. I would hate to have all the food gone before you get there." He winked as he made his way down the hall in sweatpants and FBI T-shirt.

She slammed the door shut and set down the mug, pulling on the sweatshirt and changing to jeans. Taking one last look in the mirror, she added some coverup to her dark eyes and added mascara. Grabbing her coffee and phone, she headed downstairs.

"Gage, cut it out!"

As she turned the corner, Greer chuckled seeing his mother smack him with the spatula. Gage turned with a piece of bacon and sat at the table.

"I see I'm not the only one you pester," she teased, sitting across from him.

"Oh dear. Mark, you see how your pestering has messed with your son?"

Greer chuckled as she leaned back with her coffee.

"It's a sign of endearment." Mark winked at her with a tilt of the head.

"You sore?" Gage smirked from across the table, and she shook her head.

"You're older than me, Gage. You sore?"

Mark chuckled. "She's got you there."

"What is going on?" Janet turned, looking between them.

"Just a friendly game of basketball. Greer here played in college."

"Oh, that's amazing. What degree do you have?"

"Forensic anthropology," she murmured into her mug as she took a sip.

Mark set down his tablet and grabbed his mug. "That's quite a specific degree. Why did you switch to the police?"

She cleared her throat and started to speak, but nothing came out.

"Mom, let me get the food."

Gage stood and grabbed the plates of food from the counter and set them on the table. The doorbell rang, and Mark stood.

"I'll get that." He squeezed her shoulder as he walked past.

Gage brought her a plate, then took his father's seat, pushing the tablet to the side.

"Your dad was sitting there."

"I'm hoping you're not saying you would rather his company than mine?" he whispered as he leaned over.

Instead of looking up into his eyes and having to provide an answer, she grabbed a biscuit.

"I'm hungry."

He scoffed.

"Hey, man."

A large man taller than Gage entered the room. A smile spread across Gage's face as he stood.

"Hey." Gage gave a guy hug, then held out his hand to her. "This is my acting partner Detective Greer Bennett. This is Max, my older brother."

"Nice to meet you."

"GiGi!"

A chorus of yells and screams came from the entry as two blonde-haired girls ran into the room, heading straight for Janet. She set down the utensils and turned with a grin, giving hugs and kisses as the girls showed off their nails to the woman.

The room become smaller and smaller as another woman entered, obviously pregnant.

"Detective," Max furrowed his brow as Gage was busy with the girls.

"Just call me Greer." She forced a smile as Max nodded.

"This is my wife, Pam."

"Nice to meet you."

She nodded as Pam sat next to her with a huff.

"Sorry. I don't mean to be so rude, but I'm exhausted."

She chuckled as she watched the girls. "I bet."

Pam grinned and grabbed a biscuit from the bowl. "So, how long are you here for?"

"We're working on a case in this area, then we head back this evening."

Pam nodded, her gaze apprising Greer. "Let me just apologize if Gage has been annoying. It's a Sullivan trait, I'm afraid. I can only imagine having to work with him every day."

Greer only nodded, not sure what to say. Chaos filled the room until all the bodies were pushed and corralled to the table. Gage slid in next to her while his father raised an eyebrow and sat on the other side of him.

The table was large, but with so many, it seemed smaller. Gage scooted closer, his body pushing up against hers as they took hands to pray. His fingers worked their way between hers as she gently took Pam's hand.

"Father, thank you for a full table and full hearts. You've blessed us with so much, given us more than we could ask for. Watch over Greer and Gage as they finish their mission here, protect them from evil and guide them safely home. Amen."

"Amen," she repeated as she released the hands.

Gage gave her a squeeze before he finally let go, and she swallowed the lump in her throat. She had pretty much lived with Paige those last three years of high school, but even then, they never sat at the table like a family. It was a concept that made her uneasy, but she did need to find a way to eat before their busy day.

Looking down, her plate was already full. Gage gave a wink before passing the tray back around.

After breakfast, she excused herself and went upstairs, needing some space from the chaos of family. Pacing the room, she hit the green button as Rick's name flashed across the screen.

"Yeah?"

"Hey, you okay?"

"Fine, just, what do you have?'

He sighed. "G, what's going on?"

She groaned and fell into the chair. "I'm just overwhelmed." She kept her voice down, realizing that sound seemed to travel through the rooms. "The entire family was at breakfast, and meeting everyone at once ... I'm just out of place."

"Surely it wasn't that bad."

"It wasn't bad. I'm just uncomfortable, Rick."

"Greer, you have to get over yourself with this."

"If you start pushing, too, you'll not like where it leads."

He chuckled. "Wouldn't dream of it. Seems I don't have to if he's doing his own."

"Rick."

"Okay, look, I picked up some info after looking into the daughter. Jacqueline Bolstero was arrested last night for possession. She's in the Cook County jail."

She straightened. "Has she posted bail or called anyone?"

"I called down there and explained the situation. Guy I talked to said she's a regular and usually spends a few days, then gets bailed out. If you get to her today, Officer Wrenshaw said she would still be there."

"If you were here, I would kiss you. I needed that lead."

"Easy now. Wouldn't want Paige to get jealous."

She scoffed. "Go get some rest. I'll let you know how it goes."

"Be careful, Greer."

"Always."

She threw the phone on the bed and grabbed her clothes. Finally, a lead, or someone who could give them a solid lead. It was something for her grasp onto, and she realized it was something she probably should do alone.

Grabbing her phone, she texted Gage.

> Need to talk when you can. No rush.

> Be up in five.

Plugging in her curling iron, she took off the sweatshirt and set it on the bed. Dressing into a button-up shirt, she slipped on her black work shoes. A knock sounded.

"Yeah?"

Gage slipped in.

"Rick called. But I think I need to go alone."

"Seriously?" His glare made her pause.

"He found Jacqueline Bolstero. She's in county on possession charges. I want to speak with her before she gets released."

He sighed and leaned against the footboard. "You really think there's a connection, don't you?"

She bit her lip and stepped in front of him. "Gage, she knows something. Even if it just confirms the fight with the gun, I have to talk to her. If you want to be there, that's fine. But if not, stay here with your family. Spend some time with them."

He shook his head. "I'm here to work. I'll take some time the week of the funeral, whenever that'll be." He stood and she took his hand.

"Really, if you want to stay, it's okay."

"Greer, Dusty is in the wind. You think he won't be looking for you?" His green eyes turned darker. "Yes, you can take care of yourself, but he's not messing around now. No more warnings. You need someone to watch your back."

She nodded, biting back the need to correct him.

"Give me ten." He left the room.

The slam of his door echoed.

"God, give us some guidance and give Gage some peace. We need answers."

SAYING THEIR GOODBYES, Greer frowned at Gage's changed demeanor.

"I'm sorry you couldn't stay longer." Mark shook her hand with both of his.

"I'm sorry too." Her focus on Gage, she nodded. "Pray for him. This case is hard."

"We've been praying for a long time. When he switched to Homeland, we hoped it was a change for his future, that he might want to come home."

"He didn't?"

Mark shook his head. "This is the first we've seen him since he got shot and was in the hospital."

"That was almost three years ago."

"Dad, see you soon."

His father gave Gage a hug and whispered something in his ear. Gage only nodded and patted him on the back.

"Goodbye, Greer. Please come back and see us." Janet gave her a hug, and Greer froze, patting her back and forcing a smile.

"Thank you for letting me stay here, ma'am."

Janet laughed and let her go.

As they headed to town, she leaned back in the seat.

"That bad, huh?"

"Not bad. You're lucky."

He nodded.

"And a jerk."

"What?"

"You haven't been home since you were injured? What's

wrong with you? Those are your parents. Your brother and his family, your nieces. How can you *not* go visit them?"

"I told you, it's been ... a challenge."

She scoffed and crossed her arms, more irritated than she should be. But he had no idea what it was like to not have a family.

"You just don't understand. It's my fault."

She turned to watch his strong jaw flinch.

"It's my fault Rachel's gone."

"No, don't do that."

"Greer."

"Gage." She raised her voice. Trying to calm herself, she took a breath. "Look, I realize everything with Rachel is hard. Okay? I can empathize with that. I'm not downplaying it. But you have a family that loves you, that wants you around and cares about you. Not everyone has that. Your guilt? It's in your head. You're not even the oldest, I figured that's why you were carrying it around."

"What?"

"Usually, the oldest carries that sense of responsibility. But you ... you seem to carry it all on you—just you—as if you could control anything about the situation."

"I could've. If I had gone in there and pulled her out—"

"Then Bolstero would've killed you and imprisoned her."

His face and neck turned crimson. "You don't know that."

"And you don't know it would've ended the situation. You act like that would've solved everything, but you know that's not how it works. This entire thing was Rachel's decision. I know Buchannan probably had some influence too. But it wasn't your place to fix it."

The silence settled in the cab, and she sighed. He could never move on if he held on to this guilt he didn't deserve. Did he want to be miserable? It was obvious the decision to stay was hard for Rachel, and she really thought she needed to take care of those kids. Anthropologically speaking, it as a nurturing, mothering instinct that Rachel probably developed, knowing those kids were in trouble and knowing she needed to help.

Pulling out her phone, she typed a text to Dr. Shaver.

> Did you figure anything more out about the finger?

> No. No other bodies exist on the lot. It could belong to another body that didn't make the trench. I've logged it as such.

> Thanks for the update.

> You're welcome, glad to assist.

She smiled and sat down the phone. The life she could've had as a doctor of forensic anthropology was a future she often wondered if she should've followed.

"Good news?"

"Just that the finger Dr. Shaver found is either our killer's or someone else who didn't make it into the grave. She's completed her findings."

"The mystery man?"

She shrugged. "We'll have the dentals to match whenever we get a name. I guess I should see if Rick wants to navigate the Alex Smith angle." She pulled out her phone again, texting Rick.

"Sorry."

Her gaze snapped to him. "Why?"

He shrugged. "As much as I want an answer, I'm not sure I can handle the truth."

"You don't have to apologize for that, Gage. Finding out is, scary." She finished her text to Rick and set her phone down.

"You want to go into detail?"

She shook her head. "Nope."

"Greer."

"We have a case." She glared until he nodded and sighed.

Letting him down again, she wondered why he kept trying. She was terrible to him, making him feel bad and keeping her own secrets. But then again, she wasn't pushing everything.

Yeah, like that was fair.

She pulled back her hair, tied it in a knot on top of her head, and blew out.

"Hot?'

"No, just thinking things out."

"Me too."

Watching his pained face made her reach across the console and take hold of his hand. His gaze cut to hers.

"We're really close to an answer. Don't give up yet." She leaned back and watched the snow fall around the SUV.

"Wasn't planning on it."

36

The stench inside the holding cell made Greer's nose wrinkle. In the corner, a balled-up figure sat on the floor. "Jacqueline?"

"My dad's getting quicker." She lifted her head. The woman still had a baby's face, except for the smeared makeup and bruise across her cheek. "You're not a lawyer."

Greer shook her head. "Nope. I'm a detective."

Jacqueline scoffed. "Not giving up nothin' to a detective. Even one who knows my dad."

"How do you know I know your dad?"

"I don't go by Jacqueline anymore." She said the name with an airy voice.

"Then what do you go by?"

The girl stood, eyes narrowed as she drew closer to Greer. "Get me some caffeine, and we'll talk."

"Done."

Greer stepped aside as the guard released Jacqueline and led her to a small interrogation room with a live video feed. They watched on the screen from another room and Gage shook his head.

"She's a child."

Officer Wrenshaw shrugged. "She's legal. At only seventeen, she took out a new name and severed ties with her father and mother. In my system, besides Jaqueline Bolstero, it says Kennedy James."

"James is her mother's maiden name. She's tied to her mother, still has feelings for her."

His jaw set, he barely glanced down at her before nodding.

Taking the two bottles of Mountain Dew into the room, she set them on the table by the wall, then handed her one. Jacqueline had relented to the chair in the corner.

Pulling up a chair, Greer sat as close as she could get to the girl. "So, what's your new name?"

"You don't know?" The girl took a long gulp as Greer shook her head. "Kennedy. Kennedy James."

She nodded. "Interesting. Like Jaqueline Kennedy?"

Kennedy grinned and nodded. "Yeah, she's dignified."

"Okay, that works. James?"

Kennedy took another drink and then set down the bottle. "It's my mom's maiden name."

Greer leaned back in the chair.

"Look, I'm not a snitch, and I didn't do nothing last night. I don't want any trouble."

"I don't either. This isn't about being a snitch, information, or last night."

Kennedy eyed her a moment. "You're not from around here. You have an accent."

She chuckled. "So far, you're the first person to comment. I didn't realize it was that bad. I'm from Tennessee. I'm a detective there."

"Why're you up here?"

"I wanted to tell you a story. You got time before you go back to holding?"

Kennedy nodded. Hopefully giving her a choice would make things go smoother.

"I was called out several days ago to a small, rural town. I realize you think I'm country, but this town is small, and they were clearing some land to build a store. As they were digging, they found some remains."

"Like people?"

Greer nodded. "There's not much left, just bones. Using their teeth, we were able to identify three."

She waited as Kennedy took another drink, then set down the empty bottle.

"That's the story?"

Greer shook her head and leaned in on her knees. "The two women led me to Chicago, where they lived and worked."

Kennedy's eyes went wide. "Oh?"

"I think you might know one of the women."

Kennedy started to cry, wiping away the tears angrily as she tried to hold back. "I ... I doubt it."

"Rachel Sullivan was found."

Kennedy's face paled as she balled up in the chair. Giving her some time, Greer waited out the tears and the anger. Kennedy's hands fisted, hitting her leg as she wept.

After a few minutes, Greer leaned forward and intervened, taking hold of the girl's hand. "Why are you hitting your leg, Kennedy?"

The girl wrenched away and wiped her face, smearing even more eyeliner and mascara down her cheeks. "I remember Rachel."

She nodded and sat back on her chair. "She was your nanny?"

Kennedy nodded. "I liked her," she whispered. "She did stuff with us. I used to have nightmares, and she would ... she would make them go away."

"I don't know much about her. Did she like being with you and your brother?"

She shrugged. "I thought so, but then she," Kennedy shook her head. "I'm not supposed to talk. I'll lose everything."

Greer sighed and leaned an elbow on the table to hold her chin. "Lose what? What is it you'll lose?"

"*Humph.* I guess you think I have nothing," Kennedy spat the words.

Greer shook her head. "I think you have a lot. But someone is telling you that you don't."

Kennedy's face scrunched up.

"You're much stronger than what they want you to believe. Tougher, braver, and I think you know the difference between right and wrong."

"I'm not a head case."

Greer shrugged. "Never said you were."

Kenney narrowed her glare. "Social workers used to come in here, try and help me. They think I'm stupid or drugged out all the time. I don't do it all the time. My mind, I sometimes just need something to calm down."

Greer nodded. "I know you're smart, graduated a year early and hired your own lawyer to sever ties with your father."

"He's a jerk."

"I agree."

Kennedy straightened. "How do you know?"

"He tried to attack me in his restaurant. He didn't do a very good job."

Kennedy chuckled, wiping her nose with her sleeve. "Why were you there?"

She shrugged. "I thought maybe he killed Rachel."

Kennedy's face went pale again. "Wh-what did he say?"

"Nothing. Just ordered me to leave." Greer leaned in again. "The thing is, I think despite being with your mom, he had feelings for Rachel, feelings she didn't reciprocate."

Kennedy just stared, her mouth hanging open.

"So, when she told him no, he killed her. What do you think about that?"

Kennedy sat back. "You can't prove any of it."

She shrugged. "Maybe not, but I intend to try."

"You think you can do that?"

"I'm going to try. He's slick, and he's devious. But I think I can. Do you have a way to contact your mother? I think she might be the person I need to speak to."

Kennedy shook her head and sat up. "No, mom is, um. I mean, she can't talk."

"Why not?"

Kennedy's shoulders dropped. "She doesn't talk anymore. When Rachel left, she stopped talking. Dad sent her away. I never get to see her."

"I bet you miss her."

Kennedy nodded. "But I can't. I'm not allowed to talk about any of it, and if he finds out, I lose everything."

"Who finds out?"

"Him."

Kennedy was losing her courage.

"I wanted to share something else." Licking her lips, Greer took a breath. "We found a gun in Rachel's friend's house. It was fired seven years ago."

Kennedy's eyes widened, and she covered her mouth.

"It has blood spatter on the end, and we're running the DNA. The story my partner is pushing is there was a fight and your mother shot Rachel."

"No! That's a lie. She did it, Rachel shot my mom!"

"Tell me what happened. Was it an accident? Were you mad?"

"I ... mom had the gun, and then ... the bullet, it hit the glass lamp. It shattered all over me." Kennedy ran her fingers down her glossy black hair. "Rachel screamed and tried to tell her it was a mistake. She didn't accept the things. I saw her put all these things in Dad's study, boxes of necklaces and rings. When mom tried again, Rachel—she tried to stop her." Kennedy trailed off and cried again.

Taking the box of tissues from the cabinet, Greer handed them to her and scooted closer. "Kennedy, what happened after that? Rachel left, upset and crying. Your mom was injured?"

"I called Dad. He said we can't call the police." Kennedy took the offered tissue and wiped her face. "He said he'd take care of all of it. That I wasn't supposed to talk to anyone. Mom said she would be okay and come back. But after that, Dad wouldn't let her back."

"What did your dad do?"

Kennedy shrugged. "I never know what he does. I don't want to know."

"When Rachel came back to say goodbye, what happened?"

Kennedy wiped her red face, raw emotions bleeding through her eyes. "H-how did you know she came back?"

Greer shrugged. "I would. She cared about you and your brother too much to just leave. It was a bad idea to come back after all that. She knew it could cost her her life. But she loved you."

Kennedy nodded. "I loved her."

"What happened? Was your mother there?"

Kennedy shook her head. "Rachel came in the back with her key. She found us upstairs and hugged us, crying. I didn't understand. I told her she wouldn't be in trouble, and she could stay. I wasn't mad, I just needed her. The nightmares were back, and I needed her.

"When she left, I followed her down the steps and to the door. A man was there, I saw him through the window. He was watching. Rachel started to run and then she fell. I hid."

"What happened after that?"

Kennedy shook her head. "I looked out the window, and

Rachel was there on the ground. Dad was leaning over her. I ran out and told him what I saw, asked if she was okay. Dad's face, it went red and he yelled at me. He had never yelled at me before."

"The man—what did he look like?"

Kennedy shrugged. "White guy, brown hair with a beard. He was big. Bigger than my dad." Her voice quivered. "Rachel was gone a little while later, and Dad sent mom away, sent me away. I just never understood why."

Straightening, Greer sighed. "Your dad should never have done that to you."

"Yeah, well, now that he knows I've talked, he'll probably make me disappear too."

"Not going to happen." Greer stood. "I'll be right back."

Stepping out of the room, Gage leaned against the wall, his head in his hand.

"What now?" Officer Wrenshaw questioned.

"We need to get her statement and get her into WitSec."

"What? For that? She just said her father didn't do it." Gage glared up at her.

"Yeah, but her father killed Rachel's best friend."

Officer Wrenshaw shook his head. "You have proof?"

"I will."

"I'll keep her here, try and get a counselor called in."

She nodded and stepped back into the room. "Kennedy, I want you to write down what you saw, all of it and give it to the officer. We can get you away from your father if you want."

Kennedy stood on shaky legs. "But where will I go?"

"Witness protection."

"That's like, a new life, right?"

Greer nodded. "It is. Would you like a new life?"

Kennedy gave a sliver of a smile. "I-I've wanted one for a long time."

Greer smiled and gave her a hug. "Get to writing. Officer

Wrenshaw will keep you in here until it's all ready. But the thing is, if your dad sends a lawyer, you have to decide to walk or stay."

Kennedy nodded. "Yeah, I guess so."

Feeling a pull on her heart, she rushed through the paperwork on her end and made her way outside to find Gage.

37

The small park seemed like a good place to sit and think. Then it started snowing.

Gage's mind was on overdrive. Hearing Kennedy spill the words like it was nothing, like it took nothing for her to say. Even though she was a child at ten years old, why couldn't she have said something seven years ago?

"Hey." Greer sat next to him, and he found himself needing some space. "Talk to me."

"Not now."

"You're the one who told me last night to talk."

"Yeah, well it doesn't seem to be working does it?" He stood with a grunt and shoved his hands in his coat pockets as he made his way down the trail.

Greer walked beside him, silently. She let him have his space as she kept in step, following him down the trail that apparently wound all the way to the lake.

The breeze coming off the water was frigid, but he ignored it. He needed to move, he needed to do something before the pain ate him alive.

When he finally stopped, Greer paused, her arms wrapped around her middle, her head down.

"Good grief." He stepped in and wrapped her up, guiding her away from the water. "You should've gone back to the vehicle. I just needed a minute."

She nodded but didn't answer.

When they got back to the station, he helped her into the car and started it up, pushing the vents toward her. Her nose and cheeks were bright red.

"I'm sorry."

"Stop," she said as she shivered.

"Greer."

She glared, and he turned his focus to the parking lot. Backing out, he pulled onto the road and drove, having no idea where to go.

"You made a promise I don't think you can keep. Prosecuting Bolstero for Gabby's murder ... I don't think it'll happen."

"I'll get him."

"Not to put too fine a point on it, G, but you were wrong about the daughter."

Her glare cut deep. But as much as he wanted Bolstero in jail, this wouldn't do it. They needed proof, not just a guess.

They parked and headed up into the offices. He followed her in silence. Once in their conference room, she threw her bag and coat on the chair and sat down, shoving gloves on.

"I'll go check on the fingerprints."

"Yeah, sounds like a plan." She started looking through the book once again.

He made his way to Ari's office, collapsing in the chair.

"What's that look for?"

"You have no idea."

He retold Kennedy's story, and Ari nearly choked.

"You know who the man is?"

"We think it's Dusty. He's attacked Greer once, shot at her, missed and hit her partner, and now, we think he's the one who killed Rachel. We think she was shot, it just didn't show on her remains. Maxwell said he was a hired hand to protect Gabby."

"Man, sorry. What's the plan here?"

"Greer wants her in WitSec, but without proof that Bolstero is involved ..."

"Yeah, that might be a tough sale. But we did trace the gun used on Mrs. Maxwell."

"Oh yeah?"

"Came back stolen—from Lexington."

"You're kidding." Gage took the file and scanned it. "Just breaking and entering, huh?"

"Yeah. Report said some cash went missing, guns, and an older car."

He glanced up. "Send this to my buddy down there, Rick Myers. I want to know if the bullet from the first miss on Greer matches."

Ari nodded and started typing when Gage's phone rang.

"Sullivan."

"Hey, man. Got a match."

"Jason. Took you a while."

Jason huffed. "It's been two days."

Gage closed his eyes. Had it only been that long?

"Tommy Rhoades. He was busted last year for home invasion. Got out a few months ago."

"Great, thanks man. I owe you one."

"Next time you're in Indy, I plan to collect."

He hung up and texted the info to Rick and Ari. "Start looking for this guy. He's the link to the shooter we think is Dusty."

"Got it. I'll start looking for possible accomplices. If he lives in the area, he's mine."

As Gage stood to turn, Greer came running inside, the book to her chest.

"What're you doing?" He glared at her and the book she had covered in the evidence bag.

"I found it."

"Found what?"

"Probable cause." She laid the book out, and Ari came around to the desk. "I skipped to the last entry and found a few letters." She took a breath. "This one is to Gage from Rachel."

Her eyes met his, and he leaned over her shoulder as she read.

"Gage, Don't blame yourself. I had to leave. Things were scary, and I wanted to tell you, but you would try and fix it, like usual. Normally, I like that, but this is too dangerous. Hermann Bolstero is demented. He wouldn't take no for an answer, and Agent Buchannan wouldn't either. It's either go to jail or do something I can't morally do with Bolstero. I'm leaving, Gabby will cover for me, and when I feel safe, I'll come back. Tell Mom and Dad I love them, Max too. Love you, Gage. Rachel."

He straightened and paced, wiping his eyes.

"Go on, Greer." Ari's voice sounded.

Gage appreciated the space.

"This one is Gabby's to her boyfriend Harrison. Harris, please forgive me for leaving. I need to help Rachel. She's the only one who understands what I've dealt with my whole life. By now, you know my brother is caught up in the Bolstero cartel. He even hired someone to watch over me because he fears for my life. Although lately, I'm worried he's changed allegiances.

"If we don't show, find Bolstero and ask about the Carman account. I've been keeping tabs on his business in case we needed something to go to the police with. I love you, and I'll see you as soon as I am able."

Greer sighed. "Both these have envelopes with addresses.

One to Gage and one to Harris. She didn't finish Harris's letter. I think she was interrupted and then hid the book. There's a pen mark here going down the page."

He turned and noticed the hasty writing and the pen mark.

"I can use this. Let me get in touch with my boss and see where we can go from here."

Gage nodded at Ari and left the room, needing some more air.

GREER WATCHED GAGE LEAVE, a pull on her heart making her ache.

Ari stood at his desk on his phone. He leaned back with a nod. "Go find him."

"Last time I did, I had to follow him around the lake, and I nearly froze to death."

He chuckled. "Look, he just needs some time to process."

"What about the book?"

"Torrance is on her way to take a look."

She jumped up and made her way out the door, hearing Ari's laughter as the door shut.

Going back upstairs, she rushed to their conference room to grab her coat and paused to see him leaned in the corner, his arms crossed.

"Hey."

He nodded and grabbed her coat. "Come on."

She groaned as he turned her, and they headed out of the room. "I don't want to walk around outside again." She slid on the coat and buttoned it up as he led her from the elevators and down a breezeway to another building.

"Where are we?"

"Cooperate offices."

Leading her through another set of doors, she smiled as an

indoor park came into view. Trees, skylights and bench seats wound through the building.

He led her to the sidewalk, and they walked along, his hand drifting down to hers.

"I'm sorry about what I said."

She shook her head. "Look, we both have some issues with talking."

"But I *do* want you to talk to me."

She sighed. He squeezed her hand and pulled her to one of the benches. Sitting down, he pushed in next to her, pulling her hand to his lap.

"Greer, this thing. Hearing about Rachel, what happened, I can't understand it. It seems so wrong, and I could've stopped it."

"She told you she was worried for you. She loved you, Gage. She wanted to protect you."

He glared over at her. "It was my job to protect her."

"Why?"

"She was my baby sister." His deep voice resonated in the large space.

"And you were her big brother who would run into the situation full tilt without caring if he died or not. She had the right to protect you."

His mouth dropped as he shook his head.

"Gage, don't do this. Don't take away what she's tried to do to protect you."

He leaned forward, dropping her hand.

"I get it." Letting out a sigh, she closed her eyes for a moment. "I, my dad—"

"Don't, Greer. Not because you feel like you have to."

"You really think I can be manipulated by you?"

A sliver of a smile edged out as he leaned back in the bench.

"I don't really remember him. He left when I was six. My mom said he found someone else, another family." She took a breath. "I'd been working the past year after getting my degree. I had worked with the police off and on, things were good, and I had started working on my doctorate. I had just finished recovering some human remains."

He wrapped his arm around her shoulder as her gaze drifted to the space in front of them.

"I sifted through the dirt, taking samples and bagging practically everything. Then I found a wallet."

He pulled her chin up, those green eyes gaining her focus.

"It had my picture in it from first grade. That's when I realized the initials on the front were his."

"Greer." He sighed and pulled her into a hug. "That's what made you change."

She nodded. "Every time I started a new project, I couldn't get it out of my head. Then I started speculating more and more, thinking more about how they got there instead of just identification."

As sad as she was, she had cried herself sick over the years. There weren't any tears left.

"Did you find out why or how?"

"No. I looked into it when I first started as a detective, searching through records and things, trying to make a connection. But there was no motive. My mom always assumed he left us so she never filed a missing persons report or anything."

"Did you tell her what happened?"

"I told her I discovered he had passed away. I didn't want to go into detail. She just assumed it was after he left us, not the reason he left us, and I didn't correct her."

She sat back to focus on him. "I still struggle with not knowing what happened. But even though I lost my earthly father, I have faith in my heavenly Father. Someday I might learn what happened, but until then, I can't hang on to it anymore. It's too much to live with every day. I have accepted that God has it all taken care of."

He took her hand and held it to his chest. "I'm so sorry."

"I'm just glad we were able to get so far with Rachel's case."

"Well, even now, after learning more about what happened, it doesn't make it better. I don't feel like it's all over."

She nodded.

"Greer, if there's anything I can do."

"You're doing it." She winked and sat back, chewing on the inside of her cheek.

Although her father's death had been in the back of her mind for years, accepting the mystery was just something that never sat right. Until now. It wasn't an ache she wanted to carry anymore.

"What're you thinking?"

"Just working things out."

"Things like what?"

His green eyes pushed into hers.

"How about we go eat?." She cleared her throat, and his eyebrows rose.

She stood, pulling him up and heading back to the door. His hand found hers once again, and she hung on. Walking to the SUV, he opened her door and let her inside, then shut it.

Now that the case was wrapping up, and the dominoes were falling, the tension would be even worse. They had nothing left to focus on.

Well, they had Dusty.

Gage backed out of the lot and took off down the road. "What do you want to eat?"

"I don't care. You know the area. Pick someplace." She pulled out her phone, hoping to be busy enough he wouldn't start the conversation she figured was rolling around in his head. "What's this text from Rick? Who's Tommy Rhoades?"

She glanced up to see his jaw flinch. Calling Rick, she

noticed Gage completely focused on driving and not on anything she was saying.

"Hey."

"Who's Tommy Rhoades?"

"Oh. Didn't Gage tell you?"

"No, he's a little out of it. Give me the details."

Rick chuckled. "I got an email from Agent Munoz that gave me the serial number off a stolen gun from here. It's from the same house that the car came from, the one you shot out the glass. The bullet meant for you matches a homicide from there, a Mrs. Maxwell."

"What?"

"There's more. The bullet from my shoulder matches a missing rifle from the same home invasion. And Gage sent me an ID from the gas station footage that identifies Tommy Rhoades as being our mystery man. Munoz said he was in Chicago and would take care of it from his end. I think we got our guy."

Her jaw clenched as she processed all the new information. "How many fingers does he have?"

"What?"

"The finger from the trench. It has to be the killer or an extra body dump, I suppose, but I'm guessing killer."

"There's nothing about nine fingers."

Then how was Tommy Rhoades connected, and who had only nine fingers?

"So, you guys headed back?'

"We've got a few loose ends here, but we'll probably head back tonight."

"Stay safe. That Rhoades guy doesn't look like much, but if he's turned killer, you need to be careful."

"We need figure out the relationship between him and Bolstero. Otherwise, how does he connect?"

"Maybe he's been recently hired by Bolstero to clean up the case now that the bodies have been found."

"Maybe."

"I'll see you when you get back. Let me know if you figure out anything else."

"Yeah, talk to you later." She hung up and glared at Gage. "Thanks for the heads-up."

"Sorry. I've been distracted."

She nodded and shoved the phone in the cup holder.

"I want to talk."

Her body instantly tensed. "Oh, about what?"

"Just listen, Greer. Don't answer, just listen."

"I'm not very good at that." She smirked, but his jaw went taught. "Fine."

"I don't know why you're pushing back so much. But the thing is, this can work."

"Gage."

"Listen."

She clenched her jaw closed.

"There's more than just attraction between us, and for the life of me I can't figure out why you're refusing to see it for what it is. Don't you think all of this came about perfectly timed?"

"So, you're trying to say that God put all this together?"

"Yes."

"Gage, I just don't—"

"What? What is it Greer? Did that EMT guy screw up so bad that no one else has a shot?"

She sighed. "He wanted to get married after dating for a month."

"Seriously?"

With a shrug, she sat back. "There was something he was holding back, something he never would tell me about. Too many secrets, too much unsaid."

"What was it?"

"He, uh, he apparently wanted access to an inheritance and was tired of waiting."

"What a jerk," Gage mumbled.

"He didn't even mention whether or not he loved me. I mean, I knew something was up, but I had no idea it was something so ridiculous."

"I guess I don't get why you're taking it out on me."

"I'm not."

"Yes, you are. You think I'm hiding something, just like he did. I'm not really hiding anything here, Greer."

She bit her lip and turned away. She hated it when he was right.

"What's it gonna take to get a date with you?"

She shook her head. "I don't think you want to get involved with me."

"I just asked."

She groaned as they headed toward a bridge. "I'm not walking by the lake again."

"Not the lake. A restaurant by the lake."

"I guess I can handle that."

"Greer?"

The sound of a revving engine made her turn toward her window. A scream escaped her lips as the headlights of a truck slammed into the side of the SUV.

38

C*link.*

Greer searched the remnants of her memory as she tried to wake.

Clink.

The metallic sound edged into her brain, causing her to moan.

"Greer?"

Dizziness engulfed as a rush of sounds came through. Her body ached and burned.

"Stay asleep."

The hushed whisper sounded familiar.

"Stay asleep. Don't wake up."

Gage?

Her mind engaged, the memory surfaced. The car, the hit, Gage. Stiffening, she groaned at the pull on her shoulders preventing her from sitting up. Her head fell forward. It took all her ability to straighten. The strain was too much. Vomit lingered in her throat as her world spun around and around.

"Don't, Greer. Go to sleep."

Gage's hushed tone made her sigh. Why was he telling her that?

A loud creak and a slam made her jump as the sound both startled and pulsed pain through her head.

"Ah, she's finally waking. I was wondering if she could make it on her own. That hit looks pretty bad."

A familiar male voice brought her out of her stupor. He had them. Whoever it was that had threatened her, had them.

Emotionless, she kept her body as limp as possible, working to ignore the pain pulling and tearing apart her shoulders.

The sound of a thud followed by a grunt from Gage made her stiffen.

"You won't be so tough after hanging there for a few more hours," the gritty voice sounded from behind.

What? Was Gage hanging?

Her head was jerked and she stifled the moan she wanted to release.

"Let her go."

Gage's request was met with a chuckle.

"Just so you know, neither of you are getting out of here. I'm not the type to play around. I was trained by the best, and after I'm done, all you'll ask for is a bullet."

Her head was released, and it fell forward. Her whole body felt as though it would fall to the side. The world turned as dizziness overwhelmed her.

But right now, she needed to assess. Right, assess. Her fingers flexed and moved, discovering metal handcuffs around her aching wrists. Okay, that's not impossible. She'd never actually done it, but she knew enough about the human body to understand how to dislocate her thumb and slide them off.

With her long-sleeved shirt on, she couldn't tell, but the chair she assumed was wooden. Maybe she could break it? Everything smelled earthy—rotted wood and damp air, dirt and cold all around. She shivered.

"She's waking." Another male voice, different.

That's not good. One man, perhaps she could free herself. But two?

Her head was lifted and what she assumed were smelling salts were pushed under her nose. She gagged and gasped for air. A low chuckle rumbled.

"Yeah, she's good."

"Then I'm out."

A deep sigh sounded. "You should learn the ropes, Tommy. It'll be good for you."

"Not happening. I can't watch you do that stuff."

The sound of a door slamming made her flutter her eyes. Finally opening them, her numb bare feet were on the floor, her ankles taped to the chair legs.

"Now that we're all here and awake, let's get started."

Her head was lifted again and a blurry form finally appeared. As her vision straightened, she saw the man who attacked her outside the police station.

"What?"

He let out a laugh that pierced her aching head. "I tried to warn you off. I don't take pleasure in my job, but I do take it seriously. I hoped that you would shut down the case, leave it alone." He shook his head. "But you just couldn't walk away."

"Why?"

"Oh, come on now, Detective. I think we both know why."

"She doesn't know anything. Why do you think we're still here?" Gage's strained voice sounded behind her. The man stood.

Without a word, another few hits sounded. Gage's grunts echoed in the room. She had to get loose. With Gage's background, she assumed he would've gotten away if it had been possible. But if he was hanging ... She took a breath and winced, swallowing her fear.

"So, we're all here because I need to know exactly what you told Bolstero."

The man settled in front of her again, pushing into her space. She turned her head as he reached out, his fingers working to unbutton her top. Knowing she had a tank top on underneath, she opened her eyes and studied the room.

There were concrete walls and a concrete floor, wooden beams that crisscrossed the ceiling. A pull made her turn back.

He had pushed her sleeves down then stood, disappearing behind her. Suddenly, her arms were lifted behind her back, unleashing her scream as pain split through her shoulders. He pulled the shirt down to her cuffed hands then dropped them. Burning, piercing pain radiated down her arms.

"Greer?" Gage's breathy voice echoed.

She took several deep breaths, trying to keep from passing out. At least now, her hands were covered. Pushing on the thumb joint, she worked to get the right amount of pressure.

Something cold laid flat against her cheek. Straightening, her eyes opened.

Dusty held a large knife, pressing the flat side to her skin. He pulled it back and she spotted the space in his grip. He only had four fingers on his right hand.

"I need one of you to start talking. The thing is, I know you met with Bolstero, a couple of times actually. So, I need to know what you said."

"We don't even know who you are." Gage's words were heavy.

Her head turned.

"You want to see him?"

"No." Gage's airy words echoed.

Dusty gripped her chair and turned her around. The image of Gage hanging by his arms, shirtless and bloody made her gasp.

"I'm fine."

His eyes cut through, and she nodded, tears blurring her vision and running down her cheeks. A lump swelled in her throat.

A sharp pain in her arm made her grimace. The man stood with the knife, a trickle of blood running off the end.

"This will go better if you scream. It'll make him talk more." He stepped in closer.

Already crying, she pushed hard on her thumb. Feeling the dislocation, she squeezed her hand through the cuffs. As much as she wanted to release the pain in her shoulders, she couldn't let go yet.

"What did you tell him?"

"I-I don't even know who you are. I was just trying to find out if he killed Rachel."

Dusty furrowed his brow. "*I* killed her. I have a hard time believing you don't know me." He stood and made a slice across Gage's stomach.

"No!" she screamed.

"Tell me what you talked about!"

Dusty was escalating.

She had to give him something, give her time to figure out how to get loose.

"We ... we talked about the bodies we found. There were four. We have only identified three. Bolstero is our suspect—"

"Greer."

She peered up at Gage and shook her head as she worked the cuff of her shirt over her wrist to free her arm completely.

"What else?"

"I talked about Rachel. She worked for him."

"You think I don't know that? Did you give him my name?" He pointed the knife at her as she shook her head and shrunk away.

"No, no. We don't even have your name. What did you do? Did you kill all of them?"

"I had orders, and after finding out Bolstero had a price on my head because of that stupid Martinez, I decided to send him a warning."

"But we thought Bolstero did it," she murmured.

Another sharp pain cut across the back side of her arm. She muffled a scream.

"Bolstero wanted me out of the picture for taking out his friend. I sent him a warning with that nanny. I had plans to get to you here, but too much attention showed at Maxwell's. When you met with Bolstero, did you tell him about me? I want an answer," he hissed.

Closer, she needed him closer. Shrinking back, she allowed herself to cry, allowed the fear to overwhelm her as he leaned in.

"Don't completely lose it, Detective," he sneered in her face. "I'm not done with you."

The ice-cold blade touched the side of her face as he pushed up close. In an instant, she shoved her left hand between her and his arm, pushing the knife away as her right arm wrapped the shirt around his neck.

He pushed her back, making the chair fall and her body slam into the ground. But she kept the tension on the shirt as she rolled to her left, trapping his right arm. Tightening the grip on the shirt, his left hand pulled at her arm, then hit at her back.

His movements lessened as she rolled him to the side, landing on top of him. Her arm and weight on his head as she reached for the knife on the floor with her left hand. Cutting the tape on her ankles, she pushed the chair off.

Knowing he was good at his job, she searched the room, trying to find something to tie him up with. It wouldn't take much to overpower her if he woke up or if he was faking.

As she reached for the roll of duct tape, he pushed up, sending her flying off his back with a scream.

He grunted and lunged forward.

"Greer!"

She kicked out and then used the knife still in her hand, landing several blows to his torso. He stepped back, holding his bleeding chest as he dropped to his knees then fell forward.

Rolling to her side, she worked to stand, her vision blurred, and her feet aching as she swayed.

"Greer. The wall. Right. Go right."

Following Gage's directions, she felt along the wall, finding a pully. Unlatching the trigger, his body fell. She staggered to his blurry form.

"I'm, I'm sorry. I couldn't stop it," she whispered.

Gage pulled her in and held her for only a second as he took the knife. Sitting back, she took even breaths, trying to keep from passing out.

"Greer, latch the door. You've got to get up."

She nodded and crawled toward the steps. Pushing her legs under her, the stinging pain of the blood rushing back to her feet burned like pins and needles. Crawling up the steps, she pushed the bolts in place and stumbled off the steps, falling into Gage's arms.

"I've got you, babe." He pulled her up and moved her to the far side of the room.

"Dusty?"

The other man's voice came through the door. She stiffened.

"Dusty, answer me or I'm blowing the door."

Gage pushed her into the wall. "Stay here and don't move."

She nodded, grabbing his face and pulling him close, kissing him gently. He pushed his forehead to hers. With a squeeze of her hand, he was gone.

SHAKING off the feeling of Greer's lips on his, Gage slipped around the corner and hid down low next to the steps. The crashing sounds of gunfire erupted and splintered the door, sending wood everywhere as the reverberation echoed in his brain.

Yelling, Tommy burst into the room, a machine gun blazing. Bullets ricocheted everywhere.

As he stopped to gape at Dusty, Gage lunged from his hiding spot. Using the knife, he cut the gun strap across Tommy's back, sending him to his knees.

Gage hit him over the head with knife butt and grabbed the rope they had used on him. Binding the legs and arms of both men, he rushed back to where he left Greer.

His breath left his body as he saw her balled up in the corner, bloody and passed out, her eyes closed, and her breathing slowed.

"Come on, babe. I've got you."

Pulling her into his arms, he felt calm again, a peace that had been missing for what seemed like his lifetime filled his soul.

She roused. "I can't, I'm too dizzy."

"I know, I've got you."

He tied the strap on the gun and left it hanging across his shoulder. Lifting her gently, he kissed her forehead as she nestled against his neck.

"Let's find a way out of here."

Climbing the stairs, he kept on guard, worried someone else might appear. However, after the gunfire and with Tommy coming in the way he did, he assumed if someone else were here, they would've showed by now.

Climbing another staircase, he slowly edged around the corners, until they arrived in a kitchen. A large table sat in the middle, chairs all around the room and a fireplace that sat empty.

Scanning the walls, he didn't see a phone in the wall, no plugged-in cell phones, meaning they were off the grid. Hats and coats hung up by the door and a diesel truck sat just outside.

"We're getting out of here."

He laid her down on the table, then pushed on a pair of boots. Finding them too small, he pushed on another pair and then tied the small boots on Greer. Shoving a hat on her head, he grabbed a coat and put it on, wrapping the other around Greer's shoulders.

His energy bottoming out, he groaned as he lifted her again.

"You, okay?" she asked.

"Yeah, we're going home. And I'm expecting a date out of you, Greer Bennett."

Her airy chuckle made him smile.

Opening the door, he scanned for anyone else, but the area was empty. Rushing to the truck, he opened the car door and pulled himself inside.

"Lay down, honey."

She complied, and he pushed her legs out of the way to sit. The keys were in the ignition. He started it up, turned around in the small yard, and headed down the driveway.

"I'm cold," she whispered.

He turned on the heat full blast. "Just stay with me, G. Your head. I'm worried you've got a really bad concussion."

He blew out a heavy breath. As amazing as he knew she was, to see her in action, to take out that man while dizzy and obviously hurting was remarkable.

Man. Ari was right, women like her don't come around often.

The driveway ended, but he didn't recognize the area and had no idea which way to turn. Deciding to go up instead of down, he turned left and picked up speed.

"Greer?"

He patted her legs.

Pushing down on the accelerator, he sped down the road until he finally spotted a bridge, tall sky rises all around and he blew out with recognition. The Outer Drive Bridge. They were on the outskirts of town.

Pulling into a gas station, he leaned over and locked her door.

"I'll be right back." He kissed her head, then slid from the seat, leaving the truck running.

Pushing through the door, he ignored the stares. "I need a phone, call the police."

"What?" The woman behind the counter nervously gaped at him.

"Call nine-one-one and get the police here now! I need a phone."

A man held out his cell phone, and he called Ari.

"Hello? Who's this?"

"Get help here now."

"Gage? Where are you?"

"Lock on this cell, get an ambulance here now. Someone is calling the police, but Greer, she's hurt, has a bad concussion."

"We're on our way, don't move. There's already a search helo in the air, I'm sending it to you."

Ari's words echoed in his mind, spots entered his vision as the adrenaline coursing through his body ebbed. He handed the phone back and stumbled outside to get into the truck with Greer.

As he sat down, he barely had the energy to pull her up into his lap, cradling her head and studying the matted blood on the right side of her head.

"We made it, Greer. We're safe."

A deep breath escaped her lips. Leaning over, he kissed her gently, making her eyes flutter open for just a moment before they shut once more. His fingers swept across her jaw, feeling much too helpless now that he finally had her in his arms.

39

The smell of cold and dirt filled her senses. She pulled at her arms, but they wouldn't move. Tied up again? But she, she got away, right?

Someone gripped her hand and she pulled. She had to fight to get away.

"Greer."

Gage's voice made her still. He sounded, different. His cologne engulfed her senses and she smiled.

"Now, open those eyes, babe."

Her mind engaged. She felt a soft bed under her body and her hand being held tightly. It took much more effort than she imagined to make her eyelids finally rise.

"What?" She grimaced at the burn in her throat.

"Easy. Don't try and move so much," Gage whispered as he rubbed her arm.

"What happened?"

Her eyes finally focused. Darkness made up the room as a low glow highlighted the pitted ceiling.

"We got out. Thanks to you."

She groaned and closed her eyes. Nausea swept through,

and she took a deep breath. As the wave ceased, she opened her eyes and found Gage leaned in, his green eyes watching.

"You remember the wreck?"

She closed her eyes. "The wreck. Yes. Someone hit us. Then I was ... hurting." Her eyes opened, and she took in a breath. Gage. He was hanging ... "Are you okay?" She tried to roll but let out another groan as her body was completely against the idea. Pain pulsed through her shoulder.

"Stop moving, I told you." He sighed. "You have a bad concussion, and your shoulders are pretty bad."

"You were hanging." She swallowed the bile rising again as he sat on the bed, holding her hand in his lap.

"I'm fine."

"You got cut."

"So did you. Stop worrying. Although now, I think I definitely owe you." He pushed her hair back, smiling as he swept his fingers over her cheek.

"Can I have something to drink?"

He shook his head. "Ice chips only. Want me to sit you up? It's gonna hurt."

Mumbling yes, the bed started to rise. She closed her eyes, working to ease the dizziness.

"Ohh."

"Easy, babe."

She smirked at the nickname. Taking a deep breath, she opened her eyes again, focusing on him standing next to her with a cup. He held up a spoon.

"I can do it."

"No, I'm not sure you can."

Her eyebrow went up, and she made her arms move to take the cup from him. He sighed and held the bottom as she spooned the cool ice into her mouth.

"Remind me never to say you can't do something."

Letting it melt, she swallowed and let it ease the burning in her throat.

"When, when can I go home?"

He sighed. "Greer, you're going to be here for a bit. I'll be here too."

She furrowed her brow and tried to ease the emotions that were working their way up. He leaned in and wrapped her up gently in a hug. She gripped his shirt and cried, her body aching, and her head pounding.

"Just rest. I've given Ari the basics so for now, that will suffice. He'll wait until you're ready." He kissed her forehead.

She wiped her eyes "I don't want to go to sleep," she whined, feeling like a child.

Taking her hands in his, Gage kissed each one, then leaned down. "I'm not leaving. You're safe here. Get some sleep."

His green eyes made her sigh.

"Why are you here?"

The question came out before she could stop it. She was too tired and hurting to control that side of her brain.

Gage just chuckled. "Why do you think?"

"I can't think. You shouldn't take advantage."

He laughed, filling her with something other than fear and worry. His smile made her smile, made her happy.

"I think I need all the edge I can get." He leaned over again, sweeping his fingers over her cheek. "I care about you too much to walk away. I'm here for the long haul, and even you can't push me away."

She closed her eyes, breathing him in and letting her nerves settle. He wanted to be with her. The thought no longer came with fear and worry.

A gentle kiss landed on her cheek. She opened her eyes. Gage stared down as she reached up and ran her fingers over his stubbled cheek.

"I thought you said I should rest," she whispered.

He shrugged. "I thought you were." His hand held the back of her neck, his fingers running gently over her sore muscles as his left hand held her upper back.

"And now?"

He ducked his head and eased closer, gently kissing her lips. "Now you can go to sleep."

She pulled the front of his shirt, bringing him down and kissing him hard. When she finally released him, he pulled back, wide-eyed and breathless. He watched her for a moment as she worked to catch her breath.

"So, what does it take to get that kind of kiss all the time?" His smile grew as he leaned his forehead to hers. "Because there's no going back now."

She chuckled. "I guess we'll have to see when I wake up. I might forget about it. My concussion and all."

He grunted and kissed her cheek. "I'm not letting you forget about that—not happening," he whispered in her ear, making her shudder.

Gage sat back and took her hands once again. With a contented sigh, she closed her eyes, feeling her body ease as his hands held hers.

40

Five Weeks Later

"You have to accept it Greer. You love him, and he loves you and that's what's supposed to happen." Paige gaped at her like she was crazy.

Sighing, Greer packed her favorite dress in the garment bag. After almost two weeks in the hospital and another three weeks off work, life was returning to some kind of normalcy.

The bodies from the case had been released by the ME and Gage's parents had made the funeral arrangements for Rachel. Gage was going to pick her up, and they were to fly out that evening.

"I mean, I do love him. Things are just, amazing. I miss him and we talk all the time. But it can't be this easy, right? It's never this easy."

Paige chuckled. "You're really in, aren't you?"

She shoved more clothes for the weekend trip in her bag. "I'm not looking at marriage, if that's what you're thinking."

"Well, he might be."

She turned to stare at Paige.

"Come on, Greer. He's older than you and has been looking a lot longer than you have. We can all see it on his face. He's settled with you. Are you saying that in all the time you spent together at the hospital, it never came up?"

She shook her head. "No, we got to know each other and stuff like that. We didn't talk about future stuff."

"You need to talk to him, let him know what you want. Just don't shut him out."

"Shut him out?"

"You tend to avoid subjects when you don't want to talk about."

Frowning, she zipped up the bag. "You're a real mood killer, you know that? I was excited to get to spend time with him and his family, even though it's a more serious occasion. Now you've got me freaked out he's going to propose or something."

"Okay, time out." Paige grabbed her hands and pulled her to the loveseat in the corner. "He's not going to propose. It's the weekend of his sister's funeral. It won't happen. But he does want to spend this time with you. He loves you, Greer. Maybe that's where this conversation should start."

She nodded. "Yeah, I guess."

"Just don't balk on him, please."

"Why would I?"

"I don't know, but ..." Paige held her belly and grinned.

"What?"

"He's kicking."

Her eyes went wide as she held the side of her friend's belly and felt the kick. "He's a he?"

Paige nodded, and Greer gave a yell as she grabbed her in a hug. The secret they had been keeping for months was finally out.

"I think you're more excited than Rick was." Paige giggled.

"Well, I mean, boy or girl, I didn't care. But now I can start shopping for him. You got a name yet?"

"No. We're still arguing about that."

She grinned and knelt, feeling along Paige's side. She felt another punch. It was amazing.

"You need to finish packing."

She sighed and stood. "Yeah, yeah."

Packing seemed uneventful as she watched the smile on Paige's face.

"Marriage can be good for a lot of things. God's got a good plan there, and I think it would suit you, if you thought about it."

Glancing at the clock, she smiled. Gage would be here in less than an hour to take her to the airport.

"I've got to head out. Call me if you need to, and please be careful."

She smiled and returned her friend's hug, following her out of the house to the porch. Leaning against the door frame, she watched Paige leave. A dark blue pickup truck pulled in. A smile lit her face again as Gage got out and rushed up the steps.

"You're early." She grinned as he pulled her into his arms.

"Couldn't stay away." He smiled and kissed her gently. "Was that Paige?"

She nodded and pulled him inside. "They're having a boy!"

He smiled as she clapped her hands.

"I've been waiting to buy clothes, but now, I can go crazy." She winked and took off down the hallway. "Let me grab the rest of my stuff, and I'll be ready to go," she called over her shoulder.

Finishing up with her overnight case, she came out of the bathroom to see Gage leaned against the footrail of her bed. His arms crossed and a smile on his face.

"I thought we said no bedroom conversations."

He chuckled as she pushed the small bag into the top compartment of her suitcase. "I wanted to ask you something."

"Okay ..." She pulled the charger from the wall and coiled it around her fingers.

"Have you thought about that? Having kids, I mean."

She froze in her spot, watching the smirk on Gage's face. "I ... no, not really. Why do you ask?"

He shrugged. "You seem happy about Paige and Rick. I just wondered."

"No, I mean, I'm happy for them. They're my family. I've never had family or nieces or nephews to buy for. I'm excited, but I'm not there. I've never really thought about it."

He took the cord from her and set it on the bed, then took her hands in his. "Stop over-thinking, Greer. I just asked a question. I'm not looking for a specific answer."

Her jaw clenched as his green eyes studied her, laughter on his face. "Okay, so what about you then?" Two could play this game.

He shrugged. "I haven't thought about it. Life's been too complicated, and I was never at that point where I thought I could have a family." He wrapped her up, pulling her to him.

Her hands gripped his arms as she leaned back to look up at him. "And now?"

"I guess it depends."

"On what?"

"If the woman I want to marry wants kids." He grinned and she squeezed his arms.

"Very funny."

"What's funny?"

She tried to push away, but he held her tight. "What're you trying to do?"

"Talk to my girlfriend about what she wants."

"What I want?" Heart pounding, she worked to ease the

frustration of the same exact commentary coming from him that came from Thomas. "You want to know what I want?"

"Look, you brought it up with the baby talk and I just wanted to know what you thought about all of it." He released her, taking up just her hands instead. "I get you're gun shy. I'm not asking you to marry me. I'm asking what you want from this, from me."

Her eyes finally met his. "I ... I'm not sure."

"Okay. Then tell me that. Don't shut down."

"I'm not shutting down."

He scoffed. "You just did. I can read you now. It's taken a while, but I can read you loud and clear. I'm not Thomas. Please don't push me away."

She pulled her hands back and crossed her arms. Instead of letting her be, he moved in, grabbing her waist.

"I'm not leaving, and we're not going to be mad. I just wanted to know the answer to a question. Now I know."

"Gage, I'm not there." Guilt hit her stomach.

"Never said I was."

She started to rebuttal, but he was right. He never said he was, and she freaked out. With a groan, she threw her arms around his neck and hugged him. His arms wrapped her up.

"I'm sorry. Paige had me all worked up about it, and I took it out on you."

"About what?"

She sighed. "She's trying to prepare me for moving on. Whatever that means. I just don't know."

He pulled her back. "Know what?" His amazing eyes watched her, filled with worry and concern.

"I don't even know what marriage is. I've never really seen it. I mean, the only time I've seen it was after we moved here, and I basically lived with Paige for three years. Her parents were worried for each other and talked. They did argue some, but they were, kind." She looked up. "I just don't want to screw it all up. I like us too much."

He chuckled and kissed her gently. "I like us too."

What had she done in life for God to put Gage right where she needed him?

"So, let's get loaded and head out. We can grab a bite on the way."

Once on the road, Gage shared the information he got from Ari. "The name Gabby mentioned was some kind of scam Bolstero had orchestrated. He was using his trucking company to ship more than just legit freight. Maxwell told Gabby about it as insurance. The FBI has already launched into the scam. Maxwell claims he's willing to do what he can to put Bolstero away."

She squeezed his hand. "What about Agent Buchannan?"

"He's under investigation, and Ari's pretty confident he's going to jail. Rachel's case wasn't the only one where he had intimidated his people."

"Rick told me yesterday that Tommy gave everything up. Apparently Bolstero shot Dusty, but it wasn't fatal. When the driver went to dump them, Dusty pulled the man's gun and shot him. Dusty's finger got torn off when it got snagged in the liftgate."

"The extra body in the grave?"

She nodded. "The drivers been identified from dental X-rays. And on another note, Kennedy is getting the help she needs and is moving. The DA doesn't think WitSec is necessary, but they're keeping in touch in case Bolstero decides to take out his anger on her."

Gage nodded. At least the man who had killed so many innocent people was now dead. She let out a shiver remembering their close call. Gage kissed her hand and smiled.

She never would've made it without him.

They had time to go inside instead of eating in the car, so

they pulled into a fast-food restaurant. After ordering, she turned to see Sheriff Tillman and his wife wave.

"So nice to see you." Tillman stood and gave her a gentle hug, as did his wife. "Homeland, glad to see you took an old man's advice."

Gage's cheeks turned bright red.

"And what advice would that be?"

Tillman laughed. "I told those boys one of them better step up and not let you go. Since Rick was already taken, that left Homeland."

"Please, sit down." Freeda patted the chair next to her.

Greer set down the drinks as Gage pulled out her chair.

"Handsome *and* a gentleman. I think my husband was actually right about this one."

She giggled as Gage let out a smile.

"I was right? One time in forty-three years? I guess that's better than none."

She and Gage both laughed as Freeda playfully slapped at his arm.

"That's enough out of you. You need better manners."

"I guess you need to teach me."

She held her fingers over her lips, feeling her eyes water at the sight. Forty-three years these two had been married, and they still picked at each other. But the love in their eyes was still there.

Tillman wrapped his arm around Freeda's shoulders and squeezed. "Just wait her out Homeland. That's what I had to do with this one. It took a few months, but I wore her down."

Her face heated as Gage squeezed her leg from under the table.

"Never mind that." Freeda sighed. "So, how are you, dear?"

She must've noticed the injuries still healing.

"I'm good. We had a rough case, but it's all cinched up now."

"And the bodies?" Tillman's tone turned serious.

She nodded. "All identified and returned to their families."

"Good. They deserved a proper funeral. I'm so thankful you two were there to take care of it."

"You mean to take care of you." Freeda scoffed. She leaned over to take Gage's hand. "Thank you for rescuing my husband. You saved his life."

Gage's eyes went wide as he nodded, forcing a smile.

"Now, let's go and let these two have their alone time." Tillman stood and helped Freeda out of her chair. He gathered up the trays and nodded to both of them. "Have a good rest of the day." He winked at Gage and with a wave of the hand, they were gone.

"That was, interesting."

She nodded, avoiding looking up as she stared at her tray.

"You good?"

She nodded again, taking a sip of her drink.

After eating in silence, they went back to the truck and continued the drive to the airport.

Paige's words echoed in her head. Marriage was the path they were on. It shouldn't worry or scare her just because she had no idea how it all worked. Mark's words were the only thing she had ever learned about marriage, and she had God and love for Gage.

So, it shouldn't be an issue, right?

"Everything all right?"

"Yeah."

Gage took her hand. He kissed it, then let it rest on the middle console. He was an amazing man, loving, kind and protective. The fact he was willing to look over her inabilities so consistently made her want to be better, do better.

Attraction and lust were things she had for other men she had dated, but never this—never love. She wanted him to be happy. She wanted to make him happy and be there for him just as often as he was there for her.

The fact they were in different areas was already overwhelming and she couldn't believe how much she missed him since she was released from the hospital. Missing him every day, only getting to talk and Facetime was killing her.

Maybe Paige was right. Marriage was just the next step.

Her heart fluttered, heat filled her face.

Marriage? God, can I really do this?

41

The morning service was perfect. Gage watched as his sister was finally laid to rest. A weight lifted off his shoulders. His mother and father did well, considering, and as long as he had a hold of Greer's hand, he knew he would heal. Guilt was a burden, but it was something he was trying hard to release.

Back at his parents' home, he sat in the sunroom, looking through an album his mother had pulled out. Pictures of his sister lined the pages.

"Hey." Greer came up and sat next to him, leaning in as he wrapped an arm around her shoulders.

"Hey."

She grinned as she pointed out a picture of him holding Rachel as a baby. "That is the cutest picture."

He smiled as she pulled the album in her lap. Giving her a squeeze, she snuggled into his body and flipped through the pages. She laughed, pointing out the various pictures of him and his siblings.

"Do you have photo albums, Greer?"

She shook her head. "I asked once, after seeing all the

pictures of Paige at her house. But Mom said they were lost in the move."

Laughter echoed as she pointed at a picture of him at three or four, naked, but covered in bubbles as he stood from the bathtub.

"It's that funny, huh?"

She patted the side of his face. "You were sure a cute baby."

"I *was* cute?" He took hold of her waist, the only place he had discovered she was ticklish and ran his fingers across her skin.

"Gage, stop." Her laughter filled the room as he leaned over the top of her, holding his weight up on the couch.

She opened her amber eyes, a smile on her face.

"You're beautiful."

Her eyes went wide.

"I know I've told you how amazing you are, but you're beautiful. I hope you know that." Pushing back her hair and caressing her face, he kissed her gently.

Leaning his forehead to hers, he sighed. The prodding on his heart had been a constant stir, something he had been avoiding since he knew she wouldn't be okay with moving so fast. Their conversation in her home the other day made him hurt, and he wondered if she would ever want more from him.

"What's wrong?"

He sat up as she followed, taking hold of his hand. "Just a lot going on."

She leaned back into the couch, pulling his hand. Looking over, he smiled at the way she measured her hand to his.

"Mom wanted me to ask if you would like to come to Thanksgiving dinner? We could come up for the entire weekend."

"That sounds great." She snuggled into the space at his side.

That pull kept washing over him.

Shooting up from the couch, he pulled her up. "Let's go for a walk."

She tilted her head, less than amused. "It's November. It's snowing outside and cold."

He grinned and pulled her close. "I won't let you get cold." With a wink he kissed her quickly and pulled her up the stairs. "Get some warm clothes on."

Guiding her to the room, she reluctantly sighed as she closed the door.

"Gage?"

He turned to see his mom at the other end of the hallway.

"Yes?"

"Are you going out?"

"Yeah, just for a walk." He rubbed the back of his neck. "Greer said she'd like to come to Thanksgiving."

"Good." She smiled, her gaze lingering.

"You need something?"

She patted his arm. "You ever need use of any family jewelry, just let me know."

His mouth dropped as she chuckled. "It's been a month."

She shrugged. "I can still see love in a young woman's eyes, son. Don't let her get away." She winked and headed back down the staircase.

He made his way to his room, his head spinning. "God, You can't do this, not now. It's too soon. He slid on some flannel-lined jeans and a sweater.

After her freaking out on him in her house, the subject of marriage and futures seemed a bad idea. But as much as it was pushing on his heart, he had to tell her now. Because if she was never going to be in and never wanted more, he had to get out, somehow.

Sliding the hat over his head and pulling on his boots, he grabbed his coat and knocked on her door.

"Come in."

"Hey, you ready?" He opened the door to see her looking around the room.

Her leggings stuck out of the bottom of her long shirt and a stocking hat sat on her head, her hair hanging down in front of her shoulders.

Man, he loved her.

"You're going to get cold in that."

She put her hands on her hips. "Yes, I assumed as much. I packed my jeans, but ..." She pulled up the flap in the suitcase and pulled them out. "Here they are. Have you seen my coat?"

He leaned against the door as she slid the jeans over her leggings and pulled her gloves from the case.

"Gage?"

"Yeah?"

"My coat?" She stepped in front of him and he leaned down, receiving a gentle kiss.

"You know, you gave me a doozey of a kiss when you woke up." He smiled as the ends of her lips curved up slightly.

"Find my coat, and we can discuss that on our walk."

"Sounds good." He winked and pulled her down the hallway, her laughter echoing.

Once on the trail through the woods behind his parents' house, he took her hand, then pulled her close to wrap an arm around her waist.

He fingered the holster at her back. "You brought your gun?"

"You're telling me you didn't?" she winked.

"You feel safe with me, right?"

She paused, and he stopped next to her. "Really?"

He was picking a fight, and he didn't even realize it. "Sorry."

"Okay, what's going on? You've been acting odd, and I don't think this is just about Rachel."

He shook his head and pulled her in close. "I ..." he couldn't even get it out. The fear of her running strangled his voice.

She pushed her arms up to hold on to his neck. Pulling him down, she kissed him. Letting everything else fall way, he leaned in, holding her and deepening the kiss, wanting her to understand just how he felt.

As her hands moved down to his chest, he rested his forehead next to hers, his breath heavy and burning in his lungs as the cold air did nothing to ease the heat moving between them. He closed his eyes.

"You know I love you, right?"

Gripping her waist, he was surprised she didn't bolt. He leaned back to see the smile on her face.

"Greer?"

"I know."

"You do?"

She nodded and started to drop her hands when he stopped her.

"Not so fast. I just told you I love you. Are you running?"

Her eyebrows furrowed. "You think I would run away?"

"After the conversation we had at your house, yes."

Her arms pushed back around his neck, a slight grimace on her face that made him pull them back down. Her shoulders were still healing from the strain.

"Stop, Gage. I'm fine. Look, I know I freaked out, but I can't believe you think I would run."

"I love you too much to lose you. The thought makes me sick, and I ... I want more. If you don't ever want that, not now, but not ever, then I need to know." He swallowed hard, worry and fear weighing on his shoulders.

She gave him a gentle kiss. This can't be a goodbye kiss ...

"I love you too."

His jaw dropped.

"How can you be that surprised?" Her amber eyes were bright as they searched his.

"Greer, with everything and how you reacted," he leaned

forward and took another kiss, deeper and longer than the others.

She held on to his neck, and he breathed her in, felt her body against his. His world clicked in place.

"I want to marry you."

She paled as he held on tight. "What?"

"I don't have any other reason besides the fact I love you. I want to see you every day, I want to fall asleep and wake up to you every day. That forty-three years could be us, and I want it to start sooner rather than later."

Her mouth hung open as she continued to grip the front of his coat. At least she was hanging on.

"I'm not asking for anything but you. No other motives, no other ideas. If you want a family, we can start one. If not, we won't. I'll move to you, I've already thought about it. I'm tired of being without you every day or just talking on the phone. It's not enough."

"Gage, I know there's a lot of ... it seems to be coming up a lot." She swallowed hard. "Seeing the Tillmans," she chuckled, a good sign. "I met her at the hospital. They were so funny, she called him names, and he pestered her. I wondered how to be married like that."

"Greer, I'm moving anyway. I was going to talk to you about it this weekend. This is soon, I know it's soon. But between everyone pushing, and God—"

"God? You're going to blame God for making you propose?" She grinned, and his heart lifted.

"God's been putting it on my heart since we first flew out to Chicago. That night at your house, you left me standing on the porch, and I had no idea why. I heard you crying. Right then, God started moving something in my heart for you."

Her wide eyes glossed over, and he pulled off his glove to wipe her face. "Don't cry, you'll get cold."

Pulling her in, she gripped his body. He felt that peace return. She pushed back, then raised up and kissed him gently.

"Ask again in a month." She winked and turned.

He took hold of her hand and pulled her back. "No, wait."

She sighed.

"A month?"

She nodded. "But next time, you better have a ring and the whole proposal thing down."

He grabbed her up and smiled at her laughter. As he allowed her to slide down to the ground, he kissed her gently.

"What changed?" he watched her lips turn into a smile.

"I love you, Gage. I've never said that or felt that with anyone else. Don't think God was just working on your heart. He's been messing with mine as well. I'm not—I don't really know how a marriage works. You need to know that up front."

"Just because I watched my parents do it doesn't mean I have all the answers, babe. We'll do it together."

She nodded and bit her lip before he pulled it down and kissed her again.

"Maybe we should go in." Her gaze focused on his lips made his heart pound faster.

In a month, she would be his. His body heated as he grinned.

"I think the cold is good." He kissed her gently. "So, after a month, how long then?"

She chuckled. "I don't know."

"Let's elope."

She gave him a gentle kiss as her fingers worked into the back of his hair. "Only if it's somewhere warm."

He laughed and picked her up in his arms.

"Gage, let me walk."

"Nope, I'm good. Besides, I've got some plans to make." He pushed her up on his shoulder as she laughed and he took off for the house.

One month. He just needed one month.

EPILOGUE

The warm sand edged between her toes, and her heart skipped as she walked hand in hand with Gage across the beach.

It wasn't a real elopement, but close enough.

Before Gage and Greer headed to the Bahamas, his family and Rick and Paige attended the small ceremony at the church where Greer was saved. To come full circle, to find Jesus and the future she was so uncertain about in the same place hit home.

God was so good.

"How's the weather?"

Grinning up at a shirtless Gage, Greer enjoyed the view.

"You made the perfect choice. I'll come to the beach anytime you want to go."

Wrapping her up, he leaned in and kissed her gently.

Paige was right. God's plan was so much better than she could ever had imagined.

ACKNOWLEDGMENTS

I'd like to thank all those in my area who enjoy and read my books. There are several people who ask day to day, "When's your next book coming out?" It's been hard to get back into writing after losing my father in 2022, but knowing people actually enjoyed my books and are looking forward to the next one drives me.

God has purposed me to be here and write these stories and I'm hoping that through Him, people will find Him in all the chaos of life. He's given me more strength than I can imagine to be able to get through the past few years and continue writing.

I also want to thank my publisher for allowing me time to get back in my groove. It's been a while, but I'm ready to get back into it!

ABOUT CINDY BONDS

Growing up in northwest Arkansas, Cindy Bonds has moved from the time she was in college until finally settling down in her husband's hometown of Clinton, Arkansas.

As a child, she would accompany her father to visit a lot of men and women in nursing homes or their own homes to offer company and listen to stories of the good ole days. Most were former military, several having survived World War II.

Her father, both grandfathers, and uncles all served our country, so as she grew up, she was inundated with stories of heroes, chaos, and the burden of war.

Having listened to stories her whole life, it was easy to put pen to paper and begin her own storytelling journey. As God led her through grace and mercy in her own life, it was only natural to put it all down and include the hero types she'd heard so much about growing up.

ALSO BY CINDY BONDS:

Fighter

Book One of the Tactical Response Team (TRT)

Bexley Bowers has lost everything during her 30 years . Struggling to find her path, she's targeted and kidnapped by a crazed terrorist.

Evan Mitchell retired from the Navy only to find himself back at work, clinging to his job with the Tactical Response Team. He meets Bexley while on assignment, and a strange tug on his emotions leaves him scrambling. Bexley is too stubborn and too beautiful. He'll never be able to get her out of his mind—especially now that he's her protection.

When Bexley finds herself in trouble, can Evan's team arrive in time?

Fighting the clock and their pride, Evan and Bexley must decide which is more important—their egos or their future.

Get your copy here: https://scrivenings.link/fighter

Protector

Book Two of the Tactical Response Team (TRT)

Danica Freeman has put her past firmly behind her. She's found happiness and a place to belong within the TRT. But as her new family comes under attack, the chain of events makes her wonder if this is less about the team and something more personal.

Haiden Blake overcame his tragic childhood and found himself in the Army. Now a retired sniper, he uses his skills to protect and defend on American soil. He's found a family in the TRT, but something more with Danica. She's his close friend, as close as he can allow her to become.

Danica and Haiden leave sparks to burn, unwilling to risk it all to move forward to something more. But another attack puts Danica in danger, and Haiden is unable to protect her. At the risk of losing Danica forever, Haiden takes a leap of faith, praying God will catch them both.

Get your copy here: https://scrivenings.link/protector

Survivor

Book Three of the Tactical Response Team (TRT)

As the Tactical Response Team reels from past attacks, Jeff Powers is determined to figure out who wants them gone. But on the job, he becomes distracted by a beautiful doctor dealing with a stalker.

While helping Dr. Shelby During, Jeff falls deeper and deeper into a strange plot that puts both in grave danger.

Get your copy here: https://scrivenings.link/survivor

Rainstorm

Laurel Ashburn has a scarred past, filled with corruption and pain. After an injury overseas sends her home, she moves back in with her foster mother and to a town that hates her. Being home puts her on a path to find a missing friend. But when she's attacked over and over, who will be willing to help?

Detective Dev Hollister traded in the big city for a slower pace and less crime in rural Arkansas. After rescuing Laurel from an attempted kidnapping, he finds himself intrigued with this headstrong and stubborn woman.

While Dev's job is to protect Laurel, he wants much more than to solve the case. He wants to give her a new life and reason to stay.

Laurel must push beyond her dark past to trust Dev with her life. But after losing so much, can Laurel survive one more storm?

Get your copy here:

https://scrivenings.link/rainstorm

Hostage

Her confidence shot, Agent Macy Packer desperately wants to go back to her regular life, before she was taken hostage. To forget the pain, the fear and forget the man that helped her through all of it, then disappeared.

Kane Bledsoe is finally healed, his scars serving as a reminder of his time in captivity. But all he can think about is the blue-eyed woman that saved him. She had saved them all and left him with a burning hope.

A chance meeting and an attack prove Macy is still in danger.

Kane pushes himself into the investigation, doing what he can to provide protection.

The enemy is clear—he wants Macy.

Kane will have to decide just how far he's willing to go to protect her. Can he sacrifice himself when the time comes?

Get your copy here:

https://scrivenings.link/hostage

NEW ROMANTIC SUSPENSE FROM SCRIVENINGS PRESS

Vengeance in Vienna by Sara L. Jameson

Troubled Waters Book 3

Interpol Special Agent Jacob Coulter and his fiancée Riley Williams set out on a moonlight sail, but a sniper turns their idyllic Austrian vacation into a deadly nightmare.

On temporary assignment to the Vienna Interpol office, Jacob must apprehend a notorious terrorist financier and uncover his operations in Austria. But the financier is determined to destroy all Jacob holds dear. And that includes his kid sister and his fiancée, Riley Williams.

Opera singer Riley Williams is tired of dodging terrorist attempts on her life. When she insists on helping Jacob catch the financier and his henchmen, she gets into more trouble than she bargained for.

But the financier's tentacles of evil reach far deeper into the Austrian economy than Jacob and Riley suspected. What they uncover appalls them. The clock is ticking. Can Jacob locate them before it's too late?

Get your copy here:

https://scrivenings.link/vengeanceinvienna

Sunset over Swaziland by Shirley Gould

The African Skies Series - Book 3

Grant writer Jocelyn Millender travels to Swaziland to get humanitarian aid for the devastated, disease-infested country. When war threatens, all travel is suspended. She's trapped, scared, and in danger.

Hearing about her life-threatening situation, Austin Bendale, a decorated soldier turned security services specialist, purchases a plane ticket and comes to the rescue. But things aren't as they seem. Hidden agendas are inciting riots, humanitarian funds are dwindling, and orphans are disappearing.

When you put one determined woman and a never-say-die hero in this life-and-death situation—using her gifts and his brawn—can they ignore the sparks between them, escape the chaos, solve the mystery, apprehend the guilty, and get across the border in time?

Because the sun is setting over Swaziland ...

Get your copy here:

https://scrivenings.link/sunsetoverswaziland

Stay up-to-date on your favorite books and authors with our free e-newsletters.

ScriveningsPress.com